I0460058

Into the Garden of Gethsemane, Georgia

Laraine Herring

INTO THE GARDEN OF GETHSEMANE, GEORGIA

First published September 2013

Library of Congress Control Number: 2013945137

ISBN: 978-0-9852607-5-0

Author photo by MH Ramona Swift, ©2013

Cover by Mike Iverson

Presented by The Concentrium

Phoenix, Arizona USA

www.theconcentrium.com

Also by Laraine Herring

Gathering Lights: A Novel of San Fransisco

Ghost Swamp Blues: A Novel

The Writing Warrior: Discovering the Courage to Free Your True Voice

Writing Begins with the Breath: Embodying Your Authentic Voice

Lost Fathers: How Women Can Heal from Adolescent Father Loss

Monsoons: A Collection of Writing

Author's Note

Into the Garden of Gethsemane, Georgia arrived after a conversation with my husband about the end of life.

"Wouldn't it be great," I said, "if my characters came for me at the end?"

That question led to more questions and soon Mrs. Abigail Fisher's voice began to whisper to me, and it turned out she wasn't in particularly good standing with the characters she'd written. One of them, in fact, had come back from the cutting room floor for revenge.

What next? How does an author make things right with the characters and stories she's been charged to carry?

This thread pulled me into an attempt to dramatize the creative process. I wanted to show the sticky and often obsessive relationships a writer has with her characters, and I wanted to show what happens when those characters take on lives of their own and demand their own endings.

I hope this story is more than a ghost story and a mother-daughter story. I hope it speaks to you about the profound and necessary power of the act of writing and storytelling to change the writer's life as well as the reader's. Our stories do indeed create our lives.

I'd like to thank my fearless first readers: Gayle Brandeis, Michaela Carter and Arvin Loudermilk for their input on the manuscript, and Keith Haynes for listening to the story over and over again. Thanks to The Concentrium for designing the book and for all their countless efforts of support for my work and career for over twenty years.

Each of you helps make my stories better.

You have betrayed and sold out the talent that was granted you...

That talent is now officially withdrawn.

Enjoy your dirty money.

You will never have anything else.

You will never write another sentence above the level of *In Cold Blood.*

—William S. Burroughs, letter to Truman Capote 1970

1

From her perch on the dusty bookshelves, Pistachio Simmons, the almost-heroine of the mega-bestseller, *The Garden of Gethsemane, Georgia*, watched her author and creator, the South's Esteemed First Lady of Letters, Mrs. Abigail Fisher, sleeping alone. She peered over the cracked spine of her should-have-been book-home, shaking off the memory of the day she had been brutally cut from the narrative with a swipe of a red fountain pen.

Pistachio was surprised by the condition of the house. Over the years the walls had fallen almost in on themselves, but her creator, the author Mrs. Abigail Fisher, did not realize it. To her, the columns still shone a pristine white, the spiral staircase always a shining mahogany, the windows one pane after the other of glistening, glimmering possibility.

Pistachio watched her creator shift beneath the sheets. She was certain she had no idea she was being watched. It would be easier than Pistachio had dared to hope to slide between the half-mast eyelids until Mrs. Abigail Fisher could no longer deny her existence, could no longer not pay attention. She had waited almost thirty-seven years for this moment. She could wait a few more days.

"Sleep well, Abbey," she said, kissing the top of Mrs. Abigail Fisher's thinning hair. Mrs. Abigail Fisher brushed away a fly buzzing around her head.

The gold sticker, *National Book Award Finalist*, shimmered on the spine of the story that should have been her home. The sticker had once looked rich and thick, but now it had dulled and peeled at the corners; years of humidity had weakened the color. She hadn't given thought to how she might return to the pages, slip back into the letters and spaces, rest her head again on the pillow of a comma; she only knew she had to find a way to wrap herself again into the quilt of the narrative.

The letters of Pistachio's own rejected scenes cascaded from the peaks of her shoulders, and she felt an empowerment in simply standing on her own. No one else's words imprisoning her. No one else's story arc dictating what she could or could not do. There was a curve in her spine, a flexibility she didn't know was there until she pushed her way out of the paragraphs and onto the shelf's edge. She opened and closed her mouth, letting her tongue wash over her lips. What would she say if the words were her own? Where would she go if her own feet walked in the direction of her own choosing?

2

There had been letters, of course, written on her mother's rose-scented stationery in her shaking hand, but Elise Fisher had ignored them, at first on purpose and later from habit. The letters were designed, Elise was certain of it, to press all her buttons, to elicit the responses that her mother, the author Mrs. Abigail Fisher, hoped for, ever the writer, ever the story-crafter. They began innocuously enough with the passive guilt-inducing "It's been so long since I've seen you" lines and escalating to "I feel there is someone else in the house," to finally "Daughter, I think I am afraid," all crafted with precision and an intimate knowledge of the weaknesses of the sole audience member: Elise.

She sent letters because she could control, down to the pick of punctuation, the message she wanted to convey. And more importantly, she could avoid any deflection or reflection that might arise should face-to-face contact occur. The telephone was out of the question, the price of long-distance ludicrous. Elise had never been able to convince her that calling plans had changed.

Elise saved her mother's letters in a shoe box, thinking one day a university might want her papers. At the very least, an eBay buyer might relieve her of them, giving her some small compensation for being the failed daughter of the esteemed writer.

"Maybe she really is afraid," Elise's fiancée, Henry Wakefield, said one night after a light dinner of mozzarella and garden tomatoes.

"My mother? Afraid?" Elise could not picture her stoic mother afraid of anything.

"It's possible."

"It's not possible. My mother is impenetrable."

This was the point in the conversation when Henry would try to soften her, sometimes by tickling, sometimes by kissing, sometimes by reading poetry from her collected works of Blake. She knew he thought she overreacted to her mother. She knew he thought she was in part to blame for the distance between them. But he had no idea, only his cobbled-together stories of idyllic mothers and daughters and his own close relationship with his late may-she-rest-in-forever-peace mother to show him what was possible. Elise loved that about him, that he had a mother and a family that liked each other, chose to spend time with each other, even helped each other. She loved his belief that everyone was good somehow, even though she knew that wasn't true, especially about her.

The letters arrived daily for several weeks, the last one with the all-capitals closing: "Daughter, please come home. Sincerely, Your Mother Mrs. Abigail Fisher." Then there was silence, the mailbox an empty mouth. Henry thought she should call, but Elise knew this was the dramatic pause in the story arc. This was the place where the questions had been expertly tossed into play and she, the reader, was left with only the burning desire to find out what happened next. Elise had long ago learned to suppress that desire, having finally learned that the questions were never answered, no matter how she might have begged.

The call from the Chatham County Fire Department was an unexpected plot element, though.

"Ma'am, she almost burned the whole house down," said the man on the other end of the line, a John or a Gene or a Jerry. He must have taken Elise's silence for shock. "Don't worry. Your mother is all right. We've got a social worker with her right now. But you have to go home. She can't stay there alone anymore. She could have burned the street down."

Elise slipped into character. "Of course. I'll drive down right away. Of course. Thank you very much for calling."

John or Gene or Jerry was obviously relieved by Elise's appropriate response. "We'll keep an eye out until then," he said. "And ma'am?"

"Yes?"

"Have you been home lately?"

"Well, not in awhile," she said, trying to remember whether the last time she went home was seven or eight years ago. "Why?"

"I just want you to be ready. She—your mother—she's not in good shape. The house is—well, it'd just be great if you could come home right away."

"I'll leave first thing." Elise pushed back down the knot forming in her stomach. She had managed to avoid going home for so long.

"Thank you, ma'am. Have a nice evening. I'm sorry for the call."

"Thank you. Good evening."

When Henry came home from work she'd almost finished the bottle of Raven's Wood Cabernet. "She set the house on fire, Henry. That was more than I gave her credit for."

Henry put his Sheriff's hat on the kitchen table—a frayed centerpiece—slid his standard-issue .40 caliber pistol out of his holster and emptied the ammunition. "I can come with you." He put the gun in the lockbox.

"No you can't." Elise tapped the top of his hat. "Besides, she wouldn't let you up the stairs."

"Probably not."

"Probably?"

"OK. Not."

"Not."

"I'll be home on Tuesday. We can go get the marriage license then."

"Promise?"

"Of course." She poured him the last of the bottle. "Drink with me, my love. Just a little bit left."

"I can come with you."

"So you said. Go to work. Feed the cat. I'll be home soon."

"What are you going to do with her?"

Elise softened, stood to kiss his chin-dimple, the part of his face she'd first fallen in love with. "I don't know."

"Why don't we go look at Oz," he said.

This was what she loved about Henry. He said the goofiest, most perfect thing at the most perfect time. She needed to remember that more, when she was wondering why she was with him, which was usually due only to her crazy self-absorption caused most recently by too much time on her hands since the charter school where she'd been teaching art history and literature to tenth graders had cut her position to half-time. There just weren't enough tenth graders anymore. Families had left what was already a sparsely populated area in the Blue Ridge Mountains of North Carolina and headed east to Charlotte or Raleigh to try and find work; the more adventurous went west to Nevada, Utah or Oregon.

"It's late," she said.

"Yes, but the moon is full. I'll bet we can see the bricks."

The now-defunct Land of Oz Theme Park was located a town away in Beech Mountain. Apparently, it had been quite the experience for children in the 1970s, complete with balloon rides, a simulated tornado in Dorothy's house, and of course a walk through the poppy fields past the Wicked Witch's house on the way to the Emerald City. Elise hadn't known the remains were there when she took the job in Boone a decade ago. She wanted to get away from Georgia any way she could, and the first job opportunity that came along for a forty-something woman whose only job up until that point was daughter and personal assistant to Mrs. Abigail Fisher was in Boone at the Blue Ridge Academy for Girls. Elise never even Googled the town before she loaded up her Accord and headed northwest from Savannah.

The theme park still held a fall party each October, and the first year Elise was in North Carolina, she spotted the flier at the co-op. She thought it would be hokey, and it was, but it was also an explosion of story and color, and she found herself genuinely smiling at the earnestness of the cast members who'd returned and the zeal with which the people who attended slipped back into their childhoods. Anyone could see the path of yellow bricks didn't go very far; that the Wicked Witch's cave was not in fact filled with Flying Monkeys; that Dorothy was very far away from fifteen years old, but it didn't matter. The dream of what could be at the end of that yellow 44,000-brick path still sustained wonder.

"We can't trespass," she said. "You're a cop!"

"No trespassing, cross my heart," said Henry. "We'll just go to the overlook."

She didn't really need to pack much. She told herself she'd only be gone three days—long enough to clean out the house and get her mother established in an assisted living facility. She was aware of the callousness of her thoughts, but she couldn't help herself.

"OK," she said. "But you drive. Flash the lights. Use the siren. Make us seem important."

He grabbed her hand. "You know that's against the rules." He kissed her index finger. "But tonight, we'll go for it."

"Really?" Henry never broke the rules. Not about eating salad with the salad fork and soup with the soup spoon and most certainly not about anything to do with his job. He had walked the perfect line since his reassignment to "the boonies" as he called it. "You must be worried."

"I always worry," he said. "And whenever you talk to your mother, it takes me a month to bring you back to normal."

They got in the squad car and buckled in. Elise held her finger over the siren switch. "Can I do it?"

He nodded just enough. The siren shrieked, giving her the cover she needed to release her own scream, which she disguised as laughter so Henry wouldn't know the depth of her own fear. She didn't know how to present herself if she were afraid. It would be messy, blubbery, maybe even dangerous. After a few minutes, she flipped the siren off.

"Had enough?" asked Henry.

"Started to hurt my ears."

"The night's too pretty to yell at it like that," he said.

It was an hour's drive to the old Oz Park, and the drive felt a bit spooky in the almost-dark. The autumn moon would not be full until the next evening, but it was the pumpkin color Elise loved. It made her think of Charlie Brown and all the life encompassed in his very simple lines and curves. She'd been in this area almost a decade and still she marveled at the beauty of the Blue Ridge Mountains, even as the night shadows sketched a darker edge along the tree line. These mountains spoke to her in a way the porches and wide columns of Savannah never did. She wanted to walk through the historic parks of Savannah, stroll along the river and feel like she was walking with the happy ghosts of her ancestors, but she knew it was a trick. She knew the basements were rotted in many of the manicured houses. Too much damp and darkness will crumble anything, no matter how solid it once was.

"I don't know what to say," she said after awhile, because she thought she should give him something on this last night together.

"You might want to save your voice for home."

"There's nothing I can say anymore, Henry. You know she hears what she wants to hear."

"Maybe." He pulled into a gravel turn-off and killed the headlights. "Ready to walk?"

She took his hand and they climbed a weakly marked path. "I think this is trespassing," she tried to joke. The overlook they were walking to was where they'd first met. An overzealous neighbor who'd been watching too many 48-hour Mystery shows thought she was a serial killer and called the police. When Henry found her, she'd been sitting cross-legged on a boulder, looking out into the pre-dawn fog.

"That never stopped you before."

"Well, I am my mother's daughter."

He lifted her onto the boulder and then climbed up beside her. The oaks and pines around them shivered in the evening chill. Leaves had begun falling, making the path and the boulder slippery, but Elise knew where to place her feet, where to rest her back so she could peer down over the ski-lift line and find a glimpse of the yellow brick road.

"Is it too dark?" asked Henry.

"It glistens in the moonlight," she said. "I have no idea why. Part of the magic of Oz I guess."

"Look there," said Henry. "I think I see part of the witch's castle." He traced the peak of her shoulders with his fingertips.

"Remember how big her nose was?" she asked. "In the movie. I thought she was horrifying." She giggled. "She reminded me of my mother. I even checked her closet for flying monkeys once."

"You did not."

"I did." Elise remembered it had been just after her sister, Courtney Lynn, had died. Her father had been gone for only a few days and her mother hadn't let herself believe that any of it had happened. The house hadn't yet taken on its layers of dust and gray shadows, grimy windows and overgrown gardens. She hadn't yet begun to be afraid of what was at the top of the stairs hidden in her mother's bedroom. She was only afraid of what she believed was there, and only in that little girl way of turning every bump in the bedclothes into a monster-in-waiting.

"And what did you find?" asked Henry.

She'd found stacks and stacks of yellowing notebooks, the pages eaten by moths and silverfish. She thought she recognized her mother's looped and curlicued handwriting, but she couldn't bring herself to touch them or remove them from their dark place in the closet. The arm of a winter sweater slipped off the hangar, landing on her head. She started to scream but was afraid of being caught in her mother's forbidden things, so she swallowed the shout and hurried away from the closet, leaving the sweater on the floor on top of the Sunday pumps. She closed the bedroom door quickly behind her, but the dust from the notebooks lingered on her fingers long after she scurried down the mahogany staircase to the safety of the living room. "Nothing much," she said. "No monkeys anyway!"

Outlines of bats' wings flapped against the moon as the bats dove and swooped for insects. She loved the angles their wings made, just like the images of angels in the stained glass windows of her childhood church.

"Where do you think they go in the daytime?" she asked.

"Who?"

"The bats."

"Somewhere dark, I guess. Lots of caves and old mines around here."

She let herself sink back into him, his arms wrapped around her in the dark. He pressed his lips against the back of her neck. She wanted to turn and lay everything out on this boulder on this night looking out at the ruins of the witch's castle. But not bad enough.

"I'm going to miss you," he said.

"Me too." She reached behind her and pulled him closer. "I'll be home before you know it. Savannah's less than a day's drive."

"You can't clean out that house in three days."

She could. She would. She'd already called for a temporary dumpster to be set up in front of the house. How long could it take to pitch one item after another until the only things left were those that were stuck to the walls or buried under the floorboards? She would not be one of those people who held every object, turned it over and over, and then told a story about it. Her legs twitched. She was ready to burn down whatever her mother had left alone.

"Don't worry," she said, knowing he would and knowing she was glad of it. "Be happy it isn't you!"

He squeezed her shoulders. She knew he hated when she deflected away from whatever serious direction he was trying to take the conversation, but at least up until now, he'd played along, taking whatever she could give to him, lacking though it may be. He inhaled and she was afraid he'd finally say the words that would make her let him in. She didn't know what those words were. Over the four years they'd been together, she'd felt him getting closer, sneaking in under her edges, climbing over her walls.

"Shh," she said. "Let's just look at the moon. Imagine the cackle of the Wicked Witch. Can you hear her? She thinks she's going to get Dorothy, but she never really does."

He laughed. "I never hear her."

"Close your eyes and listen with your imagination."

"You know I don't hear things like you do. You tell me. Describe to me what you hear."

Elise closed her eyes, the scratchboard of the night sky still hovering behind her lids. This was her favorite part. "Well, first there's the whoosh of air as she flies by us on her bicycle. She's got Toto with her and he's barking and barking and barking hoping Dorothy will come find him, but she can't hear him. There's this huge tornado and she's never been in one before and it turns the whole house upside down. All she can hear is her own heart and the breaking of glass. The witch, though, she thinks she's won. She knows Dorothy will come looking for her dog and when that happens, well, you know what happens then. But right now, she's laughing, and it's deep and rich and full of every possible hope a witch can have."

"What do you think a witch hopes for?" whispered Henry.

Elise opened her eyes just enough to see her fingers balled into fists on her lap. "She wishes someone would follow her," she said, surprised at the pressure of her fists, the hot lump in her throat. "She hopes one day someone will be brave enough to scale all the obstacles and flying monkeys and pyrotechnics and help her get her castle back. She's not sure anymore quite how it got to be the way it is."

3

Pistachio surveyed the damage. Blackened walls. Some melted Tupperware. A heavy smoke smell that she rather relished. Nothing too dreadful. At least not from her perspective. She'd been aiming for a little less smoke and a lot more fire, but she reasoned these things would take some time to fine-tune. She'd been so stiff for so many years, folded in on herself in a corner of the closet, feet behind ears, wrists under hips, jaw hanging open like a pelican's hoping for something nourishing to leap in. To be fair, and Pistachio was very keen on making sure things were fair, she hadn't intended to start an actual fire that required outside assistance. The last thing she wanted was someone from the dimensional world poking in and around Mrs. Abigail Fisher's home. But it had happened, and she was going to have to deal with the consequences since she was not sure how to put things back the way they were.

She had felt liberated, pushing herself free from the mildewed notebooks where she'd been relegated for seven presidential administrations. Not to mention fifteen other books that Mrs. Abigail Fisher had birthed and sent forth into the world to mingle with readers and critics, teachers and book club groups, and more recently, gatherings on-line of people who were able to place images of the book covers on their virtual shelves and rate their merit. The world had become even more remarkable, and Pistachio had been shut out from it.

She remembered the first slice. She hadn't been able to bring herself to pull open her blouse to see the scar, but she could feel it still vibrating, especially when she coughed. Mrs. Abigail Fisher wrote with a nibbed pen, and when she slashed its indigo ink across Pistachio's first paragraph, it cut her almost in half. It was so fast, so deliberate, so cruel. She'd been just about to say something important, having figured out how to turn her thoughts into the squiggles on the page, but the cut occurred mid-breath, leaving her choking, trying to hold her two halves together.

4

When Elise left for Savannah, Henry was sitting in the wicker chair on the porch drinking coffee. The thin daily paper was open on his lap, their gray cat, Smeek, staring at him from the porch's railing. She loved how Henry took up the whole space of the chair, even though his frame was thin. He was tall, all angles and straight lines, and when he crossed one leg over the other to prop the paper up, his legs reminded her of a butterfly's wings, opening and closing in the breeze. She loved how no matter how late he was, no matter how cold it was, unless there was an emergency call from the station, he kept to the same morning routine—three cups of Maxwell House, the entire paper front to back, and a short conversation with the cat, which Elise had learned to pay attention to for clues into Henry's world.

"So it's time," he said, keeping the paper open.

"I want to make sure I can get a good start today. The dumpster should have gotten there already."

"What about the garden?"

He hadn't turned around, so she couldn't see his expression. She inhaled and tried not to waver her voice. "It's past first frost now," she said. "We don't need to worry about our garden right now."

"Not ours. Hers. All that brush. Overgrown trees, some fallen trees I bet. There'll be snakes and spiders and probably fire ants and all sorts of things. Are you at least bringing gloves?"

She hadn't thought about gloves. Hadn't thought about the garden at all, at least not while she was awake. "I don't think I'm really going to worry about that. The most important thing is to get Mother settled. We'll be able to take care of the yard later."

He still didn't turn around. "Whatever you think is best. I'm sure it's getting to be an eyesore for the neighbors."

There was no doubt about that. Even years ago, when Elise left the house for what she had imagined then was the final time, the garden had taken on epic proportions, especially the honeysuckle plant that stood, literally stood, not wrapped or crawled or crept like a vine is supposed to do, on its own, taller than a sapling pine, its branches of yellow-white blossoms stretching over a mile in all directions. It encroached on two other people's properties, and Elise had hired someone to cut it back, but the next day, the plant was back again, fuller and more fragrant than before. Fortunately, the two neighbors had opted to try to work the honeysuckle into their own landscaping rather than deal again with the reclusive Mrs. Abigail Fisher. She couldn't imagine what the plant looked like now.

"Maybe once we get Mother moved out," she said. "You and I can go back and get everything fixed up and ready to sell."

"Recession's a good time to try and sell a crazy old run down Southern house," he joked.

"Well, we could slap a plaque on it and hold tours. Come one come all! See the rooms where the great Mrs. Abigail Fisher, the South's Leading Lady of Letters, created her masterworks. Behold, the kitchen where she drank her tea. The bed where she slept all by herself, needing no one but her writing to keep her warm throughout the night."

"That's not a half-bad idea. Savannah's full of tours."

"What'll we call her house? Every good Southern house has a name."

"I don't know. I'll think about it when you're gone." He finally stood up and turned to face her. Smeek leapt into his chair. "Don't get a speeding ticket."

She wrapped his arms around his neck. "If I do, I'll just tear it up, tell them my man is a big-time Sheriff, maybe bat my eyes a little."

"You know that doesn't actually work."

"Not for women who look like me, anyway."

"I think you're beautiful."

"I know." She kissed his ear, his cheek, and finally, his lips. "I do."

She watched him for as long as she could in her rear view mirror as she drove down the hill away from the house. He'd put his hat on, and the farther away she got, the more the hat looked like part of a too-big costume; he was only a boy playing dress-up. When she could no longer see him on the porch, paper folded under his arm, she slipped her sunglasses on and picked up speed.

Although she wasn't looking forward to her destination, she was looking forward to a long solo car trip. Being in the car alone made her feel invisible in the best of all possible ways. She could, though never did, deviate from the expected course. She could stop at a roadside stand for peach ice cream or vinegary North Carolina barbecue. She could listen to the same song over and over for hundreds of miles, but most importantly, no one knew exactly where she was. She didn't have a smartphone with GPS; her dumbphone that only texted and made phone calls had served her for an unexpected number of years. She was hurtling through the in-between space in a metal and plastic pod at seventy miles per hour. It was the closest thing to flying on the ground.

This time, though, her CD player wasn't working right and kept spitting the CDs back into the front seat. She didn't want to listen to the radio and hear the ads or the news, even the kinder, gentler news from NPR. So that left her in silence, the wind of her inhale and exhale, the pop of her gum, the shifting of her body in the seat her only company until she reached the South Carolina border and saw the pigtailed girl holding up a cardboard sign that misspelled Savannah as *Savvana*. Elise drove past her for a quarter mile, then turned around in a two-pump Texaco station. Henry would be furious. She heard him in her head shouting all the dangers of picking up hitchhikers, even the ones that don't look like serial killers. "The good ones don't look like murderers," he said. "If they scared everyone away how could they kill anyone?" Elise always figured people got snuck up on in alleys or budget motel parking lots and swept into dark blue windowless vans. Henry assured her that more frequently, victims went willingly, "even laughing" to the one who will kill them.

But a little girl? *She could be a front for her uncle who's waiting just on the other side of the shoulder behind that grove of trees,* she heard in her head. Stop it, Henry. She's just a little girl. This was a rural part of the country and the recession had hit it hard. The South hadn't manufactured much in years, but as tourism had slowed and airfares had climbed and the drought, even in the swampy south, stretched on another year, crops that could always be counted on—corn, tobacco, cotton—were suffering. Childhood was anything but idyllic in these communities. Just the other day, Elise had read about a seven year old boy who hung his little sister from a tree down in the Florida panhandle. She'd ridden his bike. They arrested the boy in the middle of the night, but then what were they supposed to do?

When she pulled up beside the girl, she saw the layers of red clay on her skin from sleeping outside. Her blonde hair was stringy and sweat-packed. Elise couldn't get a sense of her age. She looked both five and fifty, if that were possible. Her body was small, but she held herself with a confident presence that caught Elise's attention. Her eyes were a vivid blue, almost purple, and when Elise rolled down her window the girl held up a battered green teddy bear with a chewed right ear and said proudly, "This is Mama Bear and she take care of me."

Elise unlocked the passenger door. "Pleased to meet you, Mama Bear. And what's your name?"

The girl shook her head, pulled the bear close. "You a stranger."

Elise's defenses folded; Henry's voice in her head warning of an ambush by marauding gypsies with axes and body bags no longer a whisper.

"I could be your friend." As the words slipped past her lips, she knew she'd gone to the predator script. She smiled wider, wanting to reassure the girl she wasn't stranger-danger. The girl stared back, unblinking.

"I'm Katrina," she said.

"After the hurricane?"

Katrina shook her head. "I'm older than the hurricane. Everybody just thinks I'm not because I'm little." She pouted a little, her lower lip turned under. "I never even been to New Orleans."

The wind picked up, twirling some of the newly fallen leaves into brilliant red and orange pinwheels. Elise forgot to look for axes and killers. "But you want to go to Savannah," she said.

Katrina nodded. "My mama there. She been asleep for a long time, but she waking up now."

"She is? How do you know?"

Katrina held up the bear. "Mama Bear, she tell me stories when it's dark. That's how I know everything I know." She pointed to the ear. "I get so excited I chew on her ear sometime but she don't mind. She say she only need one ear to tell me what she hearing."

Elise turned off the engine. "That's a very special bear."

Katrina looked at her as if she were an idiot. "She just a bear."

"Are you hungry?"

"No. I ate."

Elise was puzzled, but the girl did look well-nourished. Just dirty. And alone on a state highway on a school day. "I'm going to Savannah to see my mother too." She tried to make it sound like a good thing—like every girl wanted to go be with her mother. "Do you want me to take you to your mama?"

Katrina held Mama Bear's snout to her ear. She closed her eyes as she listened, shaking her head, then nodding. "She say it's OK to go with you. But we have to stop at McDonald's."

"I thought you weren't hungry?"

"Mama Bear hungry."

Katrina pulled the seat belt around her waist. She was too small for the shoulder strap to fit comfortably, so she just lifted it off. She slipped Mama Bear between the seat belt and her belly.

"What's your name?" asked Katrina as Elise started up the car.

"Oh! I'm sorry. I'm Elise."

"That a good name," she said, and closed her eyes, her thin fingers resting on the frayed head of Mama Bear.

5

Elise made one stop at a McDonald's with a PlayPlace, but Katrina didn't want to climb on the plastic slides or jump on the bouncing balls. She just wanted a Quarter Pounder with cheese and a small chocolate shake, which she shared with Mama Bear, even though she ended up eating the whole thing herself. Katrina chewed with her mouth closed, ate slowly, chewing each bite at least ten times, and used the paper napkin. Elise had made her wash her hands, which Katrina did willingly, after first whispering *hello* to the water, but the red stains on her hands and arms, which she thought had been mud and dirt, wouldn't come off. They didn't look like bruises. They didn't look like bloodstains or finger paint stains or anything other than the red clay dirt of North Carolina. But it wouldn't wash off. Katrina endured Elise's second and third soapings and scourings with the rough brown paper towels, but by the fourth time, she pulled her hands away.

"It's just how I am," she said. "You can't wash color off you."

Elise stopped mid-scrub. She was surprised how tightly her hands were gripping Katrina, how intent she was at cleaning her up. "I'm sorry. I didn't think it was your skin. I just thought it was a lot of dirt that got caked on." She wanted to lift up the girl's shirt and see if the stains carried on through the rest of her body, but she knew she'd crossed way too many boundaries already in the short time they'd been together. "I just didn't want you to eat your hamburger with dirty hands."

"I know," Katrina said. "It's just been enough washing now."

Elise was grateful no one had come into the public bathroom while she'd been at work. From a distance, the stains might look like bruising, and to a stranger, it would be easy to suspect that Elise had been the one who'd inflicted them. She couldn't be sure what Katrina would say if someone asked her about them. She ran her own hands under the lukewarm water one more time before leading Katrina into the restaurant. She tried to gauge whether or not the patrons, many clad in Clemson T-shirts, were staring at them underneath their baseball caps and thick round sunglasses, but she couldn't tell. Maybe they thought she and Katrina were mother and daughter. There'd be no reason not to. They're not even thinking about you at all, Elise thought. You're just another random person in another random McDonald's convenient to a freeway. Katrina was in deep conversation with Mama Bear, speaking in a language other than English. Her face was a kaleidoscope of expressions, mostly smiles peppered with the occasional shocked 'o'. After she finished her conversation with the bear, she reached for Elise's hand as they stood in line to order.

In the car, the two were quiet. Elise began to wonder if she were kidnapping someone's child, and now that she'd crossed the state line, she was no doubt committing multiple felonies. Henry would know. But Henry wouldn't have stopped to pick the child up. He would have done whatever the rule book said to do. Call social services. Call child protective services. Call somebody who makes out more forms and has more rule books and who might send the girl to a place where the caregiver wouldn't stop trying to scrub the clay stains off her thin young skin. Henry absolutely wouldn't have taken her across the state line to some imaginary destination. *What are you going to do now?* She heard him say. *Now you've got a little girl in your car. What possible explanation is going to work for that?*

She wished the CD player would stop spitting the discs back out. She wanted to hear her father's CD. Well, it wasn't really her father's, but he was on it, playing his saxophone with Miles Davis on quite a few of the live recordings. She found out about that by accident. Her father had left them when Elise was seven. He'd called and sent Christmas and birthday cards, and during her twelfth summer, she went to stay with him and a new woman in Chicago for three weeks. But then she didn't hear much after that, and her mother never offered a thing. One day she'd been flipping through some record albums and saw her father's name, *Phillip Fisher - Saxophone*, on the back, on a recording by another group she'd never heard of before or since: *The South Side*. She brought the record to her mother.

"Is this Daddy?"

Mrs. Abigail Fisher had put down the calligraphy-style pen she liked to write with and took the album cover from Elise's hands. She brought it to her nose and inhaled. "That was many many years ago," she said, which was much more than Elise had expected her to say. "I used to love this record."

"Can I have it?" Elise said too quickly.

The familiar window shade descended over her mother's eyes. "I don't need it anymore," she said coldly. "Yes, daughter. You can have it. And yes, this was your father. His music took him."

From that point on, Elise scoured record stores looking for anything her father might have played on, hoping that she could learn something about him from the arrangements of notes, the type of musician he chose to work with, the venue—anything at all that would bring him somehow into her body. She played the record too many times. The grooves wore out and eventually it was unplayable, and not too long after that record players went away. They're available again, hipster-cool, in lime green, lemon and orange colors, so she bought one for their bedroom, and every few months she conducts a random eBay search for *The South Side Jazz Quartet: Lady Luck,* looks through the music on Amazon, flips through stacks of records at garage sales and antique stores, but she'd never seen that album again. The cover was a deep forest green, the type simple, white block letters. Sometimes the album cover floats through her dreams like a screen saver, bouncing from one side of her mind to the other, holding her in place.

Katrina wasn't sleeping. Her blue eyes took in everything in the car—the automatic window button, the sun visors, the cup holders, the crumpled fast food bags on the floor, the occasional stray ketchup packet. She'd look at something in the car and then follow with her fingers, delicately tracing its edges until she was satisfied.

"Sorry the car is a mess," Elise said.

Katrina shrugged. She stretched her arm toward the steering wheel, but because she was buckled in, couldn't reach.

Elise smiled. "You want to drive?"

"How else you going to know where to take me?"

"I thought I would take you to my mother's house and—" *and what?* "And then we could get some rest and in the morning you could show me where your mama lives. It's going to be dark by the time we get to Savannah."

Katrina stroked Mama Bear's remaining green ear, pressed her lips together and nodded. "My mama waiting."

"We could call her. I have a cell phone you could use."

"She don't have a phone. I tell Mama Bear and she'll tell mama."

Elise remembered other children's mothers would sew tags into their offspring's clothes with their name, address, and phone number in case they wandered off. Her own mother never did that of course *(What child of mine doesn't have enough sense to get herself back home if she walks away from it?)* She knew the kids with the tags were embarrassed by them, but Elise always saw the perfect stitching and the block print letters as fingerprints of love.

Katrina put the Miles Davis CD in.

"It's not working, honey," said Elise.

But the CD player didn't eject its disk and the opening bars of her father's saxophone filled the car.

"He plays nice," said Katrina, and closed her eyes.

6

Pistachio sat on the kitchen table's edge, rocking her feet back and forth. Mrs. Abigail Fisher hadn't come downstairs yet and Pistachio was reluctant to go back upstairs into the bedroom, for fear she'd end up back in the corner of the musty closet once again. The fire's heat had peeled the wallpaper back, revealing several underlayers of thick floral paper, their ends curling, the glue sticky once again. She crossed her legs, shifted her weight to accommodate the table, and waited to figure out what to do. Even though she was fully grown at slightly over five feet tall, she was flat, like a paper doll, weighing just twenty-one pounds. She had a front and a back, a left and a right, but very little middle. Decades of being pressed between pages like a clover had left her stiff and uncertain. She was also lopsided, her chest having the slightest bit of expansion to it, her rib cage almost wide enough to accommodate a full-sized pair of lungs and a heart.

She had been in the early stages of developing when the cut came that sent her to the closet floor with all the other quarter-formed and half-formed creations, writhing around together among the shoes and coat hems. Many of them were dead before they hit the floor; vital organs not yet established. Some were aberrations with oversized heads or no limbs or eyes at the base of their skulls. Those characters never drew a breath, miscarriages of the story. But there were others, like Pistachio, who had developed enough before their executions to retain life even in the mass graves that peppered every writer's backyard. There were others, even in Mrs. Abigail Fisher's closet, and when Pistachio finally found another, after seasons of feeling certain of her aloneness, the possible directions for their stories multiplied.

She leapt off the table. She had no time to think about Harold right now, not now, or what may have become of him; she had to figure out what to do next—how to become three-dimensional, maybe even four-dimensional if she were lucky enough to have a reader's eyes dance over her words and bring her to yet another kind of life. Some characters were immortal, residing in various forms in the recesses of human brains all across the world, not to mention waiting for more readers in libraries, bookstores, and the web. Others had a short shelf life, relegated to the remainder table before their first year in the world. Still others only lived with their writers in computer files or desk drawers, spending their entire lives crawling around on yellowed notebook paper trying to find a way to get into the larger world.

It had been the internet that made the transition possible for all of them—all of these forgotten lives—to try again at a life, to try again to achieve their potential. When books became digitized, the characters got jolted with electricity, enough so that some of them were able to transcend their particular stories. Without hard covers pressing them into puzzle pieces on bookshelves and under beds, they were able to stretch and reach and eventually jump out of their coffins and make their own way. Pistachio didn't understand it; she didn't understand dimensions or technology or multiple incarnations. But she did understand she'd been cut, and she did understand the cut hadn't healed and even more than that, she understood that she wanted something different from her creator. She didn't want to be on the closet floor. She was Pistachio Simmons and she had things she needed to say.

She allowed herself one more passing thought of Harold (his extra-long eyelashes whispering from his flattened face) before pushing it away. Later. She'd let herself remember later.

7

Elise began feeling her usual panic as she crossed the South Carolina/Georgia state line. She always wished Savannah were deeper in, all the way to the Florida Keys so she'd have more time to transition from her current life to her old one. The worlds that stretched between the eastern North Carolina mountains and coastal Savannah were more than Elise could count. She needed more than the few miles of Georgia land to get herself ready to face her mother. This time, the panic was two-fold. She was starting to realize the magnitude of having an entire person sitting next to her in the car. An underage person. A young girl. What *had* she been thinking? What made sense several hours ago began to crash in on her as the ridiculous choice it had been. Katrina was still sleeping; the sun hadn't gotten as low in the sky as she'd hoped, and she wished she had a reason to stop at a café for a cup of coffee, but she was afraid of waking Katrina and having to tell her that she had made a terrible mistake and needed to call social services. Because that was what had happened, right? She'd made a terrible mistake. She'd meant well, as many often do, but she should have called when she first saw Katrina. She should have at least called Henry. Katrina's fingers rubbed the edges of the bear's ear and she made a soft cooing.

"God damn it," Elise said accidentally out loud.

The CD wasn't over yet, though her father's role had ended two songs earlier. She liked the last two tracks though. They featured a cello and a female vocalist who was uncredited on the liner notes.

The woman's voice, a cross between Esperanza Spalding's and Miriam Stockley's, had always evoked a tear. The woman harmonized, singing no actual words, but her voice was enough to make Elise believe she could transcend the entire world on one note. It was precisely because she was listening to that voice that Elise didn't notice the state of her mother's house. She pulled into the sandy driveway on autopilot, closed her eyes and listened for a few final seconds to the haunting voice before shutting off the engine. When she opened her eyes, Katrina had already gotten out of the car, holding Mama Bear close to her chest. Elise opened the driver's side door and started to call for her, but instead she watched.

The girl had slipped her ragged sandals off in the car, so she walked barefoot on the overgrown yard, sidestepping glass bottles and overturned wheelbarrows like she was playing hopscotch. Elise focused on Katrina, but even so, she could not deny the wreck that was once her house. Katrina stopped to touch dead leaves and run her tiny fingers over rotted wood that sprang from the sides of the porch. She whispered something to nothing, as far as Elise could see, and then waited for the response.

"Katrina, come put your shoes on." Elise closed the car door and held out the sandals.

Katrina wouldn't approach her. She stood defiantly, legs a triangle, and said, "How you know where my mama is?"

"I don't. That's why we have to call somebody. You see, I shouldn't have brought you here. It's not that I don't like you, it's just that you're obviously someone's child and they're probably worried sick about you and—"

Katrina wasn't listening. Her head tilted toward her right shoulder. In the waning light, she was almost a shadow. "I am somebody's child and she has been worried about me. I asked how you know where she lives?"

Elise took a few steps forward, but stopped when Katrina edged even further into the darkness. "Like I said, I don't. I'm not sure what you mean. Come on, honey. At least put your shoes on. There could be all kinds of rotted nails and things back there."

"My feet'll be fine. How you know my mama lives here?"

Elise looked up at the collapsing mansion, no longer able to block out its broken windows and peeling paint. "My mama lives here, Katrina. Not yours."

"That's not what Mama Bear say."

She wished desperately for Henry. He would be able to coax the girl out of the trees, slide her shoes on, and convince her that they weren't at her house after all, and Katrina would think only better of him for it. He had that kind of way with children, and Elise knew how it gnawed at him every day the way his daughter wrote him out of her life, blamed him for what happened in Boston. His notes and phone calls went unanswered, and some nights, when he twitched in his sleep, he shouted his daughter's name.

"What does Mama Bear say?"

"Mama Bear say this is where my mama is. What she don't understand is how you found it. Are you a devil?"

Depends on who you ask, she thought. "I don't think so, Katrina. I think I'm mostly nice."

The approaching dark cloaked the worst of the house. Elise had the picture in her mind of her childhood home, one of the grand historic homes Savannah is famous for. There were three floors plus a basement and a large attic with five windows. Two fireplaces, one in the kitchen and one upstairs in her mother's room, served mostly as decoration, but at one time had been the only source of heat. A wide porch wrapped around three sides of the house, and visitors, when they had any, didn't know which door to knock on. The house was much too big for her and her mother, much too big even when they'd been a larger family, and Elise didn't understand why her mother held onto it, other than the reasoning that the South's First Lady of Letters should live in a Southern mansion, complete with a parlor, a formal dining room, and at least one closed off room.

Katrina made her way toward the porch steps. There were three of them, the bottom two collapsed in on themselves. Elise followed her, stepping over the broken stairs. Katrina held Mama Bear up to the first bay window she could reach. Elise couldn't see anything inside except the graying edges of the lace curtains.

"Mama Bear says we go inside."

The child was off; there was no doubting that. Something about her didn't quite fit. Except for the red clay stains on her skin, she looked like a normal young girl. Her purple-blue eye color, though unusual, was not unheard of. She even had the requisite missing two front teeth. Her proportions were awkward, extremely long arms and feet, a shortened torso, and a severe, almost masculine jawline, but any of those could be attributed to childhood's fingerprints. It takes a human awhile to grow into its final shape.

It was then Elise caught the smell. Katrina had her hand on the screen doorknob when it hit her from behind, spiraling around her and finally hovering in front of her. The scent's fingers wrapped around her throat, holding her in place. Elise reached for her neck, but grasped at nothing. Katrina watched her.

"What's the matter?" the girl asked.

Elise gasped as the hand left her throat. "Can't you smell that? All of a sudden it came up behind me."

"I just smell the outside," she said. "Smells like outside. Outside has everything in it, so I guess it stink sometimes."

The smell wasn't a stink, not exactly. It was sweet, like a young girl's drugstore perfume, with undertones of ash and salt. And it had density, like a skunk's odor, only she couldn't see a skunk or any other creature that might be releasing its scent. She stepped closer toward the house and the scent dissipated a little. Katrina opened the screen door and pushed the thick oak door open. It had not only been unlocked, but the door had been cracked. Had it not been dusk, Elise would have likely noticed that from the driveway.

"Mama?" said Elise, stepping over the threshold, dodging stacks of molding newspapers and unopened mail.

"Mama?" said Katrina, holding Mama Bear in front of her like a compass.

The foyer mirror that had always been meticulously polished had a thick film on it. Elise saw only a shadow of herself when she turned reflexively as she had as a child to check her hair when entering the house.

"Why does Mama live in the dark?" asked Katrina.

Elise flipped the hall light switch. Nothing. Oh God, she thought. Had her mother been living without electricity? She should have come down sooner. It's only a day's drive. She just hadn't wanted to, and as she stood in the darkening entryway, she knew it was for this reason, not the one she'd always told herself. She didn't want to imagine her mother's dying. It was so unlikely for her, she'd decided it wasn't happening. Sure, the house needed repair; the yard needed cleanup, but her mother? The esteemed Mrs. Abigail Fisher was immortal. No one, not even death, would ever be able to touch her.

Elise looked at the layers of debris on the floor, and she knew the dark that had descended on the house was not from the setting sun but from something permanent. Her father's green leather chair remained in the receiving room where he'd left it decades ago. Her mother had responded, not by donating the chair to charity, or even taking it to the dump as many women might be inclined to do, but by simply closing off the room where the chair, and Elise's father, had spent so much time. She sat in it slowly, unsure of what was on the seat, or even if the legs would hold. They did, and she pretended she could smell the zing of her father's shaving cream as she sat, again a little girl on his lap while he read a story, or even better when he played the saxophone.

"For you, beautiful one," he'd say, picking up his instrument and playing a simple scale, ending in a flourish that made her jump and squeal. "For my special girl."

The notes were only in her head; Elise knew that. The aftershave long gone. Her sadness had ceased being sharp, overgrown with layers of excuses and re-rememberings until she held close the story she wanted to know: *Her father, a beautiful, mythic man, used to play her songs on his saxophone. Her father, too beautiful, too mythic, for small-town life, left to follow his muse, his dream, and because his dream was so powerful, so great, he disappeared into his dream and couldn't come back to play music for his daughter anymore. It was not his fault the dream was so big. It was not his fault. He was only the carrier of the music. He could not direct its fate.*

8

Pistachio heard the front door open. Two voices bounced off the walls. She stood straight along the wall, arms branched like a coat-rack. She didn't know exactly how to behave when she wasn't working in harmony with Mrs. Abigail Fisher's pen. Maybe she thought something and Mrs. Abigail Fisher gave her ink and that ink somehow became fuel which helped her live. She felt brittle and a little silly standing in the kitchen, arms like antlers, but she wasn't sure who was in the house and she had no idea who, if anyone, could see her, and frankly, she didn't know if she could have any kind of dialogue with anyone if no one was there to put the quotation marks around her words, holding them in sacred, suspended conversation.

The downstairs sounds grew closer. She thought if she lowered her arms she might become thinner and blend in to the walls, so she tried, waiting to determine whether or not the people were threats. Harold had told her that people couldn't see them with their eyes. People needed to see the words on the page in order to make them spring to life. "Something magic goes on," he said. "They see those lines and dots and they make a whole being with it. They make us."

"Mrs. Abigail Fisher made me."

"No," said Harold. "Mrs. Abigail Fisher planted you. Only a reader can make you be."

Pistachio had marveled at that as she and Harold folded into each other in the closet. She hardly dared utter her thought. "So if there's no readers..."

"Then there's no us."

The notebooks behind them buzzed with half-lives and entire scenes. There was even a whole lifetime, a whole novel, at the very bottom of the stack. The notebooks were too heavy for Pistachio and Harold to push them off so they could set free whoever was in the pages, but they knew it was something fierce and heavy. The buzzing never stopped. They slept each night with its thrumming; their tiny paper hearts expanding with each pulse.

9

Elise wished she had a flashlight, or at least a smarter phone that could possibly double as a flashlight if necessary. She flipped open her dumb phone to use whatever glow she could from the small screen. The oak door that had once barricaded the way into the receiving room and Elise's father's chair hung on one hinge. As a girl, she'd climb in through the window to sit in it. Elise hadn't realized the door had been already open when she stepped through. She'd just been compelled to sit in the chair again. The room seemed larger, even in the almost-dark. As Elise's eyes adjusted somewhat, she saw Katrina standing on the other side of what once had been a wall, complete with ancestral daguerreotypes and black and whites in the expected dark wood frames.

"Be careful when you come out," said Katrina. "There's a lot of mess here on the floor from where this wall fell in."

Elise was going to have to call some kind of social agency because the house was far beyond clutter. It was unsafe, so when she finally located the proper hotline, maybe she could find something to do with Katrina that would be legal and would also make Henry proud, once he got over the fact that she'd transported a minor across a state line.

"Somebody's coming," said Katrina, and she leapt over the rubble from the wall and pressed herself against Elise.

The flicker of a candle or a kerosene lantern glowed in the foyer. Elise hadn't heard anyone come down the stairs.

"It's not Mama," Katrina whispered, slipping Mama Bear into her shirt.

"Daughter." Mrs. Abigail Fisher spoke, though Elise still couldn't see her, and she spoke without the command she usually held with each word. "Daughter, I seem to have lost the light."

"Mother, stay right where you are. I'll come to you."

Katrina grabbed Elise's leg. "Don't! That's not Mama!"

"That's my mama, silly girl."

When Elise reached her mother, who was only a few steps away but had been hidden behind the door, she found she wasn't holding a candle or a kerosene lantern, but a battery operated train lantern, the kind that men used to swing back and forth to indicate the approaching locomotive.

"Where on earth did you get that thing?" Elise asked.

Mrs. Abigail Fisher handed it to Elise. "You take it. I'm tired of carrying it."

"What happened to the electricity?" *And the entire house?*

"The firestarter took it away."

"The firestarter?"

"The thing in the kitchen who started the fire. That's why you came, isn't it? The fire department called you. Told you I tried to burn the house down. You're here to take me away."

Were there daughters somewhere on the planet who had normal reunions with their mothers, maybe with a hug, a glass of wine, some clean sheets?

"The men came with the dumpster this morning."

The dumpster! Of course. That had to have been the smell she'd noticed.

"I know why you're here."

"Mother, I'm here because I love you and I want you to be safe."

"I am safe. I just have to find the firestarter and get her out of here."

Elise held the lantern, which was more of a beacon, above her head. Did all parents shrink, or did children simply get larger? Her mother had never been tall, but she'd filled every space she'd ever occupied. The woman in front of her was stooped, her hair, always in a meticulous bun held in place with a gold filigree pin, had thinned so much her skull shone through, the pin now holding the strands together in the middle of her back. She wore a belted dusty rose housecoat, and military-style boots on her feet. She'd have never imagined her mother in such unfeminine footwear, but the house was collapsing. It was no doubt practical to have steel toes. Her mother's hazel eyes swam under a milky film, cataracts she knew had been there for years, but her mother had refused to go have them treated. "I like blurry," she said once. "It makes the world easier." To complete the look, her mother had applied her characteristic orange lipstick.

"I got your letters," Elise said, because any other daughter would have held her mother, taken her to a hotel, cleaned her up and made her hot tea, but Elise had no idea how to do any of that.

Mrs. Abigail Fisher nodded curtly. "You shouldn't have come. I wrote that last one in a fugue state. I didn't mean to imply that I needed anything."

"More writing exercises then?"

"Everything is a writing exercise."

"Let's go upstairs to bed."

Mrs. Abigail Fisher turned her head away, her aquiline nose still fierce and prominent. "I don't utilize the upstairs rooms anymore."

"What do you mean?"

"The fire, you know. The smell. Just too much so I moved downstairs. And imagine my surprise when I came downstairs and found your father's chair. After all these years, still here."

"It's here because you never threw it out."

"Nonsense. I threw it out years ago and now it's come back. It's a symbol, don't you think? I adore symbols."

This woman had once sparred on Dick Cavett with Norman Mailer. This woman had launched a literary feud in the *New York Times Book Review* with Christina Fair, whose book beat Mrs. Abigail Fisher's Southern masterpiece, *The Garden of Gethsemane, Georgia*, for the National Book Award. This woman had a lifelong correspondence with Truman Capote, and wrote not one, not two, not three, but seventeen novels over the course of her career.

"Give me the light, daughter. You don't know how to use it."

Elise surrendered the beacon to her mother as she marveled at how she could be both so frail and so fierce. *Paradox!* her mother would say. It was one of her favorite literary tools. Mrs. Abigail Fisher held the light above her head, a garish and intimidating hat. The glare struck Elise directly in the eyes.

"Where is your male companion?" asked Mrs. Abigail Fisher.

"He's at home, Mother."

"He couldn't be bothered to come see me? I am frail and in quite a state, apparently."

"He had work to do."

"They brought the dumpster today. I suspect you'll be putting me in it and carting me off to the sea. I have always rather fantasized about a dramatic end. Be careful, daughter, for I have left notes all over this house and you will be found out. One way or another, you will not get away with sending me into the waves. At least dear Virginia Woolf chose the water. But I, if it is to be, shall find myself the victim of matricide. Which, daughter, I must give you credit, isn't used much anymore and is quite the universal device. Please put the beacon in my barge as well. I should truly hate to face death in the dark." She shook the beacon, casting dancing beams along the peeling walls and then lowered the lamp.

"I'm not going to put you out to sea, Mother," she said, though she was briefly thrilled by the thought of her mother adrift in a dumpster with only a beacon for company.

"We'll see about that."

"Yes, we will," Elise muttered.

The crash on the third floor startled them both, and for a moment Elise saw the fear in her mother's eyes. She regrouped quickly.

"The wind," Mrs. Abigail Fisher said. "The most extraordinary thing has happened with the wind. It has taken up residence inside the house. Did you know that an element could do such a thing? Simply splendid."

"I think that was in the attic." Elise hadn't been up in the attic since she was a child. It had been one of her favorite hiding places. There were trunks of antebellum clothes and even a family crest with a dark blue shield, a honeysuckle vine and a rattlesnake. Her mother had told her it belonged to the Scruggs, who have been in the South since before it was even part of America and she should be proud. "Who are the Scruggs?" she'd asked.

"We," her mother had said. "We are Scruggs."

"I thought we were Fishers."

Elise's father had not yet gone. Her baby sister had not yet been born.

"Your father is a Fisher, and I agreed to take his name because it would be easier for him. But we are Scruggs." Mrs. Abigail Fisher had straightened, threw her shoulders back and tapped her chest. "Lineage follows the mother. Remember that daughter. You formed in *me*."

Mrs. Abigail Fisher put the beacon on the floor. The light cast triangles across the hardwood. "I don't know as anyone can get in the attic anymore. Something appears to have happened to the stairs."

"Katrina!" said Elise, realizing she hadn't seen the child since her mother appeared.

"Elise, darling," said Mrs. Abigail Fisher. "I said the wind was living in the house, not a hurricane. Besides, dear, that hurricane was five years ago. It would be highly unusual for any of it to still be trapped in this house, don't you think?"

Elise felt the scream that had been living in her belly for more years than she could remember start to unfurl. She started to wonder: Did the dumpster have wheels? Could she just push it to the river? Was there a lid? If her mother accidentally fell (and really, who could avoid it in the state of this house) and found herself in the metal canister, would anyone really notice? Would anyone think to wonder where she went? The scream, as usual, stretched itself in silence and wiggled its lips around before returning to its cage. Snap out of it, Elise. The first murder was an accident. If you committed this one, no one would believe you didn't mean to.

"Not the hurricane, Mother. The child. Didn't you see her when you came downstairs?"

"Cataracts, dear. And it is so dark." She picked the beacon up again. "And are you telling me you have lost both your male companion and a child? You never told me you had a daughter. But that would have required you to write to me or pick up the phone and I know you've been just too busy up in Banner Elk or Boone or Blowing Rock or some B-place trying to teach literature to kids. Don't worry dear. Please, just introduce me to my grandchild."

"Katrina is not my child! I picked her up on the side of the road and—"

Her mother's terrible smile began to tug at the edges of her sunken lips. "Really? You picked her up on the side of the road? How *interesting*. That is an act of much greater bravery than I would have given you credit for. Maybe one day you'll write a story."

This time the scream beat its way past her lips. The vibrations hurt her throat. Mrs. Abigail Fisher stood straight and still, waiting until it was over.

"I see your lungs are in fine shape. You must have given up smoking, then?"

"I never smoked, Mother. You smoked. Daddy smoked. I never smoked. Maybe you started smoking again and that's how the kitchen caught fire. Maybe you forgot where you put your butt and before you knew it, everything exploded."

"Daughter, I believe the B-town where you've been residing has diminished your syntax."

Elise opened her mouth.

"Ah," said Mrs. Abigail Fisher. "I know what you're thinking. If you put me in the dumpster, I shall haunt you the rest of your days. I have never written a ghost story such as the one you'd be living."

Elise had enough. "Do you honestly think you're not haunting me every day of my life anyway?"

"There's no need for melodrama, dear. It's a cheap manipulation. Here, you take the light and go find my grandchild. I'm going to rest here for a minute in your father's chair. It's quite remarkable that it's back. Magical realism is such a hard thing to explain to the world, but it happens all the time."

Just shut up, Elise told herself. Don't give her another line. How long has she been here? Ten minutes? Twenty minutes? Her mother had quite the gift for elongating time. It was a quality book reviewers often noticed and praised. She felt silly with a train lantern inside a collapsing house chasing a child with a prescient stuffed bear. A bar from a Johnny Cash train song rumbled through her brain and she allowed herself a laugh. How Mother hated the Man in Black. "Too affected," she would say. "He's withholding too much from the audience."

10

Pistachio folded into herself and rested in the shape of an envelope flat on the floor. She was trying to calm her shaking. She was afraid she rattled. It was clear that whoever came into the house was not leaving anytime soon. She was shaking because of what had bar-reled through the charred kitchen moments ago. She didn't know what it was, only that it moved quicker than she could and didn't have the girth of a human. It was a feral thing. Scampered. That's the word. The thing was scampering and Pistachio had been mind-ing her own business trying to look like a coat rack when the thing knocked her down and headed for the attic. She wasn't equipped for this. Harold was better at the ways of the different worlds. He'd been in more of them. One night he whispered to her that he'd been a main character in at least six of Mrs. Abigail Fisher's books, but always at the last minute she cut him out. He showed her the scars on his legs, arms, and torso. He'd gone on many adventures in these stories before he was excommunicated from them. He'd know what the thing was that had knocked her over.

The stranger was coming up the stairs with that enormous light. She got to the landing and stopped as if she'd hit a wall. The strang-er was a woman, and Pistachio knew from the sharply angled nose that she was part of her creator, Mrs. Abigail Fisher. This woman was rounder, much rounder, and rather than enhance her face, as the nose did for Mrs. Abigail Fisher, on this woman, the nose sim-ply stood out, a beak in a round pie plate face. Her hair was frizzy, but her eyes were clear. The woman put the lantern on the kitchen table. Her eyes filled with tears. Pistachio held her breath, tried to squish her random shaking into the very smallest part of herself.

"Oh, Mama," said the woman as she took in the blackened stove, the curled calendar on the wall, the colonial cabinetry that was now a skeleton of itself. The crisped calendar was opened to September 1987. The table held stacks of unopened bills and letters, many now unreadable. The woman covered her nose, coughed. "At least the window's open," she said, referring to the kitchen window that had blown out during the fire. The woman slid out a kitchen chair, held the lantern up to it, picked up the chair and pressed it back to the floor, testing the legs, and then sat. The papers and bills disintegrated when she touched them, leaving her tiny fingers with soot stains. Pistachio surprised herself by wanting to unfold herself and wrap her skinny arms around this human, but she thought that would be more than she could take. The woman's mouth hung open as if she were trying to say something, or trying to cry, but nothing came out. Her face was frozen in its attempt to express itself, but Pistachio could see the tapping of the woman's feet on the floor, and she could feel the dance of sorrow and rage flowing out of them. Those emotions made Pistachio shake even more, made her frustrated by her lack of dimensionality or ability to communicate with anyone directly. The woman inhaled sharply and the exhale had a hint of a sob. She took out her cell phone and dialed.

"Henry," the woman said. "My mother is gone."

Pistachio panicked, stretched out her leg and kicked a frying pan that had fallen during the fire. Gone? If Mrs. Abigail Fisher was gone, then how would she find her story?

"No, not missing," said the woman. "But I don't know where she is."

Pistachio slid her foot back. She didn't think the woman noticed the noise.

"I found a girl. I'll have to tell you tomorrow. I have to find her now. I think she's lost in the house."

A girl? Was that what rushed past her?

"I'll call you tomorrow. I just wanted you to know I got here. The house is unlivable." She paused, wiped something from her cheek. "I have to find the girl now, honey. I'll talk to you in the morning." She closed the phone and slipped it back into her pocket.

A girl? Pistachio unfurled herself and slid under the woman's tapping feet and out of the kitchen.

11

Elise was afraid to lean back in the chair. Nothing in the house was stable. Henry had almost yelled at her on the phone. That was before she heard him change his tone to the one he used when arresting mental patients. She had somehow become her mother's daughter—crazy stories and all. The house was silent. Her mother, she assumed, was sitting in the dark downstairs in her father's chair. Katrina was somewhere—who could know in a place like this? She might have fallen under the floorboards in the attic and been swept away into an alternate reality that was probably much more healthy than this one.

"Katrina!" she shouted. A pause.

"Daughter, it isn't the hurricane! It's the wind." If her mother had held a cane, she would have punctuated the statement with three loud thumps against the rotten wood.

Elise imagined the surprise the fire had given her mother. Since she hadn't meant to start the fire, the shock of the flames would have cost her precious seconds of reaction time. The cabinet above the stove would have caught first, shattering family china. Would it have spread left and then right? Or both sides at the same time? And her mother, frozen in the middle of such heat, such wind, where would she have gone? How would she have gotten out? And why was she not burned? She wouldn't even let the paramedics take her in for a check up. She signed the required release, stating, "I'm fine," and moved on. She imagined her mother standing there, flames shrieking across the floor, fire eating oxygen until it demanded more and blew the two kitchen windows out into shards. Would her mother have gasped then, taking the oxygen out of the fire's raging mouth, and would she then have screamed? Images from films she'd seen of characters burning at the stake took over. Did people melt like the Wicked Witch when she was doused with water? Did they morph into Salvador Dali-esque creations until there was nothing but smoke? She couldn't imagine her mother doing any of those things. No earthly element was capable of transforming her into something else.

"It's not a hurricane. It's not the wind. It's a girl, Mother."

"I'm sorry, dear, did you say something?"

The lantern was powerful, and Elise imagined how strange the house must look to someone observing from the outside, a single light bouncing from room to room. But then she remembered the entire house was collapsing, and the neighborhood, a gentrified street in an historic section of town, must be furious over the state of the property. A bouncing light wouldn't make any difference to neighbors who'd probably long ago taken every reasonable measure to avoid ever looking at the esteemed Mrs. Abigail Fisher's crumbling home. They're going to have to tear it down, Elise realized. It's long past condemned.

"Daughter!"

"I'm up here, Mother."

"Whilst you have been up there dallying with the ghost of a hurricane, I have been sitting in the dark."

It's every time, she thought. Every time she has a glimmer of compassion open up in her heart, every time she feels that ancient ache of love for her mother, Mrs. Abigail Fisher slices it out and hands it back to her. "When you live in a house without electricity, you'll find it's dark half of every day."

"I'm sorry, did you speak?"

Elise and her father would have breakfast at this ruined table. They ate bowls of cereal on wax placemats with pictures of the state of Georgia and its historic Civil War battle sites on them. Her father read the paper, pulled out the comics page for her, and drank dark percolated coffee. She enjoyed orange juice in her favorite small glass with actual oranges printed on it. She liked when what was on the outside of something matched what was on the inside. Her mother would be asleep. She always slept through breakfast.

"She writes all night," her father said. "She's making stories." He smoked a pipe. After he left for good, Elise found a half-full tobacco pouch on the porch swing. She carried it to her room and placed it under her pillow and slept with its scent peppering her dreams.

"I want Mama to be awake when I'm awake," she said.

"I know," her father said. "But you have me. We're awake together while your mother is asleep. Isn't that grand? Think of the fun things we can do."

This was before the baby Courtney Lynn came. This was when the kitchen still had new cotton curtains in the sparkling window, when the house was part of one of the many historic tours of Savannah, when the world was still calling for her mother and the worlds she created in the dark.

"You left me, Daddy," Elise whispered to the lantern. "You left me and Mother is still here."

She waited a beat, as she'd always done, for a reply that never came.

"That's what I thought," she said.

"Daughter!" Mrs. Abigail Fisher shouted from the first floor. "The firestarter is down here."

"You are the firestarter, Mother."

"Daughter!"

She took the lantern and moved carefully down the stairs. This time she was the one holding the lantern above her head peering into the shadows. She was surprised at how her eyes had already acclimated. Her mother was ramrod straight in her father's chair, thin hair spiraling out of her head. She clasped her housecoat closed with her left hand, which still, to Elise's surprise, wore her wedding set. Without turning her body, Mrs. Abigail Fisher pointed to a corner of the room with her eyes. "There. The firestarter is over there."

Elise shone the lantern into the corner. China cabinet. The edge of an Oriental rug. Thick burgundy drapes.

"There's nothing there, Mother."

Mrs. Abigail Fisher pressed her lips together, then spoke. "Why is it, child, that no matter how many times I show you the world, you simply refuse to see it?"

12

Pistachio was tired of hiding in plain sight. It was one thing when there had been only the two of them, but now there was another human and another creature. She jumped out from behind the drapes. No reaction from the strange woman.

"I don't have to see you to know you're there," said Mrs. Abigail Fisher.

"Why can't you see me, Mother? I'm right in front of you. Look." She swayed the lantern back and forth. "It's me. Your daughter with the mega flashlight."

"I'm not talking to you. I'm talking to the firestarter."

"There is no firestarter."

Pistachio waved her hands in the air.

"Where is my granddaughter?"

"There is no granddaughter."

"Well, once again we are at an impasse. If I were writing this scene, I would have an unexpected character enter the room now."

And then you'd cut them out, thought Pistachio. And then you'd leave them on the floor. You wouldn't even see if they were dead. You'd just twist the pen in and pull it out and close us in the dark. She smacked the back of Mrs. Abigail Fisher's head.

"Did you not see that, daughter?"

"What?"

"The firestarter hit me on the head." Mrs. Abigail Fisher raised her voice. "You could have the decency to show yourself. My daughter thinks I am crazy."

Pistachio crossed in front of the woman's lantern, but to her dismay, her body didn't break up the beam. She was surprised by the heat of the light. She hadn't thought it would be warm.

"There, Elise," said Mrs. Abigail Fisher. "Did you see that? The firestarter walked right in front of you."

"Maybe the firestarter walked right in front of you, Mother. Or maybe you're making the whole thing up like you make up everything."

"I'm cut by that, daughter."

You don't know what that means, thought Pistachio. You don't know what that's like. The iron poker for the long-defunct fireplace shone in the lantern's glow. Pistachio imagined wielding it like a pen. She would cut Mrs. Abigail Fisher first in the abdomen, just enough. Then she would draw lines on the insides of her arms, vertical ones, not the cry-for-help horizontal cuts. She'd wait a long while before severing her head. She picked up the poker, but it was too heavy and slipped out of her thin, flat hands.

"Katrina!" said Elise.

"That was the *firestarter*."

Pistachio pressed her foot over the poker and froze. The creature was there beside the pie-faced human. She couldn't tell if the creature was a male or female, or even if it was human at all. Its eyes glowed purple in a triangular face, flat-cat ears on its head, and a body that seemed to spiral into itself; its core a pulsing amethyst. The thing carried a green book in front of her. Elise put her arms around the creature, patted its head.

"Where have you been?" asked Elise.

"Mama Bear and me went exploring."

Pistachio heard the words as a hiss, a growl that turned itself into consonants and vowels.

"You can't just go off like that. We need to find your mother."

Mrs. Abigail Fisher cleared her throat. "Daughter. Do you need a moment to finish your phone call?"

"I'm not on the phone. I'm talking to Katrina." She pushed the feral thing toward Mrs. Abigail Fisher. "Katrina, go say hello to my mother."

"That's not my mother," said Katrina.

"Daughter, there is no one with you."

Pistachio held her breath. She crouched to pick up the poker stick with both hands. If the creature made a move toward her, she would not wait. Harold had told her one night of an adventure story he'd been a part of. He'd been a warrior, riding a horse in the Battle at Antietam. He'd gotten to use his bayonet more than once before he was removed from the story. He told her if she ever found herself in such a narrative, that she was to get as low to the ground as possible, hold her weapon in front of her with both hands and then leap and thrust simultaneously with all the force she could. She may only get one chance, he told her. She could never be certain what skills her enemy may possess. The poker was cold in her hands.

"Say hello to my mother," said Elise.

The creature held out its claw, a malformed hook. Mrs. Abigail Fisher didn't reach for it. "Hello Mother," the creature said.

"No, honey," said Elise. "This is my mother. We still have to find your mother."

The thing turned, unhinged its jaw and let out a yell. Pistachio clutched the poker harder, shifted her feet in the dust.

"Katrina, honey. I told you your mother wasn't here."

The creature opened the book and began to read. "I went into the garden one day and saw the snake. I didn't know why the snake was there until it opened its mouth to bite me."

"I can't very well help you if you can't tell me more than that," said Elise.

What? Pistachio wondered if perhaps she heard something different from Elise.

"When the snake bit me, I knew I had come home," said the thing.

"I know it's not really a very nice home anymore," said Elise. "It was different once." She stroked the creature's head, rubbed its ears. Its spiral tail curled around her legs. It closed the book.

"Daughter, would you agree that we are at an impasse this evening? Why don't we sleep, and in the morning you can stab me with the fire poker and put me in the dumpster. I should like one more night of sleep before then, if you don't mind."

"I'm not going to put you in the dumpster."

"Shhh, dear. It's all right. You are only behaving as I have created you. I have no one to blame but myself." Mrs. Abigail Fisher stretched out on the floor, pulling a crocheted afghan on top of her body.

Elise shook her head, put down the lantern, and lay down next to her mother. The creature, its book tight in its hands, padded over to Elise and wrapped itself around her. Elise kissed its head and turned off the lamp.

"Daughter?"

"Yes, Mother."

"If indeed I should die before I wake, I have written my obituary. It is in the nightstand drawer in my room."

"Of course, Mother."

Pistachio set the poker down softly and lay down next to Mrs. Abigail Fisher. The author's eyes sank deeper into her face when they were closed, and her mouth, which had seemed so large, was only a thin line. Pistachio touched her white hair, the texture still silky. "Good night," Pistachio whispered, and when she pressed up against Mrs. Abigail Fisher's brittle bones, she was surprised to feel her own skeleton expanding.

13

Elise's dreams were vibrant in the way that often comes with sleep in unfamiliar places. When she was a girl, she never slept in the receiving room, and she certainly had never slept next to her mother. As she drifted, arms wrapped around Katrina, who held Mama Bear against her belly, she wanted to roll over and put her arms around her mother. She wanted to know, even if her mother was sleeping, what it felt like to press against her body and know she came from that woman and that the woman was glad about it. Still fantasizing. Still hoping for something that was never going to come. Even lying on a rotting floor in a partially burned down house didn't stop her inner child from engaging in magical thinking. Katrina's hair smelled mossy and she slept with her mouth open, right leg twitching like a dog's. If her mother smelled of anything, it was paper, the moldy kind you find in old places, the kind that hadn't been touched in a very long time. A small crash upstairs made Katrina open her eyes, but she quickly closed them and turned toward Elise. Any number of things could be falling, Elise reasoned. There's not one thing in this house that's hanging on tight.

The first dream was one of sound. Ocean waves crashing against piers. Boats creaking and snapping against thick rope moorings. A flute far off, following the cries of gulls. Elise was half-awake, or half-asleep, listening to the music. Her mother slept on her back, her feet pointed straight in the air, her nose piercing the darkness. Her breath rattled in her throat, adding the percussion.

Katrina did not snore, but she tossed her red body from one side to the other, scratching at her legs and arms as if she were covered in bugs. Elise tried to wake her once, but the child had growled, so she kept to herself.

The wind outside stroked the old porch swing into a rock, the iron chains sighing against themselves. The porch had been a brilliant white once, the swing a forest green. Elise used to nap on it as a girl. The swing was the perfect length to hold her in its cradle. The moss-covered trees stretched their arms above the porch, the moss hanging down in strands like beads. Elise liked to imagine the trees as friendly giants helping keep the house safe. The trees had turned on her too, after the murder, and they began to die off one by one. Trees that had survived the Revolutionary War felled by her act. They didn't completely fall, though. They remained standing, each year more of their bellies hollowing out for squirrels, spiders, and birds. The moss continued to hang on increasingly skeletal branches, tangling in on itself until a person needed an axe to push herself out of the house and into the world. Even before Elise moved away, the utility companies had left notes about removing the trees, blocking the wires, and other dangerous things. "These are our trees, Daughter," her mother had said. "We will not destroy them." After awhile, the power company stopped coming by. They even changed their plans about where to put a master box. "It's not in my yard, Daughter," she said proudly. "My yard rejected it."

The honeysuckle plant did not seem to reject anything. It fed on the water beetles that skated on the thin creek that ran beside the house toward the Savannah River. It fed on aluminum cans and cardboard boxes and pet goldfish and baby sisters. And it kept growing, yellow and white blossoms exploding from its arms like shooting stars scattering across the neighborhood yards. Elise couldn't remember the actual year they planted the vine. She felt heavy, her bones anchored to the floor, her skull pressed into the rug. She felt herself moving toward the plant, a strange peeling away of herself from her skin, and her weight, even though she left her bones and organs on the floor, was too much to allow her to stand, so she slipped across the floor as if it were ice. The dream's fingers were strong and they pulled her at her throat. She was heavy smoke, slipping under the front door, under the rusted porch swing and out into the garden.

The stars were a thick blanket, constellations she'd never seen before, and the moon was as bright as a stadium light. The garden was washed in cold yellow light, and Elise was reminded of grade school gym locker rooms. She could no longer see the house, not even the skeletoned sentries, as she'd taken to calling the trees that surrounded the porch, but the longer she was away from it the less it mattered. The garden was flushed with color; flowers shades or two darker than found in the world she remembered, but brilliant blues and burgundies nonetheless. A layer of peach fuzz seemed to cover everything, but when she reached to touch it with her smoke-fingers, it evaporated. As she slithered along at ground level, she saw earthworms inching up and down, the folds of their bodies an accordion. Ants busied themselves with giant scraps of bread, sometimes parts of other insects, and a nest of baby snakes, Elise couldn't determine the type, squirmed and slipped over each other. The mulch smell was strong, and she wanted to bury herself in it, cover herself in this moving, living earth until the sun struck down the icy moon.

The base of the honeysuckle vine was a thick tree stump. Without her flesh, she could circle it and slip in and out of the always-growing branches. The sweetness of the blossoms mingled with the ash of earth. She was intoxicated, Dorothy in the Poppy Field, and thought she could lie down and rest under the yellow flowers forever. An Eastern Blackneck garter snake wrapped around a branch beside her, its spotted neck as bold as a leopard's. It turned its head toward her, opened its jaw, and showed her the remains of a frog's leg still trapped in its teeth. She reached to save the tiny foot, but when she passed the snake's fangs with her non-fingers, the snake clamped down its mouth and inhaled all of her past the still wriggling frog's leg and into its belly.

She woke up panting. Her mother still slept on her back, nose in the air like a flagpole. Katrina and Mama Bear had rolled away under an end table. The moon was bright, and what curtains were left on the windows had thinned and bleached long ago. She stretched her fingers. Ten of them. All solid, if a bit arthritic. She pressed her palms to the floorboards below her. Solid. She was inside the house. She had always been inside the house. She had just been dreaming. What time was it? There was no promise of sun yet. She wished for a pillow. She wished for Henry. He would have stayed close to her, not rolled away under a table. He would have traveled with her in her dreams if he could. It was too late to call him back, try and calm him down and convince him she wasn't crazy, though her mother might certainly be. It was too late to try and assure him she had everything under control.

14

Pistachio, who used to be able to fold herself into any origami shape she could imagine, was getting fuller. In just the few hours she'd been lying next to Mrs. Abigail Fisher, the woman had begun to flatten, barely noticeable at first, and Pistachio became just a little more round. She could no longer, for example, press her foot completely against her shin. There seemed to be something new in the way. But her foot had also expanded its width, no longer a razor's edge but more of an ice-skate blade. Her legs were still two-dimensional, and she couldn't really be certain about her head. It felt heavier, but that could be just because of the extraordinary day she was having. Too many thoughts all at once. She was fiddling with the new movement in her ankle—circles in addition to up and down—and wondering if Harold's feet had ever grown like flippers when she saw Elise's fog rise from her sleeping body and slide under the front door.

She had been observing Mrs. Abigail Fisher's fog for quite some time. Hers was a pewter color. At times it whirled like a tornado; at other times it fractured from itself and the parts seemed intent on killing one another. Pistachio hadn't known other people had fogs too.

When Elise's fog left the room, Pistachio dared to cross over Mrs. Abigail Fisher to touch her. She wobbled on her newly-widened feet. Elise still slept, snoring even. Pistachio touched her arm. It was softer than Mrs. Abigail Fisher's. There was more flexibility in the flesh. Elise kept sleeping. Pistachio took care to avoid the feral thing, which now crouched under the parlor table voraciously reading its green book. The thing looked up at her from time to time with its violet-fire eyes, but didn't seem to be able to see her.

Pistachio had long contemplated the nature of the fog. She and Harold, trapped in their respective chapters on the closet floor, would whisper possibilities to each other.

"They have clouds inside them. That's what keeps them upright."

"They have wildness that needs more than their bones to contain it."

"They have secret selves that they don't even know about."

They concluded the fog had something to do with the humans' dimensionality, but beyond that, they just made up stories about what it could be.

Elise's body tossed and turned while its fog was out. Mrs. Abigail Fisher's body had always remained still, a discarded cicada skin. The feral thing muttered to itself, ears flat against its head, claw tracing the lines on the page as it read.

Pistachio sat on the music chair, the one Elise referred to as her father's. She and Harold had found this chair on their first venture out of the upper level of the house. Harold was pulled toward it, a fly to flame, and when he sat in it he seemed a different being.

"Do you hear?" he whispered.

"I don't," she said. "What is it?"

"Saxophone. A trumpet. A snare drum."

"Where are they?"

"In the chair."

"In the chair?"

"Shhh."

They crouched together, paper dolls on the slippery leather, and pressed malformed ears against the chair's flesh.

"It's in there," Harold said. "Somewhere in there is music."

Pistachio caught a trombone's bluster. "Oh! I think I hear it!"

"Listen."

She did, and over the next moments, brass joined strings joined keyboard into a rainbow of notes.

"This is a magic chair," Harold said. "If we sit here, we'll go places."

"What places? Where else is there but here?"

"I don't know. But don't you see? If you can hear another world, you can find a way to get there."

That was the first time she fell in love with Harold. It had never occurred to her to dream of places beyond what she could see. Where was he now? She stroked the chair's arms with the parallel lines of her fingers. He had been conscripted again. She knew that much. He'd left her a brief note: *She calls! I will see you again, my love!* But she didn't know what story he'd been conscripted for, if he was riding on the backs of elephants in India or dying in a foxhole in World War I or drinking scotch with F. Scott Fitzgerald and dancing with Zadie.

He'd been called up four times since they met. Each time he was gone for only a short while before returning, another wound-mark on his body, to the closet floor. Pistachio wasn't certain how to mark time accurately. She only knew he had gone before the fire in the kitchen, gone before the awards dinner held for Mrs. Abigail Fisher by the Southern Literary Guild when Pistachio first discovered she could be seen by her creator, gone before the woman and the wild thing arrived. They'd hoped of being in a story together one day, but it had been much longer than before the kitchen fire since Mrs. Abigail Fisher had called for her.

She still wore remnants of the pink party dress she'd last worn in her final half-performed scene. The moths had eaten most of it, but she remembered the silkiness of the fabric, the way the dress made her feel womanly for the first time, in spite of its pink color. She felt like she was beginning a whole life, not another half-one, and as she'd been spinning on the hardwood dance floor with gentleman after gentleman in tux and tails, she felt her knees give out, and she fell to the floor all crinolines and satin. A hand reached to pull her back up, but as she reached for it, her arms were yanked above her head and she tumbled and tumbled and tumbled, waking up days or weeks or years later in a bed of yellowed pages on the closet floor.

She pretended she could hear the notes living in the music chair, in hopes that by pretending hard enough she could bring the sounds alive. The tree frogs and crickets and hoot owls sang their songs. The wind pushed the porch swing back and forth, forth and back, the rusted chains clanging cymbals. The feral thing smacked its lips as it read its gibberish, its tongue snapping in and out like a reptile's. But there was no music. Not tonight. Maybe Harold was falling in love with another character at this very moment, touching the small of her back for the first time, waiting to go deeper. Maybe this character was fully formed, not the aberration Pistachio had become. Maybe she smelled of lavender and lilac, not of sod and molded paper.

Mrs. Abigail Fisher stirred. Elise's fog had returned to her body in a whoosh as fast as the retreat of a wave before the tsunami. Mrs. Abigail Fisher's fog had three strands this night. One was very small, and Pistachio might not have seen it if the feral thing hadn't exhaled, a deflating tire, causing her to glance across the room. The small bit of fog looked to be an unformed sunflower, its petals still closed in on themselves, waiting for light. It bowed its head at the other two strands, but they didn't offer it any hope for connecting with them. The baby fog-flower kept trying, though, until Mrs. Abigail Fisher began coughing, sucking all her fog back into her belly.

15

Elise woke to the sound of her mother's coughing. The first gray-pink of dawn was caressing the house, trickling through the sentries like dew. Katrina hummed a tune in her sleep. Mama Bear had fallen from her grip and now sat beside her staring into the room. Elise ached. She felt like she'd crawled through a thick jungle, and a memory of a dream was heavy on her—a frog's leg, a fang—but it was quickly vanishing into the mist of dreams.

"Mother, wake up. It's day."

Mrs. Abigail Fisher opened her eyes, pushed herself up on an elbow. "So it is."

"We have to get something to eat." She remembered the fire. "How have you been cooking without any electricity?"

Her mother pressed her lips together, and Elise realized she had not been eating. Not enough anyway. As the light grew outside, she saw the thinness of her mother's frame, the sunken cheekbones, the protruding collarbone. "I use the fireplace, daughter. That was good enough for many a family before electricity." She paused. "It was nice to have a fire down here in the receiving room. You know, I don't remember why we never used it much."

Elise did. Slamming doors. Quiet, the terminal quiet of the upstairs and her mother's writing rooms. The breaking of record albums that had been her father's. The covering of the baby's cradle in black gauze and carrying it to the dump. One day there might have been laughter around the fireplace. Elise couldn't tell if she was inventing the memory or not. Her father, thick black hair on his head, tossing back a gin and tonic, laughing at a joke she might have shared from school. She chose to believe the memory and filed it tight away.

"You didn't like to be down here, Mother," she said. "You said the room was cursed."

"I said this room was cursed? I am not capable of cursing a room. It either is or it is not."

Elise needed coffee before the conversation continued, but she had no idea how to make coffee over an open fire, and she wasn't sure it was safe to light one. Had the chimneys been cleaned in the last fifty years? Had her mother even opened the flue?

Katrina woke up. "Somebody coming," she said.

"Good morning, honey," said Elise. "Nobody's coming, I'm afraid. At least not until I figure out a way to call them. I'm going to have to charge the phone in my car. Do you want to come with me? We'll go to Hardee's and get some sausage biscuits and some coffee."

Katrina shook her head. "Somebody coming. We have to wait." She held up the bear. "Mama Bear say it."

"We'll come right back. We've got a lot of work to do over the next few days."

"You're talking to yourself again, daughter," said Mrs. Abigail Fisher, who had come to stand, holding her robe closed with one hand, pressing her hair flat with the other. "I'll get the fire going."

"No! It's not safe to burn anything else in here. Can't you see? Everything is flammable. One spark and the house could fall to cinders. For all we know, there's still some live sparks in the walls from the kitchen fire."

"Well if that's the case, then the handsome fire marshal did not do his job very well. He assured me that everything was safe. He didn't even tell me I had to move out, but I could tell he wanted me to. It's splendid, isn't it, getting old? You finally have enough fortitude to state what you want."

Elise did not remember her mother ever faltering when it came to stating what she wanted, but she let it go. "The marshal called me, Mother. You have to get out of this house, and we have to do it now. Well, now after I go get us some breakfast."

"Somebody coming," said Katrina.

"Shhh, honey," said Elise.

"I didn't say anything," said Mrs. Abigail Fisher.

"I'm talking to Katrina."

Katrina smiled, revealing the wide gap where teeth should be. The receiving room faced east. The sun's light had turned yellow and the whole room illuminated, the dust dancing in the rays. Elise saw her mother through the gauze of dust.

"Do you really not see this child here, Mother?"

"There is no child there, daughter. Stop trying to pick on an old woman. It's cruel. I am fragile. That's what the fire marshal told you, wasn't it? Poor delicate Mrs. Abigail Fisher. Did you know she used to be a writer? Did you know she took on Norman Mailer in the *New York Times?* Vicious thing, aging is. Vicious indeed."

Elise held out her hand and Katrina took it.

"I'm holding her hand right now, Mother. Do you see it?"

"You think I'm fragile and a liar."

"Somebody coming now," said Katrina, and when the loud knock cracked against the front door, Elise let out a sudden gasp.

16

"Elise!" Henry shouted from the porch. "Open this door."

Elise shook Katrina loose. She was disappointed in herself that she'd started to believe something frightening was happening. She knew this house. She knew who and what lived in it and who and what didn't live in it. Any surprises that could startle her happened decades ago.

"Henry!" She opened the Victorian door. He held a cardboard tray with three Starbucks coffees. A bag of bagels rested on the porch. She pressed into him too quickly. He almost dropped the coffee. "You look awful."

"Thanks." He stepped into the foyer, and Elise could tell by the quick way he swallowed his saliva that the house's condition appalled him. It took him a full minute to raise his gaze to hers. "I drove all night. Thought I could get a shower here, but that's clearly not possible."

"I actually haven't tried a shower yet. But it's not that bad." She found herself defending the house. "There was a terrible fire, you know."

"Yes, I know. I can smell it."

Henry entered the receiving room, gave a passing nod to the collapsed wall. He put the bag of bagels on the table.

"Daughter, my non-son-in-law has arrived," said Mrs. Abigail Fisher.

Elise had forgotten everything for the moment Henry arrived.

She'd pushed down the small-child part of her that had wanted him to come and overpowered it with the part of her that clearly came from her mother. "You didn't have to come," she whispered.

"What?" said Mrs. Abigail Fisher. She was sitting on the fainting couch. She'd tied her robe closed with its belt, and her bare feet looked like a young girl's under its hem, pale and unbruised.

"Did you hear yourself on the phone last night?" he said. "How could I not come? I shouldn't have let you drive down alone in the first place. This house always makes you crazy."

"It does not!" she said too loudly. She felt irrationally defensive of it. This house was hers, inside her in a way that nothing else could be. This house made her.

"Clearly it doesn't," he said with a short smile. "You're as rational as the day is long."

Katrina had knocked the bagel bag onto the floor and was sharing a poppy seed one with Mama Bear.

"There's the girl," Elise said.

"Where?"

"She is crazy, non-son-in-law," said Mrs. Abigail Fisher. "She's been trying to convince me there's a child in this house. Elder abuse, I tell you. Come closer, young man."

Henry took off his Sheriff's hat and bowed his head. "Yes ma'am?"

Mrs. Abigail Fisher thumped his forehead with her middle finger. "He'd be a good actual son-in-law, daughter," she said. "He's ripe."

"Ma'am?"

"Mother!"

"Somebody here," said Katrina. "Mama Bear smell it."

"It's Henry, Katrina," said Elise. "He's my friend."

"Somebody else." Katrina scampered back behind the couch,

leaving a trail of bagel crumbs.

"Closer, young man," said Mrs. Abigail Fisher. "I have to tell you about a murder."

"Mother!" Elise almost tripped on the frayed Asian rug. "Everyone isn't interested in your stories." She'd been so little. The baby had been so little.

"It's not a story, daughter. You see, non-son-in-law, my daughter here is going to kill me with that fire poker and put me in that industrial dumpster in the yard. She'd planned to do it this morning, but your fortuitous arrival has altered the plot, though I suspect only for a chapter or two."

Henry raised his head and stepped back a pace. Elise began to catch her breath. "Ma'am," said Henry. "I doubt very seriously Elise is going to kill you."

"You consider me unreliable," she said. "You are a novice. You do not yet understand how skilled I am."

"I don't doubt your gifts, ma'am." He offered her a coffee. "It's black, no frills. Just as you like it."

Mrs. Abigail Fisher smiled and took the paper cup. "A good actual-son-in-law, daughter."

"Henry," said Elise. "Let's go on the porch."

"Where's the girl?" he asked. "I left a message for social services last night. They should be calling back once the office opens this morning."

Katrina giggled from behind the couch. She raised Mama Bear up so her green face peeked over the back. She pulled the bear back down when Elise noticed it. Elise rubbed her eyes. Could there be no girl? That's absurd. She had the receipt from McDonald's for two meals. She hadn't eaten them both had she?

"Might I have a bagel?" asked Mrs. Abigail Fisher.

"Of course," said Henry, smiling wide. "I brought them for you. I remembered how you enjoyed your carbohydrates in the morning."

"You are indeed my actual-son-in-law. Perhaps my daughter will realize it one day."

"Mother!"

Katrina giggled again, hiccupping for a few breaths.

"Let's go outside, honey," Elise said. "You must be exhausted. Take some of the coffee."

"I had a few cups on the way down," he said. "But let's go outside. It'll be nice to watch the sun rise. Get out from under the dark here."

Elise didn't say anything, but she noticed how the rubble from the fallen wall glittered in the new dawn, and how the dirt on the floors had twirled into patterns as beautiful as any museum painting. She caressed the doorframe lightly as they went onto the porch and she felt the house in her belly responding. *I made you.* It said. *Take care of me.* Elise saw the snapped floorboards on the porch and the strips of peeling paint as wounds. A broken hornet's nest hung from the ceiling. She touched one of the splinters, pressed its point into her skin. "I feel you," she whispered.

"What?" said Henry.

"Nothing. Just thinking. Let's sit awhile and watch the dawn."

17

Pistachio watched Mrs. Abigail Fisher chewing her bagel. She took tiny bites, chewing with her mouth closed. Pistachio was agitated. There were too many creatures in the house. She and Harold used to dream of finding more characters to talk to, but Pistachio had never imagined they would appear like this. What books did these new ones walk out of? Did Mrs. Abigail Fisher create them all? Or was there another creator somewhere else? These thoughts were hard to assimilate. If there were other creators then there were whole new worlds that she didn't know about at all. Maybe these were worlds that Mrs. Abigail Fisher didn't know about either. Harold would know what to say. He was so good at hearing what no one else could imagine.

"Firestarter," said Mrs. Abigail Fisher softly. "I know you're here."

Pistachio held her breath.

"You can't hide from me."

Pistachio exhaled.

"Don't. Not anymore. I am tired."

"Don't what?" said Pistachio.

"Ha. I knew you were there."

Pistachio pressed her lips together.

"Don't play dumb. You're not dumb. I made you."

Pistachio reached for the fire poker. The other two humans were on the porch. The feral thing was hiding somewhere. It could be over in just a moment.

"Is it you I must fear? And all this time I thought it was my daughter who would do me in." Mrs. Abigail Fisher finished the last bite of bagel. "Come now. You haven't thought this through. If you kill me, what will happen to you? Do you honestly think that if I were dead there would be anyone left who cared what became of you? Would there even be a you?"

Pistachio kicked the poker away. She was confused. Mrs. Abigail Fisher always tried to confuse. She used words that meant different things and she strung too many sentences together. Pistachio had already been thinking too much.

"How could there not be a me?" she whispered.

"Ah. Good. Stand forth."

Pistachio wobbled to the center of the room. Her feet had widened even more in the past few hours. Mrs. Abigail Fisher squinted, reached for the reading glasses around her neck and peered through them.

"I can't see you."

"I'm right here."

Mrs. Abigail Fisher took the glasses off, rubbed her eyes, put the glasses back on. "Stand forth."

"I am standing."

"I hear you, but I can't see you. Go stand near the window."

"But they'll see me. On the porch."

"No they won't. They have other concerns."

Pistachio stood in front of the dirty glass, the edges of the lace curtains tickling her spine. She could see herself, her angled arms and stick-thin shins. She didn't see a shadow, but she did see a self.

"Are you there?" asked Mrs. Abigail Fisher.

"Yes."

"Why can't I see you?"

"I don't know."

Mrs. Abigail Fisher stood and crossed to the window. She waved her arms in front of Pistachio. "You're here?"

"I am."

Pistachio held out a hand and caught her creator's wrist.

"Do you feel me?"

Mrs. Abigail Fisher froze. "I feel you."

"Now what?" asked Pistachio.

"I don't know."

The feral thing scampered across the room, knocking Pistachio to the ground.

"Where did you go?" asked Mrs. Abigail Fisher. "I lost you."

Pistachio was hurt a bit by the impact. That thing. What was that thing? It comes and goes as it pleases. It clearly sees her.

"Firestarter?"

"I fell," Pistachio said. "That creature knocked me over."

"What creature?"

"The one that came in with Elise."

"You can see it?"

"Can't you?"

"My daughter is a storyteller, too."

"Some stories are true."

"Where are you?"

"On the floor. I'm trying to find that thing."

"There is no thing."

"You are wrong, Mrs. Abigail Fisher. You are wrong."

"You know my name."

"Of course I know your name. You ruined everything."

"I?"

Elise and Henry came back in. He had his arm draped loosely across her shoulders, but she kept some space between them.

"Mother, I thought we heard something. Did you fall?"

"Do I look like I fell, daughter?"

"Mother, this has to stop."

"What? I have not done anything. Non-son-in-law? Did she tell you of her plan to kill me?"

Henry cleared his throat. "She is not going to kill you. Besides, I'm a deputy, right? She wouldn't try that with me around."

The joke fell flat.

"I guess it's nothing to laugh about," he said. "I just think you're being unfair. She came all the way here to help you."

"She came all the way here to destroy me."

Pistachio stayed low to the ground, slipping up under Mrs. Abigail Fisher's feet. She found herself aligned with her creator. She touched the back of Mrs. Abigail Fisher's legs, tracing the blue veins toward the knee. Mrs. Abigail Fisher scratched. "Stop it," she hissed. Pistachio kept touching her thighs. "Stop it!"

"Mother?" said Elise. "What are you doing?"

Mrs. Abigail Fisher was spinning and stomping.

"Ma'am," said Henry. "Come sit again."

Pistachio giggled.

"Shut up!" said Mrs. Abigail Fisher.

"Mother. Don't be rude to Henry. He's only trying to help."

"I wasn't talking to Henry." She stopped and spun the other way, taking larger and more powerful leaps.

Pistachio gained more courage and began to tickle her arms, creeping her fingers down her spine and back up. Mrs. Abigail Fisher spun, swatted madly, and finally collapsed on the floor, panting. Pistachio howled.

"Mother!"

"It's the firestarter!" said Mrs. Abigail Fisher. "She's gone crazy."

Pistachio rolled on her back, legs in the air, trying to catch her breath. "I'm not the firestarter."

"Who are you?" hissed Mrs. Abigail Fisher.

"I'm your daughter," said Elise.

"I'm not the firestarter," said Pistachio. She sat up, wrapped her hands around Mrs. Abigail Fisher's throat. "I'm Pistachio Simmons."

Mrs. Abigail Fisher clutched her throat. Pistachio felt the frailty of her fingers as she tried to pull herself free.

"I'm Pistachio Simmons," she said again, louder. "I take it you remember me."

Mrs. Abigail Fisher ripped at her throat. Pistachio released her, surprised that her fingers had enough strength to have held her creator's throat for so long. Her body was changing and expanding without her consent.

"Mother!" said Elise. "What's wrong? Are you having a heart attack?"

Henry pulled his cellphone from his pocket.

"Put that away, non-son-in-law," Mrs. Abigail Fisher said. "I am fine."

"You're not fine, Mother. You just performed some crazy ballet and you can't breathe."

Pistachio stared at her hands. She saw the half-moon of a thumb nail beginning to form.

"It was the firestarter. She is trying to kill me."

"I thought I was trying to kill you."

"See how in danger I am? When I am dead, non-son-in-law, see to it that you investigate everyone." She glared at Elise. "Suspect everyone."

Henry's phone rang. He answered, then covered the mouthpiece. "Elise. It's social services. Where is the girl?"

18

It was barely nine in the morning and Elise felt like she couldn't go on another minute. There was no place to get her footing. She wanted to go out to the honeysuckle vine and find the snake, see if she could pull the frog's leg from its mouth, see if she could slip into its belly once again. Maybe Henry was right. Maybe this house and her mother did make her crazy.

"I haven't seen her this morning."

"Elise," said Henry. "You realize what this sounds like, right? You picked up a girl that no one but you has seen. You brought her into this house where you lost her and now that we can get some help for her, you have no idea where she might be." He removed his hand from the mouthpiece. "I'm going to have to call you back, Sandy. I'm sorry." He snapped the phone closed.

"She slept right here with me last night. She and her bear."

"She and her bear," said Henry.

"I have not seen her, non-son-in-law. Yet I see you, so clearly I am not blind."

"Clearly," said Henry.

"I'm going outside," said Elise. "You're free to leave whenever you want to, Henry. You shouldn't have even come." But she was ever so glad he had. "Mother and I have this under control."

"This? What this?" said Henry, but Elise had pushed past him through the front door and out into the yard.

The dew still clung to the grass. Her feet were bare and she worried only briefly about stepping on rusted nails. The honeysuckle vine seemed very far away, though she could see its petals.

"Elise!" called Henry from the porch.

"Just stay there," she said. "I have to go."

"Go where?"

Go find her, she thought. I have to go find her. But she knew Henry wouldn't understand. She wasn't sure she understood. The path to the base of the vine was well-worn, and she wondered if her mother hadn't been taking care of this one small element of the yard. Had she hobbled out here in slippered feet to brush away the twigs and leaves? Impossible. They had never even been out to the vine together since they first planted it in the sandy soil. Sometimes she thought she would have liked for them to visit it, but that only took place in her imaginary world where she and her mother talked like regular people, only in her imaginary world where they were each able to speak the truth and in the speaking forgive each other. But those fantasies stopped appearing much by the time Elise was a teenager, and they'd all but disappeared as she'd entered midlife and beyond. Acceptance, she told herself, over and over, acceptance. She simply must accept her mother. She will not get to do the things she'd wanted to do as a girl. She would not ever have the cookie-baking-PTA-mother that her friends had, but maybe her friends didn't have that person either and it was all a big illusion. Her mother was unusual. Maybe that was all she could expect.

Elise had spent many hours with her imaginary Oprah in her head trying to come to terms with her relationship. She had tried an actual therapist, but he hadn't been as nurturing as Oprah, so she returned to the Chicago set in her mind, the heavier Oprah (the thinner one was not nearly as comforting) and she told Oprah all about it. This was only partially crazy, she told herself, because her mother, The South's Leading Lady of Letters, had been a go-to guest on Oprah's show back in the nineties. She led a book talk segment in which she spoke briefly about the plot and spoke longly about the shortcomings of the writing. It was her favorite kind of book talk because the audience was unreachable through the camera lens. She could say anything and no one would contradict her. To her mother's credit, she never trashed an Oprah pick, at least not on Oprah's show. Elise liked to believe that her mother enjoyed being around Oprah too. Her soft curves and easy tears were the opposite of what she was capable of. When Oprah interviewed Mrs. Abigail Fisher about her long career as a writer, Oprah tried her bagful of tricks to get a drop of salty emotion from her guest, but she never could.

The Oprah in Elise's head could get her to cry just by giving her a hug. She was the best imaginary therapist ever, and she smelled of peanut butter cookies. And she wasn't crazy. Lots of people talked to people in their heads. In-her-head Oprah never told her to rob a bank or worse, so she had to be a force of good. She hadn't ever taken in-her-head Oprah for lunch at a McDonald's. She knew in-her-head Oprah was in her head. Was Katrina her imagination leaping free of her skull and dancing on the side of the road? It was clear Henry thought so. It was one thing when her mother couldn't see her. But Henry wouldn't trick her just to watch her squirm. He carried crickets and spiders out of their house and returned them to the yard.

The imaginary Oprah had been silent ever since Katrina showed up. Could Elise be fracturing into bits just like her mother had always told her she would do? "Your great-aunt Gladys," her mother would say. "One day she was carving up a turkey for dinner and the next minute she was a captain in the Rebel Army. Held her whole family hostage with the carving knife for a day and a half. No one could convince her they weren't Yanks sent to pillage the silver." Her mother would pause, pretend empathy, before finishing the story. "There wasn't anything to be done then, you know, so they had to put poor great-aunt Gladys into the attic where she spent out her days in army boots wrapped in the Confederate flag. She died saluting General Lee. It runs in the family, Elise. You keep your imagination all wrapped up in your brain. If you don't give it some place to go, after awhile it will snap."

Elise had many a nightmare about poor great-aunt Gladys, bayonet in hand, saluting a long-dead defeated general. Then she thought her mother was making it up because it was a good story, and every old Southern family had to have a crazy lady in the attic. Her mother didn't want to be the crazy lady, so she made up Gladys. But what if she hadn't?

She stepped on an overturned bottle cap. It was from a bottle of Tab. Elise pressed the cut with her fingers. "No tetanus, no tetanus, no tetanus," she said. Now she was talking to her feet. Imaginary Oprah wasn't enough. There had to be imaginary Katrina and now imaginary diseases attacking her flesh. It was a nick, not even a cut, and Elise continued down the path to the vine. She didn't turn around to see if Henry had gone back inside, to see if Katrina mocked her from an attic window. Maybe she had eaten two Quarter Pounders with Cheese at the McDonald's. She had been voraciously hungry. No. There was the bear. There was the red skin. There was the conversation. The girl even fixed the CD player somehow so it would play her father's album. Elise reached the vine and stopped, pressing her toes and heels deep into the ground. *I am here.* She thought. Grounded. On this earth. On this day. It is morning, October 21, 2009. *I am here.*

19

Pistachio was befuddled. She thought she knew the script. She'd always known what to do before, the intentions from Mrs. Abigail Fisher's pen sliding into her brain and talking her into performing the role on the pages. She'd been the willing puppet, until the morning she figured out how to break free and make her own motions in the scene. When Mrs. Abigail Fisher realized that and cut her, she had thought that would be the end of it and she would languish in pieces on the closet floor. But other cut characters were called back up, some quite frequently, and turned into other kinds of characters against their wills. Some were forced to commit atrocious acts and when they returned to the piles of shoes and papers on the floor, they were shattered, often unable to talk for weeks or months about the things they'd been forced to do. One poor soul, who had been forced to be an executioner in Mrs. Abigail Fisher's blockbuster *Inheritance*, simply couldn't endure and hung himself using old shoelaces. He didn't know how to tie the knot properly, so it took much longer than it should have, but his will was fierce. He had never been able to get the screams of his victim-characters out of his head. Martin, Pistachio thought. That was his name. Martin. "May your next author be merciful," she whispered, the traditional prayer among the characters.

She knew that Mrs. Abigail Fisher was not one of the merciful ones. She sacrificed her characters to the needs of the story over and over and over again. Some of the bloodied and bruised ones who returned said she was Machiavellian, sadistic; others said she also had no choice; she was simply doing what she was required to do by the narrative, which was larger than all of them. But now that Pistachio was out of the closet and starting to grow depth and breadth, would the old rules apply? Poor Martin had been unable to endure his role, and there were others who hadn't been able to answer the next call when the pen dipped into their home again. One of the more common reactions to Mrs. Abigail Fisher's final two books was that she seemed to recycle characters from previous works. This was frankly true, since by the time her sixteenth and seventeenth novels were being written, very few of her allotment of characters were willing to enter into the story.

Henry stood in the foyer, hat in hand, rocking from one foot to the other. He wasn't one of them. He wasn't a Fisher, and it was clear in his discomfort. Her creator, on the fainting couch not fainting, had always known exactly where she belonged.

"Firestarter," whispered Mrs. Abigail Fisher.

"Pistachio."

Henry's phone rang and he stepped out onto the porch to talk. He'd no doubt get more humans to come here. Pistachio couldn't handle any more players, at least not until she understood the script. She used her newly-forming girth to brush past Henry and take his hat from him. She imagined how confused he would feel when he saw his hat floating and dancing in thin air. She put it on her head, and though it came almost to her chin, she loved its weight on her bones. She loved that she could hold and utilize something from another world. She'd never seen Mrs. Abigail Fisher directly until she emerged from the books a few nights prior. She knew her voice, for she often muttered to herself when she wrote, and she knew the shape of her right arm from squirming under its shadow on the page. Henry closed his phone mid-sentence. Pistachio tried to empathize with how he might feel, seeing his hat suspended in air, but all she could do was laugh. It would be funny, wouldn't it? A Stetson hat bobbing up and down like a wayward apple in a Halloween tub.

Harold had told her how often humans struggle with accepting the story in front of them. "They make up all kinds of crazy things to explain what's right under their noses," he said. "They say they have great faith, but they have none. They cannot take one step forward or backwards if they don't have a story to explain what they're doing and why. What a confined way to live. It's easier for us, don't you think? We were made for surrendering." Pistachio hadn't understood what Harold meant, but that wasn't unusual. He'd seen so many different kinds of stories. He was even in an anthology once, *Best Southern Stories 1973*, edited by none other than Mrs. Abigail Fisher, who agreed to edit only if she could include a story of her own. He had a chance to be with characters from twenty-five different authors. It turned him into somewhat of a Che Guevara when he returned.

She saw poor Henry through the window trying to find the story that made a hat weaving around the room by itself make sense. She did feel sorry for him, but not enough to give him his hat back. It gave her substance. She stood taller, felt more decisive.

"Thank you, Pistachio," said Mrs. Abigail Fisher. "Now at least I know where you are."

Pistachio stopped moving.

"It's OK. My daughter is outside. I know who you are. I'm relieved, actually. I thought I was truly slipping into dementia. You rattled me the other evening at the awards ceremony."

This is a trick, Pistachio thought. She uses these tricks all the time. She has a character pretend to be nice and the other character falls for it and then winds up dismembered in a forgotten creek somewhere in an old moonshine county.

"I guess a part of me knew it was inevitable," said Mrs. Abigail Fisher. "It's natural to want to meet the woman behind the curtain, so to speak. If I were you, I'd have done the same. What I don't understand is how you're so mobile, how you're able to make so many moves without me." Her voice was calm and measured, but Pistachio knew she was afraid. Her sentences grew longer when she was uncertain. It was one of the many smoke screens she had to confuse people. When the great author was confident and certain, she spoke in short, declarative phrases with implied subjects. "What do you want, darling? I can give you anything."

"Elise!" Henry shouted, running out of the house. Pistachio lost sight of him when he passed the sentries. She still wanted to laugh, but felt she needed to maintain the advantage with Mrs. Abigail Fisher.

"He's a nice non-son-in-law," she said. "But he doesn't understand the way the house works. Men of the law frequently lack imagination."

Pistachio remained quiet.

"Come sit near me, dear. Tell me what you want. I've got at least one more good story left in me before my daughter kills me."

Pistachio had thought she knew exactly what she wanted. It was supposed to all miraculously work out now. She thought she wanted to be full, to be round and fleshy and to have been allowed to finish her narrative. She had thought she wanted revenge for her early and clearly miswritten demise in *The Garden of Gethsemane, Georgia*. That book was meant for her and she had been just about to explode on the page (metaphorically of course) into the most compelling character of all literature. But even more than that, she had things she was supposed to tell Mrs. Abigail Fisher, and the only way she had a voice was through the chapters. She wasn't sure now that she wanted to tell her creator anything, but she seemed hard-wired to speak. She was confused. She had thought she might kill her if she had the chance, but she realized she was not made to be a murderer and she wasn't sure she could go against her essential nature. This woman on the fainting couch was not the woman who wielded the pen in her bedroom in the dark hours of night. This woman was thin and growing thinner. This woman's hair was so fine it was almost see-through. This woman's voice still held power, but it was shaky. Pistachio could tell by the way the woman's gaze leapt from corner to corner that she was uncertain, even as she beckoned her closer. Stay away, stay away, stay away, she thought. The woman has killed everyone, some many times, some in ways they don't even realize.

"Pistachio, dear, don't be afraid. I know you can see me. Do I look like someone who can hurt you? I'm just an old woman now." Mrs. Abigail Fisher's gaze focused underneath the brim of the hat, but Pistachio had taken the hat off and held it off to the side, just to see what the author would do. Pistachio turned the hat upside down. "You know this is not going to make Elise and my non-son-in-law feel better, don't you? That boy is already planning to tear this house down and all of us with it. We need to work together, you and I, to preserve the setting."

Pistachio sat in the music chair. She left the hat on the floor just because she could. She thought she felt the chair vibrate a little, a beat of percussion, but it was probably her imagination, or her widening body growing some more. She'd been surprised at how noisy growth could be. "You've been mean to us," she said at last.

Mrs. Abigail Fisher had been looking at the hat. She startled to hear the voice behind her. "Don't you find it mean to keep moving around all the time? I have precious little time left."

"You just used us," Pistachio said. "You didn't listen to us. As soon as one of us had something to tell you, you cut off a leg or an arm or a head and you sent us away." Maybe she could hurt Mrs. Abigail Fisher after all. The anger from seeing body after body discarded to the floor after years of service was starting to bubble.

"I did no such thing. I gave you life. I gave you experiences you would have never had before."

And suddenly, a truth Pistachio did not know existed slipped past her thickening lips. "We were here before you. You did not give us anything. We were here before you picked up a pen for the first time in Zanzibar. We were here before you had your first conversation with Capote or Mailer. We were here before you ever thought you could write a sentence, much less a story, and we have been misused." Pistachio wished for the hat. She was flushed from putting so many of her own words together so quickly.

"How do you know about Zanzibar?"

Pistachio panted, afraid she'd caused herself a heart attack. The cosmic irony, should she actually die at this moment, would make Mrs. Abigail Fisher far too pleased.

"Pistachio, how do you know about Zanzibar?"

She didn't know how she knew, only that she and thousands of other characters had been swarming around Mrs. Abigail Fisher since she was born, when she was still Abbey. She remembered the cloud she was a part of, a glowing pulsing group of beings. They had all been light once, and she remembered being excited to be a part of the hive, excited to have been zinging around a person who was capable of doing justice to them, but her memory faltered after that.

"I want Harold back," she said.

"Harold?"

"Peter, Barney, Rufus, Claudius—you've called him lots of things in lots of stories, but his actual name is Harold. You'd have known that if you'd have asked."

"Peter, Barney, Rufus, Claudius?"

"And Ernie. You called him Ernie once. He hated that."

"Ernie? In *Passage to the King's Throne?*"

"His name didn't fit. And you had him tossed off his horse and stomped to death by the cavalry. It took me months to work his bruises and broken bones back to normal. And then you called him up again, and he was glad to go because he was your character. He was yours! And you have misused us, Mrs. Abigail Fisher." Pistachio put the hat back on and stood up. "You have misused us."

20

Pistachio had to stop on the landing to catch her breath. It was harder to navigate the stairs with her increasing body. She had not anticipated that more space would mean more weight. Her throat hurt as well, unaccustomed to so much speech. She passed the charred kitchen with only a passing regret for the damage and climbed the half-flight higher to Mrs. Abigail Fisher's bedroom. The oak double doors were open. They slid on tracks, and Mrs. Abigail Fisher had once been fond of opening and closing them with a flourish after one or more of the people she lived with had let her down in some way that left them puzzled. Pistachio herself was puzzled, perplexed, perfuddled, perklimpt. Her access to words was limited when she wasn't near her creator. She stopped trying to think about her experience and instead was going to be fully in her own scene and see what happened. She pushed the doors open wider and stood in the doorway, each arm against a door, each foot solidly on the worn red carpet. She felt taller than she'd been on the closet floor. Taller than when she started the kitchen fire. Taller even than when she'd just been downstairs.

Mrs. Abigail Fisher's roll-top desk was in the turreted window where it had been for decades. An old Underwood rested on the floor beside the desk, and an ancient word processor, not yet a computer, was next to it. The desk was covered in papers, and there were fountain pens in multiple colors strewn across them. Her chair was more of a perch, a tall, thin wrought iron stool with a red velvet cushion in the seat. The chair's back was thin—two twists of iron. When Mrs. Abigail Fisher sat in the chair, she merged with it, her own narrow spine a perfect accent to its coldness and efficiency. All the curtains on the turret's windows were closed except for the center window's, which were opened wide, their green brocade held in place with thick gold tassels. There was a small window seat, with dusty green cushions and yellowed paperbacks on it. Pistachio had never seen Mrs. Abigail Fisher use that seat. It might have done her good, she thought, to sit in the light from time to time. Rather than the expected rows of oval-framed ancestors (those were in the hallway), her bedroom walls were pinned with notes for her books—maps, diagrams, questions, photographs clipped from magazines. There were layers and layers of them. On some of the notes, the handwriting was prim and neat; on others it was jagged, like angry waves. She didn't recognize anyone in the pictures on the wall. She'd been looking for Harold's face without even realizing it.

"Hello?" she said.

The room said nothing back.

The bed was unmade, as it had been every day since Phillip, Mrs. Abigail Fisher's husband, left. Pistachio remembered that day well. The years of slaughter hadn't yet begun and most of the characters lived in relative ease in the light around Mrs. Abigail Fisher's head. She was Abbey then, though, Pistachio remembered. She was Abbey and she hadn't yet developed the angled peak of her lips that in later years would terrify undergraduate students in writer's workshops across the country. After he left, the Reign of Terror began and the characters who had once been open and excited to speak with her, grew closed-mouthed and shrunken, so much so that Abbey had to bully them into participating in the narratives she concocted. Pistachio had been a newer character then, hadn't known such change was possible in a creator. In the immediate months after Phillip left, the carnage had been unbearable. Not a day went by without limbs and heads being tossed into the room, making their way eventually to their new resting place in the closet. The golden cloud had gone, and none of the characters were quite sure when that had occurred. One day they were in the light. The next day they were in darkness. There had been something that occurred prior to Phillip's leaving that was important. She could see its peeling edges around the corners of the room, but she couldn't remember clearly. He didn't just walk out for no reason. She did remember that Phillip had stood beside the bed, just about where she was standing, saxophone case beside him, and watched Abbey sleep for almost an hour. He was dressed, a three-piece suit and a dashing hat, and he stood there so still and so quietly that Pistachio and the others had thought his fog had gone, leaving only his shell in the room. But finally he moved, adjusting his hat, lifting his sax case, and reaching over Abbey to delicately push her hair, which had been thick and auburn then, away from her face. He traced the caves of her closed eyes and the arc of her nose, and then he kissed his fingers and pressed them to her lips. She didn't wake up, or at least didn't reveal that she was awake.

"Good-bye Abbey Sapphire," he said. "Every note I ever play will be for you." And then he was gone, and within moments her eyes opened, she sat straight up, and began the killing that very morning.

21

When Elise reached the honeysuckle vine's base a quarter-mile from the house, she was exhausted, not from the distance, but from the emotional effort it took for her to break out of the house's hold. When she was a girl, she visited the plant quite a bit, talking to it and bringing it gifts. She named the vine Benjamina, but that name didn't stick. It had helped for a time for her to talk to it, pray to it if she were being honest, and in order to do that she needed to give it a name. She couldn't speak to what was underneath it. She couldn't speak to what had made it grow so thick and wild, what had made it cultivate a wonderland of birds and bees and insects and reptiles. She'd tried some of the tricks she learned during the few times her mother took her to a church.

"Dear Benjamina, I'm Elise Fisher and it's been three months and four days since my last confession." Or, "Hello, Benjamina, it's me Elise. I pushed a boy on the playground today, but he called me a name first." Or, "Forgive me, Benjamina. I knew not what I did." None of the prayers had any effect, at least not that she could tell, and as she grew older, she stopped visiting Benjamina and stopped, so she thought, feeling guilty for whatever it was she didn't understand, though that wasn't the truth either. She did understand and she'd just found a way to turn guilt into disconnection, maybe even, she worried, into disassociation. Where could Katrina have gone?

The smell hit her first, as it always did—its sweetness tinged with bitter earth. In her dream, the branches had created something resembling an awning, a protective cover. The vine before her now was tangled and twisted, branches winding in and around themselves until they were knots. The knots were homes to black birds, small and large, that shrieked as Elise got closer. There had been crows around the plant when she was a girl, but these birds were different. They had compact black bodies, large yellow beaks and red feet. When they flew out of their nests together, they were a swarm, not a flock. The vine's reach was long, stretching over property lines and spanning the creek that still trickled beside it. The vine had been a friend to her once. Now she could see its teeth.

"Benjamina," she whispered, falling to her knees. "Forgive me."

The black birds flapped and shrieked. The creek bubbled. The wind seemed to originate from within the unusually thick trunk of the vine, shaking its arms rattling them like chain mail. She grew cold from the inside out and hoped that Henry had not done what she'd asked and was on her way out here to find her. He was right. The house made her crazy. Her mother made her crazy. Everything about this trip was a terrible idea.

The smallest of the black birds landed on her shoulder. It was tinier than a hummingbird. It didn't make a sound, just cocked its head from side to side, opening its pinky-nail of a beak and sticking out a pinched tongue. It was so small. Elise was afraid to move, but she extended a finger and the bird jumped onto it, its weight no more than a penny. The more she studied the bird, the more colors she saw in its wings—shimmering emerald and a flash of neon pink under the canopy of black. It leapt back to her shoulder and then to her head, tangling its feet in her hair.

"What do you want?" she asked, feeling foolish and eight years old again when talking to the animals and the trees had made perfect sense. Then, they had talked back. Maybe not Benjamina, but the creatures that lived inside of Benjamina had buzzed and chirped and chattered around her so that she felt for a moment or two alive, and she felt that by understanding how alive Benjamina was, she might somehow believe that Courtney Lynn was still alive. There. She'd thought it. She'd formed her sister's name again. The wind quieted and the bird stopped scratching.

"Courtney Lynn," she said. "Courtney Lynn."

The bird hovered above her head, then darted into the tangle of branches.

This was ridiculous. This whole morning had been ridiculous.

"I brought you your coffee," said a small voice behind her. Elise spun around and screamed. Katrina, hair wild and damp, held a paper Starbucks cup in one hand, her green Mama Bear in the other. "I know Mama Bear is just a bear if she doesn't get her coffee." She smiled wide and Elise noticed the girl had lost some teeth from yesterday. Her gums were too red.

"Where did you come from?"

"Inside," said Katrina. "Where you left me."

Elise took the cup. It was solid and warm and real. She took a sip. Hot. Sumatran. Definitely Starbucks. "Thank you."

"Don't leave me inside."

Katrina's arms had become bones. The red flesh that had overpowered them yesterday had fallen away.

"Your arms," said Elise, trying not to scream again. "What's happening with your arms?"

Katrina shrugged. "It happens sometimes. Sometimes I go from being one thing to being something else. Don't be afraid. Mama Bear has something for you." She dropped the bear on the ground, where it lay face up, button eyes unblinking. "Go ahead," said Katrina. "You pick her up."

Katrina's voice was growing softer and sweeter, even as her bones shone whiter. Elise felt the earth take hold of her feet. She was afraid to look down, lest she confirm the roots of the vine weaving a net around her toes. The wind had stilled and there was no bird sound.

"You're not here," Elise said quietly, then louder again. "You're not here."

"What are you talking about?" asked Katrina. "You can see me, can't you?" Her smile had grown lopsided, like she'd been given too much Novocaine.

"I can see you."

"Then why do you want to pretend that I'm not here?"

Mama Bear sat up, lifted off the ground, and landed back on Katrina's bone-shoulder.

"What's that?" asked Katrina, leaning in to the bear. "She say you're not ready, Elise."

Elise still couldn't move her feet.

"She say you're too late or too early. Both are the same." The bear slipped down the front of Katrina's dress, her head sticking out of the collar as if she was in a pouch. "I hope you liked the coffee."

Elise tossed the contents of the cup over her shoulder. "You're not real!" She pulled her feet off the earth with too much force and fell backwards into the warm wet coffee. The paper cup rolled on its side behind her. "Katrina! Katrina! Where are you?"

"I'm not real," a voice whispered around her, swirling up the dead leaves. "I'm not real, I'm not real, I'm not real."

"Katrina!"

The black birds erupted from the vine, sending spacklings of honeysuckle petals down around her. Clouds had gathered over the house, but she was washed in sunlight.

"Benjamina," she crawled toward the vine. "Forgive me." Benjamina, as always, remained silent. The birds settled, a few returning to the ground to peck for seeds and worms. Elise folded into herself, forehead resting on knees, and cried. She couldn't remember the last time she'd cried, not without a purposely sad movie or soundtrack to poke her a little into releasing. This was a disembodied sort of crying, where she watched herself from another part of the yard shaking and coughing. But then she returned to her body with a jolt as the dry heaves came and she had to move to her knees and vomit up air. Thin fingers wrapped around her neck again, just as they'd done when she first arrived at the house. "You're not real," she said again. "You're not." The fingers didn't choke this time, but rather stroked her throat, her lower jaw, the base of her spine. The wind tickled her ears, lifted and played with her hair, brushed her dry lips. The fingers became arms that hugged her as she sobbed and struggled to push them away.

"Shhhh," said the wind. "Shhhh." The arms grew into shoulders into spine into hips and legs and feet, and though she couldn't see them, she felt how solid, how alive, the body was. It pulled her to her feet. "Come back inside," it said. "You're too early or too late. Too early or too late." Elise choked more sobs. "Shhh," said the wind.

"Where did she go?" asked Elise.

"I'm not real," said Katrina. "You said I'm not real."

"Where are you?" Elise rocked against the invisible body, listened to the disembodied words, and felt like she could scream loud enough to bring Henry running, even bring her mother out of the house. The body held her closer, squeezing her ribs too tight.

"Am I real?" it said. "Do you feel me?"

The rocking became swaying and soon they were dancing a waltz across the yard. One-two-three, one-two-three, one-two-three-one.

Elise rested her head on its shoulder. Its breath was hot and there was the hint of teeth, sharp as a mosquito bite. The clouds had parted and the whole street was paved in sun. The house, even in its decay, shone, and Elise remembered her father on a wooden ladder trying to paint the turret a dark red. "It's what your mother wants!" he shouted, but she'd been afraid, so afraid he'd fall from the ladder and break his back or worse. She'd been frozen to the earth, just like today, and she'd been mesmerized by the movement of his arms and hips as he stroked the paint across the wood. One-two-three, one-two-three, one-two-three, one.

"Daddy! Be careful!" she'd shouted, holding up her hands to shield her eyes from the sun. "You'll fall!"

"Don't you worry, Lisee-girl. I can't fall if I move with the music. I can only fall if I miss a beat."

The paint dripped down the brush and onto his shirtsleeves. He didn't care. The sun was bright. The house was full and loved. His little girl was watching. Or that's what she liked to remember.

"Can't you hear it, Lisee-girl? Close your eyes. Don't try to see with the wrong things. When you open them, the house will be magnificent."

And she had squeezed her eyes shut, turned away from the house and her swaying father, and listened. He whistled. He hummed. The paintbrush swished across the wood. One-two-three, one-two-three, one.

22

Elise wrapped her arms around the body holding her. Her eyes were still closed.

"Hey, honey, shhh," Henry said. "What happened?"

"Henry?" She opened her eyes. The music was gone. The coffee cup on the ground stirred from the wind.

"You called for me. I heard you scream."

He smelled so familiar, so safe and clean. This was not his world. Even in his darkest days, he dealt with criminals and the kind of dark that lives in the external world. He understood corners of bars, empty parking lots, and deals spoken in code. He understood the shadows he could see. She wanted to wrap him in a blanket and lay him down on clean sheets and try and convince him this was just a dream. He was back in their cottage, thirty minutes from the Yellow Brick Road. He was home with Smeek and his morning paper in the Blue Ridge Mountains. He was not thinking about any sort of darkness, the kind you can touch or the kind that touches you. She had not wanted him to come here. She had not known how to show him this side of her life, the side that she now knew had never left her, had never stopped governing every choice she thought she was making. Damn all of it. His face was unshaved and his facial hair was graying. He still had a solid jawline and a nose and ears that kept their stray hairs at bay. She had washed this shirt for him. She could tell because it smelled of Bounce, and he never remembered to put the fabric sheets in the dryer.

"You screamed," he said. "And my hat. It's dancing all over the house. You're going to think that I'm crazy."

She let out a hoarse laugh. "Me? Think you're crazy? There are many things I might say, but that's not one of them."

"But my hat—"

She picked up the Starbucks cup. "This cup? Katrina brought it."

"Well where is she?" Henry looked odd to her without his hat. His skull had the texture of a tennis ball beneath her fingers.

Elise shrugged. "Where is anybody around here?"

"Your mother is still inside." He scratched his head. "How long has it been since she left?"

"I don't know. I honestly didn't know it had gotten this bad. The house though, it has always held us close. I had to get as far away as I could, and I'm just figuring out there's nowhere far enough. The house isn't out here. It's in me."

"You're just tired, Elise. You don't talk like that. You sound all self-helpy. The house is clearly out here. There will be an explanation for all of this, but first and foremost, we have to tend to your mother. We have to get her out of here."

She knew he was freaking out about his dancing hat. How could he not be? His world did not have a space for dancing hats. "Mother won't go," she whispered. "There's no point in trying."

"The house isn't safe. And I think she's—now don't get upset—I think she's starting to, you know, lose her self."

It had won. Just like that. She hadn't been prepared for a fight, and now that she was here and stronger from having been away, she knew she could never beat the house. It was too clever. Perhaps it wasn't even trying to win. It knew it didn't need to. It knew she'd come back eventually, and when she did, it had planned to roll up the porch steps, raise the branches of the sentries, and seal them both off. “Mother is fine,” she said, and knew it was true, though she wanted to believe she had snapped. “If she’s seeing a firestarter, then there’s a firestarter.”

“But she doesn’t see Katrina.”

“Neither do you.”

Henry shielded his eyes as he looked at the house. “I believe you see her,” he said slowly. “I believe you believe.”

“That’s not enough. The house wants more.”

“Let’s go into town. Walk around. Maybe even go down to the ocean. Get some salt and sea breeze and all the other good things that happen at the ocean. We can find big shells and hold them up to our ears like we did at the Outer Banks. Remember?”

She did. They pretended to have a telephone conversation through the conch shells. She was on one side of a small dune; he was on the other. The breeze had been a wind, and sand kept getting in their mouths as they shouted over the top of the dune.

“Can you hear something?” he’d asked.

“Yes! I can hear something.”

“Can you hear me?” he’d asked.

“Yes. Can you hear me?”

“Yes.”

They cracked up. It was hard to have a profound conversation into a seashell, but Elise loved the weight of the shell in her hand, the smoothness of its interior against her cheek.

“Elise?” he’d asked.

“Yes?”

“I can hear you.”

She laughed again. “Yes.”

“No really.” He turned his back slightly to her. She saw him lower the shell for a minute and then pick it back up. “I hear you and you hear me. I think we should get married."

The sand blew sharp into her open mouth. She nodded but she didn't speak. He leapt over the dune and embraced her. "You hear me," he said again.

I can't, she thought, but she kissed him back. *I can't.*

Elise stepped away from Henry. The black birds fell silent. "I can't leave, Henry. Not now. Not anymore."

"We'll come back! We'll just take a break. Let me call social services again. They can sit with your mother and then we'll all just make this decision together."

Henry was a boy, earnest and accommodating. His fingers held an imaginary hat in front of his belly. He didn't know what to do with them, all empty and useless.

"This isn't your decision to make," she said. And then she almost said, *you aren't family,* but she stopped herself, though it was both true and not-true at the same time. She needed more coffee. Some food. The sun spread its light wide across the yard. The wind kissed the honeysuckle vine causing the ornaments and glass bottles hanging on its arms to make music.

"What are those?" asked Henry. "Did you hang them there?"

She hadn't, and she hadn't seen them before, not when she lived here, not in her dream last night, not in her quest this morning. She shook her head.

"They're pretty," he said. "It's like a Christmas tree."

The music was behind her. She was afraid to turn and see it. Afraid that Katrina was under the branches, hitting each bottle with a stick to make a sound.

"You think your mother did this?"

She lied. "I can't imagine."

"Look, they're old fashioned bottles." He moved closer to the vine, which seemed to have sprouted more limbs in the short time she'd been standing there. That wasn't possible, she told herself. That wasn't possible. The vine is just a plant, part of a larger ecosystem. Probably related to kudzu or ivy or maybe even moss. It's just a plant. "These are old Coke bottles from the twenties. Wow. And all this colored glass. They're quite an unusual shade of blue, don't you think? Like Milk of Magnesia bottles."

"Don't touch them," she said sharply.

"Why not?"

"Just don't. Come away from there. Let's go back in the house." She swatted at a mosquito. The black birds were silent.

"It's some kind of tradition," he said. "Hanging bottles in the trees. I remember seeing something in a magazine in an airport or something. *Southern Living* maybe."

"Why were you looking at *Southern Living?*" She brushed at the mosquito. "It's just folk art," she said. "You know we've got all kinds of traditions down here that don't make sense anymore."

"I'm a cultured guy," he said.

One of her mother's more recent letters had mentioned the *plat eye,* a term Elise hadn't heard since she was growing up and hanging out with a girl from the Lowcountry. It was a Gullah term for the evil spirit of somebody who wasn't buried properly. She'd forgotten that meaning when she read the letter. She'd looked it up and re-read the letter when she was alone. She'd shown every other letter to Henry. They'd even laughed a bit about some of them—her mother's flair for the dramatic, her overt manipulation of their emotions. But this letter she kept to herself.

Daughter, you are ignoring my solicitations for help. I will not keep asking. Instead I will tell you the story and leave it to you, gentle reader, to determine how to feel.

There is a plat eye here. I have feared this day for some time. My dear father, whom you never knew, had many contradictory qualities. One of them was his ability to reconcile the things of the spirit world with the theorems of science. He saw no opposition between the two worlds, and perhaps because of his inherent contradiction, I learned of the power of story. I am only now realizing this as I write to you. A story must hold conflicting ideas, otherwise it is a treatise. Thank you, father, once again.

I reached out, believe it or not, to old Cornelia from the Island. I told her I was doing research for a book, and she told me, as she always does, to get it right if I'm going to use her people. She gave me bottles and told me to hang them over the mound. She told me to do other things, but I am not prepared to share them with you. What I am prepared to tell you is this: There is a plat eye living in the house. The bottles came too late to keep it outside where I had hoped it would stay. I suppose I should be prepared to do the other things Cornelia told me to do, but I am not yet ready for that denouement. You know how this works, daughter; whether you have become a woman of science or a woman of story, you know how this works. It is coming for me, and I must make my peace with that. But it can't take me until it sees you. Don't ask me how I know this. Just trust me. If you have never trusted me before, trust me now.

I am not surprised, daughter, that it is here. I am more surprised that it has taken so long, and I do wish I were in better shape to deal with it. Please come home.

I remain,
Your Mother
Mrs. Abigail Fisher

Elise felt the letter was more of her mother's fictions. How was she to tell when all her life had been shaped, manipulated, and cajoled into serving one or another of her mother's precious books? The line between fiction and reality didn't just blur in her life. It was gone, and her mother was quite unconcerned about it. "There is only the story," she would say over and over again when Elise would be angry over a lie, or an omission of her mother's. "Don't quibble over the details."

23

Was there ever a time when the room had been light? Pistachio wondered if she had dreamed those times, when so many of the characters had bounced cheerfully like rubber balls from one story to another, one great love to another, eager for the next game. "Swing me, Daddy! Swing me!" young Elise would say back before things turned and there was no one left to do the swinging. The characters had felt like that. "Pick me! Pick me!" They never knew where they'd end up, only that it would be amazing, covered with dripping sentences that shielded them and pushed them forward. During the mandatory two-year rest periods between narratives, they would share stories about where they'd been and who they'd seen. They'd try to outshine each other with big-fish stories and tales of rescuing the pretty girls. They'd sleep together in puppy-piles and cuddle-puddles and dream of where they might go next.

Pistachio had been crouched in the corner of the room, batting at cat fur piles in the rising sun. Phillip had left, and she didn't yet understand what that meant. Her turn was coming soon. Abbey had finished what the critics were calling her masterpiece with *The Girl With the Red Balloon,* though sales hadn't matched critical acclaim. She wasn't troubled by that yet. She was young, still Abbey, not yet Mrs. Abigail Fisher, and wicked talented and she believed then that critics were more important than readers. She believed that if someone said she was good (and Pistachio seemed to recall the review that had sent her soaring used the word "genius" in it) then she was good. The rest of the world would take care of itself. Pistachio was in line for the follow up, the "much anticipated" sequel *The Garden of Gethsemane, Georgia*. She'd made it through the audition process, which took place at night after Abbey had gone to sleep. Somewhere in her dreams she conducted elaborate screen tests for the characters who would win the parts in the next book. She placed them in untenable situations, made them read alliterative iambic pentametered dialogue over and over again, made them twist and twirl and dance. Pistachio had been practicing all these things. She was ready for her lead. And the part, she was sure the part had been created just for her.

"Go, dear one," her friends had whispered as she slipped beneath Abbey's eyelids on her audition night. "Show her who you are."

Pistachio breathed deep, promised herself she'd remember to speak from her diaphragm as she'd been practicing, and took the dive. There were two other girls waiting in the dark velveted backstage. One was a redhead, who Pistachio instantly dismissed. She knew how much Abbey hated redheads. The other though, had the kind of body that made for compelling book covers, and her hair seemed to have been woven from her scalp into a flowing tapestry of gold. Pistachio's own brown (OK, dishwater blonde) hair was greasy from her nervous sweat. She tried to straighten her spine, stand taller, but the blonde girl was taller without effort, walked on heels made for circuses, and had a mouth that could only utter sweet things. The backstage area smelled of plaster and old paint. The musicians auditioning for the soundtrack were tuning up in the pit. The harpsichord player was off-key. The drummer kept trying to dominate the warm-up, and the conductor was on the phone. There was no woodwind section.

"Did you see the script yet?" asked the redhead. Pistachio felt badly that the girl had no chance.

"I didn't think anyone knew the script ahead of time."

"She said she did." The redhead pointed at the blonde.

"Hey," said Pistachio, walking up to the book-cover girl. "How did you get hold of the script?"

The girl looked down a perfect nose as if she'd seen a particularly amusing bug. "I asked."

"She's lying," said Pistachio. "You can't ask for it ahead of time. That's just not possible. I mean, if everyone knew what the story was before they got involved with it, how could they be authentic in it?"

"I don't know." The girl extended a pale, veined hand. "I'm Lucy."

Pistachio felt protective of the frail girl. "You know she doesn't like redheads."

If Lucy were offended, she didn't show it. "My agent said to come anyway. Sometimes the unexpected is the one that fits."

"I'm Pistachio. I have been waiting for this role my whole life."

"How do you know if you haven't seen the script?"

"I dreamed it."

Lucy nodded. "I did too."

They turned their attention toward the book-cover blonde. "She can't get it," they both said simultaneously. The blonde was uninterested in them. She crossed her legs. The seams of her stockings were perfectly centered along the backs of her thighs. Her circus-shoes stayed on her feet, and when she breathed, only her shoulders rose, and even then just a touch.

"She can't be breathing from her diaphragm," said Pistachio.

"I don't think she has a diaphragm," said Lucy.

"Next!" shouted the woman behind the black curtain.

The blonde stood, smoothed her red body-sleeve of a dress, cut her eyes at Pistachio and Lucy. "Good luck, you two," she said, and disappeared into the next act.

Pistachio paced. Lucy sat on a metal folding chair and recited a mantra. Pistachio couldn't hear the words. So many wonderful things can happen if you get chosen for the right role, and the right role actually becomes the right book. Why, there were characters whose names everyone knew—Rumpelstiltskin, Othello, Pinocchio, Anna Karenina, Mr. Darcy, Scarlett, all the Little Women—these characters grew bigger than their words, bigger than their covers and pub dates, and they touched something previously untouched in people. If a character gets these kinds of roles, they never die. Yes, they become trapped in the role. They're too recognizable as Peter Pan or Daisy to get to breathe in another story, but oh, Pistachio wanted to understand what that might feel like. To know that long long after the creator of the story died she was one of the creations that lived on. It was unthinkable, and yet it happened, over and over again. All the elements had to be in place, and Pistachio was feeling lucky.

The blonde returned, head held even higher if that were possible. Pistachio wondered how those heels could support those hips. "See you on the shelves," she said, leaving a trail of Chanel No. 5 in her wake.

Lucy continued to mumble her mantra.

"What are you saying?" asked Pistachio. "Shouldn't you save your voice?"

"It's nothing. Just a prayer."

"She's too much of a stereotype," said Pistachio. "Abbey will never pick her. She abhors clichés."

"Everyone's a cliché," said Lucy. "The surprise comes in how we choose to use it."

"That doesn't make any sense."

"Next!" came the voice from behind the curtain.

"That's me," said Lucy.

Pistachio suddenly hoped that Lucy might get the part. Well, not *the* part, but the supporting role. "Good luck," she said.

Lucy smiled, her oval face a pale egg. "May those born to write, write. May those born to read, read. May we characters always honor both writers and readers, and never forget we need both to live."

"What?"

"That's the prayer. My uncle taught it to me."

"Wow. Who's your uncle?"

"Edwin Drood."

"Oh my goodness." Pistachio couldn't help herself. He was a legend. "Who killed him?"

Lucy shook her head. "I can't say."

"Next!"

"I have to go," she said. "Remember the prayer."

Pistachio was alone in the hall. It was the most horrible of fates to be a starring character like Edwin Drood, only to have your story unfinished because your creator died. What sort of limbo must that be? Other creators try and take your character and make it theirs, but it never quite works because a character belongs only to one creator. It's just the way things are. There's an allotment of potential characters given to every author. A character can no more jump ship than an author can steal the character of another. Sure, they can try, and they may write some interesting things. But they won't have the actual characters. They can't. They weren't theirs to use. All the characters learned this from the very first story they were in. They owed allegiance to their creator; they were nothing but scraps of senses without her. This was what they had all learned, and this was the way it had always worked. Pistachio was confident in the arrangement and felt that if she just followed the rules as they'd been laid out for centuries, immortality would be hers.

Lucy returned quicker than the blonde. "Remember the prayer," she said, but she didn't make eye contact.

"Next!"

"Wait!" said Pistachio. "What's she like?"

"You've seen her before, right? In her room. At her desk."

Pistachio nodded.

"She's not like what you saw."

And then Lucy was gone.

"Next!"

Pistachio inhaled deeply, shrugged her shoulders to pop her spine, and released. *Diaphragm. Diaphragm. Diaphragm.*

Behind the black curtain was a single wooden chair. A spotlight bathed it in a harsh white circle. The stage floor was scuffed from the heels of hundreds of characters. Pistachio couldn't see into the audience.

"Sit!"

She sat in the chair. Crossed her legs. Thought of the blonde girl with the perfect seams. Uncrossed them and tried to sit taller.

"Name?"

"Pistachio," she said.

"Pistachio what?"

"Pistachio Simmons."

"And what do you do, Pistachio Simmons?"

"I—" *Diaphragm.* "I tell stories."

"I tell stories," said the voice.

"I meant that I participate in stories. I make stories come alive."

“I make stories come alive,” said the voice.

“I’m sorry. What do I do?” asked Pistachio. Her shoulders had slumped.

“You do what I write.”

“Yes, ma’am.”

“Are you ready for your own story?”

“Yes, ma’am.”

“Why?”

“Because I don’t know anything.”

Silence.

Silence.

“Ma’am?” whispered Pistachio.

“I will be in touch. Good day.”

But you haven’t heard me sing! She thought. You haven’t seen me dance or watched me cry. You don’t know what I can do. The moment was over though. Her biggest audition yet and she didn’t get to perform her monologue or even give her credentials.

“Good day,” said the voice.

“Yes, ma’am.” But she sat there. She couldn’t convince her body to stand and leave.

“Is there something else I can help you with?” asked the voice.

This. Now. This is it. She cleared her throat. “Yes.”

“Well?”

The house was pitch dark. Pistachio couldn’t even tell where the body attached to the voice was sitting. The spotlight was hot. Sweat dripped down her un-seamed legs.

“You need me,” Pistachio said.

“I beg your pardon?”

“You need me.”

“And why is that?”

"I can see where you're going. I can take you where you can't see."

Silence.

"I'll be in touch," said the voice.

"Yes, ma'am." Pistachio stood and left the stage.

When she tumbled back into the darkened bedroom, she was disappointed there was no welcoming party. She had been imagining too much, already placing herself in the role first of ingénue and later of femme fatale. She saw the yellowed dissertations on the complexities of her character already filling the stacks of libraries around the world. It was dangerous for a character to think too far ahead of the story. The character's job was to remain grounded, rooted from one word to the next. The creator's job was the visionary. Pistachio only knew of one character who had wrestled free and managed to live beyond the scope of the author's imagination. No one ever mentioned his full name. He was just V, and the story goes his creator shot himself in the head. That wasn't enough information to narrow it down. Pistachio didn't understand why so many creators killed themselves. There seemed to be, to her mind, no greater thing to be. But perhaps it was difficult having all of the characters living in their heads. She'd heard Abbey more than once shout to an empty room. "Shut up!" she'd say, after tossing a page into the trash. Or, more frequently, "What do you want from me?" Pistachio could hear all the competing answers to that question, but by the way Abbey pressed her index fingers against her temples, Pistachio thought Abbey couldn't hear at all. Or maybe she heard too much and couldn't tell which one was most important.

The bedroom was more quiet than usual. Abbey slept on the right side of the bed, her side. She never even strayed a foot or wrist onto Phillip's side, though he'd been gone for months. She slept as rigidly as she stood. Abbey's breathing was smooth; not even her eyelids flickered. Pistachio wondered where Lucy lived, if she was even in this house. Could a creator call characters from beyond her realm?

"Lucy?" she asked the dark. "Are you here?"

Nothing, but that was not unexpected. Pistachio decided to strut around the room a little, maybe practice her speeches to classrooms and book groups. Maybe even try on Abbey's lace-up boots. The shoes were too big for her, too wide, and her flat, narrow feet slipped and slid on the insoles. She tripped on the laces and was headed for a fall right across Abbey's stiff legs when Harold caught her.

"What do you think you're doing?" he asked, holding her wrist. "You want to wake her up?"

"No! I just wanted—"

"You just wanted what? To see what it felt like to play god? We're not made to do that. You know the rules."

"I know," said Pistachio, her half-written awards' speeches vanishing. "It's just that, don't you ever wonder what it would be like?"

"No!"

She took the boots off, replaced them in their spot in the closet. "You're lying."

"I don't wonder, Pistachio."

She couldn't fathom how he wouldn't have the questions or the curiosity. He was a star already and Abbey hadn't even begun to touch the apex of her career.

"How is that possible? You're famous. You've been everywhere."

"I haven't been everywhere, but that doesn't matter. I am sure I don't wonder because I want to keep being in stories. I want to keep trying new things and seeing new places. We can't leave the garden, Pistachio. This is where we have been planted. We're lucky. Our creator has talent. We have a chance. Why would you want to destroy it? A character is an open vessel for the creator. We become what she wants us to be. It's always been that way and the world is full of great literature. It's our job. It's a sacred thing."

Pistachio sat on the window seat. Harold was right. She hadn't even been in one story yet. He'd been all over the world. He kissed the top of her head. "Is that what it takes to be famous?" she asked. "Do I have to stop wanting and just pretend?"

"I don't know." He smiled. "Right now, 3,218 people are reading about me. 41 people are writing some kind of paper about me. 27 teachers are talking about me. All those versions of me out there. Sometimes I wish I knew who they were."

"They're you," said Pistachio. "Aren't they?" She'd always thought that she would somehow fracture off into as many selves as she needed to accommodate a wide readership.

"I'm right here. The person they're talking about is someone different. I'm different to each of them. I'm not really sure how that works, but I know that whatever I am underneath all the different names and adventures and lovers, comes back here every time. I find myself just like you, wandering the room wondering what happened to all of us and why I can only see the ones, except for you of course, who were in my most recent story. The Harolds who are out there in the bookstores and classrooms? There's a tiny piece of me, maybe, but I think those Harolds are mostly the readers' Harolds. I don't know how to have any effect on what the readers think."

Pistachio knew from conversations she'd heard in the bedroom that they were not far from the ocean. She'd like to see it sometime. She'd like to hear the waves. She could smell the salt in the air. On nights when the winds shifted west, the sea-air made its way this far inland. The scent pricked something inside her. She wanted to walk the dunes in moonlight. She wanted to hold a shell to her ear and hear an ocean a continent away. She wanted to see glow fish and sand crabs and maybe even find an unbroken sand dollar.

"Maybe she'll write me a part by the sea," said Pistachio. "You can run the lighthouse and I can walk along its edges waiting for my lover to return from his ill-fated voyage. I will walk forever, of course, and you will long for me from the top of the lighthouse. You will contrive ways of speaking to me, even going so far as to invite me for brown bread and wine, but I am unmoved. One morning you emerge to go into town for food and you find me, half in and half out of the water. The tide is going out, and I am being carried out to sea, where I will mingle with the bones of my lover. My hair is stringy and wet. My dress is stuck to my legs, and you speak first—my love, my love—and then you howl because it is all you can do, because there are no words for what you feel for me, and as you howl, the ocean reaches up its watery arms and with a big wave, bigger than expected at the waning tide, I am gone, leaving you to walk the perimeter, unable to distinguish the salt from the sea from the salt of your tears."

Harold laughed. "I'd leave the writing to her," he said. "But you do have a flair for the melodrama."

"It's not melodrama." She pouted. "It's a story."

"No, it's not a story. It's emotional trickery. But let's not fight. We're here together. Maybe for just tonight. What if in the morning she knows what she's going to do and you get the call? You can't resist it when it comes. You'll be utterly and completely swept away. Surrender is your only choice."

Pistachio knew that wasn't true. She was a good enough performer to pretend that she surrendered, but she would never, not ever, turn over the part of her that wants to walk along the ocean's edge. She would never turn over the part of her that wants more than her creator was capable of imagining. "Let's just wait and see if I get the part," she said. "It's all just wishing right now."

"Let's go downstairs," he whispered in her ear. "We don't want to wake her up. She's deciding right now what she's going to be doing tomorrow. Don't risk changing the outcome."

They slid down the banister like children, suppressing a laugh when they plopped in a pile on the first floor. "We'll wake up the girl," said Pistachio.

"She's awake," said Harold. "She doesn't sleep much anymore."

Pistachio didn't ask how he knew. "Should we ask her to come with us then?"

"No. She's not our creator. It would be too much."

They crept to the study where Phillip had once composed his music. "I miss the saxophone," Pistachio said. "It sounded like crying, but the good kind of crying, you know? The kind that makes you glad to be alive."

"She's outside," said Harold.

"Who?"

Harold was looking out the bay window across the porch, past the sapling trees that Abbey had just planted, out toward the creek. "Elise. Abbey's girl. She's out there in the dark."

Pistachio cupped her eyes and peered through the glass. There she was. The girl was only four. Her pajamas were stamped with yellow ducks, and they were supposed to be footed, but Elise had cut off the feet and rolled the legs up to her knees. She was holding a stuffed sock monkey, thick red lips and long tail visible in the moonlight.

"Should we go get her?" asked Harold.

"No. Shhh. Watch her."

"We can't just let her be alone out there. It's the middle of the night."

"You try and leave the house," she said. "This is our world. We can't be out there."

"I thought you wanted to be everywhere," he said.

"I do. But right now I can't."

"What if she gets hurt?"

"She's already hurt. Look at her."

Elise's thin shoulders stooped forward. She dragged the monkey along the dirt as she walked slowly toward the creek.

"She knows where she's going," said Pistachio. "She's been sneaking out ever since her daddy left."

"But what if she gets lost?"

"She's already lost too," said Pistachio. "Sometimes you have to walk around quite a while before you find out how to get unlost."

"It's harder for them, I think," said Harold. "Without a creator to give them the words how do they ever make the right choices?"

Pistachio wasn't sure that would be harder. It seemed harder to have to pretend so much. To always have to be what someone else determined you would be. She wasn't sure where these rebellious thoughts were coming from. She hadn't even had her first big role. It was what everyone dreamed of. There was something wrong with her. She was an aberration if she wanted more. "We're lucky, I guess," she said. "To not have to worry about knowing."

Harold put his arm around her shoulder and kissed her neck. "Tonight we don't have to know anything."

Elise disappeared into the moonlight. "Where does she go, I wonder?" said Harold.

"She goes to see the baby," said Pistachio.

"What baby?"

"Their baby girl. She died and she's out there now under the honeysuckle. Every night Elise goes to see her." That would be the most unbearable part, Pistachio realized. When their people go, they don't come back in another story. They don't run into you in the closet or a darkened bedroom floor. They just go, and the ones that are left seem to spend all their days trying to bring them home.

Pistachio hadn't thought about those moments in forever and ever. She and Harold had watched Elise for what seemed like years. He would get conscripted from time to time, sometimes for a short story, other times for a novel, but he'd come back and they'd watch her, gathering things from the yard and bringing them inside to her room, which was quickly becoming a winter garden of stones, branches, leaves and dried flowers. She'd leave around eleven o'clock when her mother began working in earnest in the turreted room, and she would return just after midnight with another piece of the earth for her growing collection. She didn't sleep much, the little girl. She lay on the bed with her eyes open, talking. Pistachio and Harold hovered outside her door sometimes, but they couldn't see whom she was talking to. Pistachio assumed it was another character who just wasn't visible yet. The house was full of them. They could be standing right next to a whole village from a novel's chapter, but they wouldn't know it unless they'd been in the same book. "They can't usually see us," said Harold.

"I don't think she sees anything," said Pistachio.

"Who's she talking to then?"

"I think their world must have things we can't see."

Little Elise would sit on top of unwashed sheets and move her lips and rub her fingers over invisible prayer beads.

"I wish we could give her words," said Pistachio.

"It's not our role," said Harold.

But they watched over her nonetheless, caricature-characters of guardian angels, at least until one of them had to go fall from the sky.

The woman downstairs with Mrs. Abigail Fisher did not look like the little girl in the room with the dead earth. Not on the outside anyway. Pistachio was ashamed that she hadn't recognized her when she first came back, but she had been so intent on getting Mrs. Abigail Fisher's attention that nothing else mattered. Pistachio paced the bedroom floor. The girl was old, older anyway than Mrs. Abigail Fisher had been when she'd conscripted her. She muttered words, still, and rubbed her thumb and index finger together when she was nervous. She'd been here over twelve hours now and hadn't gone into her childhood room.

Pistachio sat on the bed and dared to imagine herself as Mrs. Abigail Fisher, toes pointed straight to the vaulted ceiling. She dared to imagine being the one who created the worlds. The mattress sunk under her weight. She'd never experienced that before. Her space, her form, was growing. Her feet now each had five separate toes, instead of a graphite swoosh for all of them. She could rotate them on ankles that had a full ball and socket. She held the gray cotton blanket to her nose, but smelled only dampness, no unique human scent.

On the morning Pistachio had gotten the call, she'd been downstairs watching little Elise not-sleeping. Harold had gotten called up a few weeks earlier. He hadn't been able to send her any notes this time, so she had no idea where he had gone. She didn't miss him much, though. She was thinking about her own immortality, her book cover, what color the award seal would be and where it would be placed across her body. She hadn't seen Lucy or the blonde seam-legged character since the auditions. Maybe one of them had gotten the role after all, or maybe Abbey, who was not yet Mrs. Abigail Fisher but had turned the final corner toward that place, had decided to change the story entirely. That happened sometimes, and it was always a shame because characters had sold their houses and uprooted their families only to find out the job had gone. It was risky for all of them these days, freelancing with no guarantee of continued work. The older characters sometimes talk of a creator's loyalty, back in earlier days when everything was apparently in sharper color. But they only knew stories. Even the older characters were only Abbey's older characters. They knew nothing of a world before her. All the stories were hearsay.

But then the call came, and it was like nothing she could have imagined. Her whole body felt warm, and the back of her neck was held in a soft but firm grip. She was walked up the stairs and into Abbey's room, where the woman was bent over her roll-top desk, scratching at a ream of paper with a fountain pen. Pistachio walked beside the woman, who kept scratching at the paper. The grip on her neck tightened, and she was pushed to her knees.

"Are you ready?" asked the woman, still looking at the papers.

"Yes," said Pistachio, speaking from her diaphragm. She forgot about little Elise in the bedroom praying with open eyes. She forgot about Harold who could be getting gangrene in a trench in France or making love to the blonde seam-legged girl in Manhattan. She remembered for a split second Phillip and young Abbey in upstate New York at Zanzibar and the way they'd danced to his music in the courtyard.

"Surrender, Pistachio," said the woman.

Pistachio bowed her head and lied. "I surrender," she said, and the grip on her neck released and she was sucked into the nib of the fountain pen and suddenly awash in indigo ink.

When she was able to open her eyes, she saw many characters floating in the dark ink. They were inside a cauldron, the contents of which shifted and roiled as the woman pressed the pen along the pages. Pistachio worried about her skin. Would it stain such a dark color? She swam over to an older woman, gray hair in a bun held with a crystal clip. She was treading ink.

"Have you been here before?" asked Pistachio.

The woman increased her paddling. She held her spine utterly straight.

"I'm Pistachio."

"Gertrude," said the woman. "I have not been here before. Isn't this a new book? I said I would not do another sequel."

"I mean in the ink. Have you been in the ink?"

She stopped paddling and stretched into a plank, floating on the mild waves. The ink washed over her legs and shoulders, but it didn't seem to leave any behind.

"Why doesn't this stain?" Pistachio asked.

"Because it's not the red ink," said Gertrude. "Once you've been in the red ink, it's a part of you forever." She kicked her feet, splashing Pistachio with dark blue. "See? It's our water. Ink is where we belong. Tallyho, Pistachio!" she laughed a little, and swam away, bun remaining in perfect place on the back of her head.

Pistachio heard whisperings over the rocking waves, but she couldn't see anyone else. It was true. The ink splashed over her and dissolved into water. She dunked her head under the ink, opened her mouth and swallowed. Cool water.

"It's coming!" someone shouted.

"She's about to burst!"

"Get ready!"

Characters emerged from the ink, bellies flat against the surface, arms pointed straight in front of them, ready to dive. They looked like swordfish, ink glistening off their spines. There was a great shaking in the cauldron and then a pressure. The ink, with all the characters in it, rushed forward toward the tip of the pen.

"Here it comes!"

The wave began behind her. Instinctually she arced into a diving position. When the force hit her feet, she couldn't have prevented the birthing if she'd wanted to. She was about to be squeezed through the pen's tiny opening, ink-water pulsing against her back. Ride it out, she thought, and when she saw the smallness of the hole, she tensed up. She'd never fit! How could she be expected to become so small? She twisted herself, feet in front this time, and pressed back against the surface of the pen. She couldn't do it. She thought she could, she thought she wanted it, but not at this price. Not at the price of her form.

She heard distant screaming from the other characters. The pen lifted and shook, tossing everyone left and right against the edges of the cauldron. The pen slammed against the page, lifted again, slammed back down. Pistachio had nothing to hold on to. Her feet weren't strong enough to fight the pressure from the ink against her back. Her right foot slipped.

"You've got to turn around!" she heard from somewhere in the waves. "Your head has to go through first!"

"No!" Pistachio shouted, but she was quickly losing the grip with her left foot.

"She's going to shake you loose!" someone said.

"Just turn around!"

"No!"

Pistachio's left foot joined the right and she was now stuck up to her knees in the nib. It was too tight—a vice. She'd be cut in half before she had a chance to become whole. Ink washed over her shoulders. She swallowed some more, choked it back up. Her feet were cold. She wanted to stay in the ink, even if it meant losing her feet.

The ink was warm and in motion. Wherever her feet were was cold and dry. The pen was lifted again, and the shaking was the worst yet.

"You've already made her angry," someone said.

"You're going to end up red," said another.

"Just turn around!"

"I can't," Pistachio said, now wishing she could pull her feet back in, assume the beautiful glistening swordfish pose and slip through the hole like she was meant to do. This had been her moment. Her entrance to the story, and she had become afraid. What if she got sent back and never called up again? Harold had often talked about this moment of emergence, but he never mentioned how tiny the passage was. How could he leave out something so significant? Her torso was tossed against the sides, and she thought she might just break in two anyway. Would her feet get to at least have a walk-on part in the scene? Her right foot slid a little more into the cold. She tried to push her left one along side it. The shaking intensified. Her arms lifted above her head and she became as thin and flat as possible. The ink was so warm. Her feet were so cold.

"She's not going to stop shaking until you get through," someone said.

Pistachio wiggled against the nib. Her hips were too wide. She was about to try and pull her legs back into the ink again so she could turn around when hands wrapped around her ankles and pulled her, screaming onto a blinding white page.

She was flat and exhausted; the page was slippery and bright. She lay spread-eagled, breathing the cold. The ink had evaporated from her flesh and she wondered what would replace it. Would she dry out without it? She tried to stand but was struck down. She cast no shadow on the white sheet. She heard no other voices. The pen's nib hovered above her, and she rolled into a tight ball to avoid getting stabbed. The pen just waited. She rolled left. It followed. She rolled right. It followed. She was about to try and kick it away when it moved closer, opened its mouth and sucked her arm back into it. She was pulled across the whiteness, up and down, over and under, leaving indigo marks on the paper from her movements. She was letters. She was words. She was paragraphs. Ink was poured into her throat and she bled it back onto the page, scene after scene, chapter after chapter. She forgot she was Pistachio. She forgot about the world inside the pen. She forgot about Harold and the world before the pen. She was movement. She was dancing. Her thoughts disappeared and were replaced by someone else's words. She stretched and contracted. She cried and laughed. She was a story now, and she had lost all concern for anything else.

When Harold found her again months or years later, she'd been gutted and left for dead on the closet floor. Her belly was cut open, her breasts were sore and full, and her arms had been severed and were lying next to her body. He had just returned from a victory at Sharpsburg ("Stories are wonderful," he'd said. "Lee's victory was decisive. We took Maryland.") and was excited to share his tales of a re-visioned War of Northern Aggression. "What if Sherman had never burned Atlanta?" he asked. "That's the story's question."

When he saw Pistachio on the floor, he was still in character, shouting for a medic and some whiskey. "Hold on, Pistachio," he said. "I'll put you back together."

She couldn't speak. Each breath pushed more of her ink onto the dusty floor. Harold tore his shirt and wrapped it around her belly.

"How could she do this to you?" he asked.

"I—" She tried to speak. "I don't know where I was."

"You were in a best-seller, my darling. Everyone knew it. We were all jealous of where you were going to end up, even me, I must confess. I wanted you to have this role, this moment, but then I wanted you back. I wanted you to be waiting for me to come back from the battles. But I never thought she'd chop you up like this. I never imagined."

He held Johnny Walker to her lips. "Drink, my love. I'll find someone to put your arms back on. Medic! Medic!" She swallowed two large gulps. He wiped her lips.

"I don't remember, Harold," she said. "I don't remember my story."

24

"Don't worry about your hat," said Elise. "It'll stop dancing eventually."

Henry stepped away from her. He was eyeing her like he eyed his arrests, with a hint of aggression and fear. His nostrils flared. Elise had to stop herself from laughing.

"I told you not to come," she said softly. "I told you."

"I need to call somebody," he said. "It's what I do. I can make all this better. Look, I know you're not crazy. I really do. I don't understand what's going on, but I understand you. Listen, when my partner was killed when I was in Boston, I saw him everywhere. I couldn't get in the squad car without seeing him sitting there, eating that damn bagel with the stinky fish-thing on it, railing about something in government. I even started talking to him after awhile."

That was more than Elise had heard in one breath about his partner, William. He never talked about it. It was all before they met. It was before he was force-transferred to the North Carolina mountains. It was before his marriage ended and he found himself in mandatory rehab for ninety days. It was before his band lost their recording contract because he had been too drunk to show up for the scheduled and three rescheduled studio times. She knew all this, and she said the mean thing anyway.

"That's because you were guilty."

His arms, that were about to try and hold her again, flopped against his sides. "It was an accident," he said low.

"That doesn't make the guilt any different," she said.

She knew he wanted his hat. He wanted to smash it onto his head, pull the brim down low, and disappear into that identity. He wanted to remind the world that he had some authority. Without it, he was just a balding boy, who was, rightly, furious. She cared, she wanted to care more, but right then, all she could do was leave him in the Georgia sun a few yards away from Benjamina and the glistening bottles, and hope when all this was over, he'd find a way to make it alright.

"If you go back in that house, I'm leaving," he said. She was almost at the porch steps. About to slip between the sentries and go back inside. *Stay. We just need time,* she thought but couldn't say. She'd become her mother without even noticing. "I mean it," he said again. He won't go. He'll walk down the street. Go to the beach. Go to a 12-step meeting. But he'll come back. It's what he does.

Katrina was on the porch swing. Her arms looked better. The skin had stretched back over the bone. Mama Bear was in her lap. She sang softly, "Hush a-bye, don't you cry. Go to sleep, little baby. When you wake, you shall have, all the pretty little horses. Hush a-bye."

"Shut up!" she screamed at Katrina, who shifted to whistling. She heard Henry's footsteps walking away. "No, not you," she said, but she'd already stepped onto the porch and the sentries had stretched their branch-arms together until the porch was wrapped in trunks and timber. "Not you, Henry," she said again, but she knew he couldn't hear her or see her anymore. Black birds dotted the branches.

Katrina held out Mama Bear. "Do you want to hold the baby?" She smiled. No teeth. Bright red gums. Her clavicle popped the thin cover of flesh. Elise pushed the bear back hard enough to rock the swing. Katrina laughed. "Rock a-bye baby, in the tree top. When the wind blows, the cradle will rock. When the bough breaks, the cradle will fall—"

"Shut up!" She pounded on the screen door, which had become latched from the inside. "Mother! Mother are you in there?"

"Down will come baby."

The black birds skipped from branch to branch carrying orange and red berries. Two flew to Katrina and rested on the swing behind her.

"Mother!"

"Daughter?" Mrs. Abigail Fisher's voice was soft. "I see you must have received my letter."

"Mother, please." Elise felt something break off inside her belly. "Let me in."

The latch lifted, and Mrs. Abigail Fisher, with wild hair and open robe, stood straight.

"I sent you a letter."

The swing rocked back and forth. Elise heard Katrina's whistling.

"You see her then, right? On the swing?"

"No, child."

Elise wanted to stomp her feet and scream. She was four, she was eleven, she was seventeen. She was tired, absolutely once and for all furiously tired, of this game. Mrs. Abigail Fisher must have seen it coming.

"Come back in, Elise. Just because I don't see it, doesn't mean it isn't there. How have you lived with me all these years and not understood that?"

The rage bubbling in her stopped spinning. She didn't know what to do with it, so she coughed.

"Come back in. The house needs you."

Henry's hat had ceased dancing and was hanging on the edge of the banister. As more sunlight poured into the house, Elise was able to take in more of the house's condition. It was weeping, she realized, fire in the kitchen notwithstanding. The house was overcome with water. Velveted wallpaper curled up like used party favors. The insulation poked its tentacles out from holes in the walls and hung in pink clumps. The robin's egg blue shades that once were crisp and dry had molded and drooped, becoming sagging eyelids for the windows. She picked up Henry's hat and put it on her head.

"She liked that hat, there," said Mrs. Abigail Fisher.

"Henry said it was dancing all over the room." Elise almost smiled.

"She always liked to play dress-up." Mrs. Abigail Fisher held out her hand. Her fingers were too long for her palms, and they gnarled and twisted into a tiny bird's nest. "Daughter. I know that you don't like me. You may even be trying to kill me. I haven't seen your Henry fellow around here in awhile. Maybe he's gone to get the shovel that will dump me in the disposal. But that is neither here nor there at this moment. Do you see my hands?"

Elise nodded.

"The skin is so thin I can see the blood moving around. It's not going to move for too much longer. Your Henry is not going to have to kill me. I know I am dying. It slows down, you see, and there's not a thing you can do about it. That blood pressure the doctors are always yakking about that matters so much? Well, blood pressure is nothing more than the force of your fire. It's how much heat you have left to keep your blood moving through all the miles of arteries and vessels it has to go through."

"Mother, I don't think that's what blood pressure is."

"Ah. Listen. There are more stories about the world than you can imagine. I have lost my blood pressure. I used to wake up and feel it exactly where you'd think—right in the middle of my chest.

And that fire pulled me out of bed, made me write, kept me alive after your father left us. That fire made me me. And I've lost it now. I can hear my own breath in my chest when I sleep. There's no pulsing, no percussion, no drum beat. There's just the rattling around of air in a cavity that is collapsing."

"It's not so melodramatic, Mother. You hate the melodramatic."

"Sit." She cleared a dusty afghan off an Edwardian chair. The swing's chains rattled. Footsteps creaked across the upstairs floorboards. "Daughter, if you just accept the house, it will stop frightening you. Come. Sit."

Elise brushed the seat cushion with her hand, then realized it didn't matter. "Mother. We have been in this place before."

"Why do you think I hate the melodramatic?" Mrs. Abigail Fisher sat on the floor, suddenly as limber as a teenager.

"What?"

"You just said I hate the melodramatic."

"Oh, I don't know. Years of you saying that, maybe. You made students cry if they made any attempt to inject emotion in their stories. Remember the lecture in Iowa City?"

"That wasn't emotion. That was gibberish. You can't force emotion."

"Hence, you hate melodrama."

"Daughter, melodrama knows what it is. It embraces itself. It is sentimentality that I cannot abide."

"Why are we here? We have to get this place emptied out. Henry will be back soon."

"Will he? I thought you sent him away."

"He will be back soon. Why are we sitting here? We have nothing to say to each other. Oh. There's this. I'm not going to kill you. No matter how much you might want me to. I'm not going to kill you and bury you in a dumpster or in the backyard or under the porch or in any other dramatic or melodramatic fashion. One day you will be gone, and I will wish—god Mother I will wish—that I knew some small real thing about you. But I don't. And it's time I grew the hell up and stopped thinking a fiction writer could tell the truth."

The swing stopped swinging. The footsteps stopped shuffling. Elise felt the house inhale; its walls arcing inward for a brief moment. Mrs. Abigail Fisher remained on the floor, her flexibility becoming rigidity once again. Henry's hat was lifted from her head. It spun, it flipped, it twirled. Mrs. Abigail Fisher remained unmoved. Elise couldn't help but stare. She thought briefly of the original Snow White film where all the woodland creatures came and helped with the housework. The hat was playing. She opened her hands. The hat came to her. She threw it back in the air. It flew from corner to corner, landing for a moment on the curtain rod. She opened her hands again. It came back. She turned it over and inside its mouth was a notebook. "What's this?" asked Elise. The notebook was weeping like the house, its pages curling and yellowed. The ink had bled from page to page in some sections, but it still seemed legible. "Is this yours, Mother?"

Mrs. Abigail Fisher didn't look up.

"Mother?"

Mrs. Abigail Fisher smiled wryly. "Well played, plat eye. Well played."

"What is it, Mother?"

"It's a draft of a book."

"Your book?"

"Yes, my book. Who else writes in this family?"

Elise opened it. The pages cricked apart, sounding like crunching leaves. "Which one?"

The hat jumped in her lap, shuffling the pages of the notebook.

"For Phillip and Courtney Lynn," read Elise. She hadn't spoken her sister's name in too many years. "Mother. Which book is this?"

"One that didn't work," she said. "Hand it to me."

The hat flipped, keeping the notebook pressed against her lap.

"Knock it off, plat-eye-fire-starter," said Mrs. Abigail Fisher. "I know what you're doing."

The hat was still.

"It's my story," said Mrs. Abigail Fisher. "You've no right to read it."

The hat leapt from Elise's lap, taking the notebook with it. It rested above the drapes, balancing on the wrought iron curtain rod. The whistling from the porch grew louder. Katrina stretched the whistle into words. "I need you!"

Mrs. Abigail Fisher at last looked up. "I hear that, daughter."

"That's Katrina."

"No. Not Katrina." She went to the door, opened it and stepped onto the porch. The shouting stopped. The swing's chains stopped rattling. "I'm going outside, Daughter. The notebook is yours."

Mrs. Abigail Fisher stood tall, chin tilted up, hair wild and frantic on her head. She allowed her robe to fall open and slip from her bony shoulders.

"You can't go outside naked, Mother."

"There's no one coming, Daughter." Mrs. Abigail Fisher stepped onto the porch. "Everyone is already here." She pulled the door closed behind her.

The hat flew from the drapes and landed on the pine floorboard. Its mouth was open. Elise picked up the notebook again. "For Phillip and Courtney Lynn," she read again. And then the epigraph: "It is very easy to love alone. Gertrude Stein." She flipped through the pages. Most of the book was written with a deep blue fountain pen in her mother's precise handwriting, but towards the end, the red ink surfaced, scratching out lines, paragraphs, pages, even pooling in several places, sticking the old pieces of paper together. There was a page ripped out towards the end, but the blue ink resumed in a flourish to close out the book. She read the final line. "In the morning when she visits, the garden will still hold its honeysuckle and weeping willows, each reaching desperately for sun and earth, connecting with neither." It was a draft of *The Garden of Gethsemane, Georgia.*

25

Pistachio held her breath. This was the moment. If only Harold were here, but she couldn't think of him now. She could only hope that Elise would read the notebook. The characters couldn't read. Fireside legend had it that once upon a time the characters had the ability to read, and not just in the language of their creator, but in all languages ever uttered. There was an epic battle, one that continues to be re-enacted in fantasy novels across the world, in which the invaders try to crush the indigenous cultures out of a fear of their powers.

According to the Book of Characters, Characters had always existed. There was no beginning or end to them. They waited for a Creator to pull them onto a page, but they existed regardless of an allegiance. They would continue to exist after their Creators became a footnote. But the Creators were jealous of the Characters' ability to read the words as they were being written. They liked the idea of power being theirs alone. If the Characters could read then it was only a matter of moments before they might start writing as well, and if that happened, well, the possibility was too horrific to contemplate. So the Creators held a summit, the details of which are sketchy still, which declared that the ability to read be henceforth and forevermore removed from the Characters' skill sets.

Pistachio never quite understood how they achieved that declaration—how they were able to get inside the souls of billions of characters and take out a working part—so she never quite believed that they had the power at all. Characters were prone to telling tales and the most reasonable explanation was that they'd never been able to read at all, but they wished they could, and it was a much more dramatic choice to have that power taken away by unseen hands. It gave the Characters something to unite them. Harold told her once that there was a single character left with the power of reading, and that character lived on an island off the coast of Japan where he was sequestered for his own safety, attended to by a council of crones. Harold liked to tell stories, too, and Pistachio liked to hear them, even though she never believed in their plausibility.

But maybe now she could sit at the feet of someone who could read, and that someone could tell her story, tell her what happened when she was cut out so violently and left for dead. She picked up the hat. Elise didn't notice. She put it on her head. She wanted this woman to see her. Pistachio pulled an afghan from the wingback chair and sat on the floor. She wrapped the afghan around her shoulders. She tried to imagine what she might look like to Elise—a hat and a shawl at her feet—but she remembered instead the little girl walking out at night toward the creek, moonlight dancing on her shoulders. "Read to me," Pistachio whispered. "Please read to me."

26

Elise felt panicked. Reading her mother's notebooks was tantamount to treason. How many times had she heard, "this is private—this is Mother's—this is none of your business," while growing up. When her father was still with them, her mother would often gather them together in the parlor and read the day's pages to them. Her father would laugh at the right times, nod seriously at others, and they both would applaud the end of each chapter. Over the years her father had become a wisp of colors and sound that danced through her from time to time. She caught his scent in the folds of old sheet music she rifled through at antique stores or felt his hand on the back of her neck when she walked the woods around their house in North Carolina. She thought of him as a child might relate to an invisible friend.

The stench of old shoes, rotted vegetables and skunk had faded from when Elise first arrived at the house, but it had been replaced by a sauerkraut and root cellar smell. She thought of the fresh overturned earth in the garden when she and her father had planted tomatoes, green beans and a few yellow squash. The earth squirmed with earthworms, ants, and spiders. "Do they eat the seeds?" she'd asked her father, pointing at a gray worm.

"No, Leesy-girl. They keep the soil full of air so it can breathe."

Years later in sophomore biology, she cried when she saw the pinned earthworms in the dissection pan. It was too much to think of how the soil was suffocating without them. There was silence on the porch. No swing chains rattling. No Katrina singing. No Mother complaining. Then there was the matter of the hat and shawl in front of her, an invisible praying figure. Its head was bowed, shoulders a rounded egg. She thought it shivered.

"You're the firestarter," she said.

The hat nodded.

"My mother sees you."

A nod again.

It didn't even seem odd anymore that she was talking to a hat and shawl. It would have been rude to ignore them, right there in front of her on the floor, and Elise was a daughter of the South. She could not bear to be rude. If she ever got out of this house again, she would check herself into an in-patient rehab center, though she wasn't sure what she would be rehabbing from—a family? Was there a special ward for that?

"Were you trying to burn the house down?"

The hat shook back and forth.

"I believe you," said Elise. "I really do."

The figure inched closer, resting its head on her knee. She felt its coolness when she reached to touch it. It was just a vapor, just a condensation of water, but it wanted her, and Elise wanted it.

"I'll read you a story," she said. "What else is there?"

27

Elise was surprised her throat was burning. She coughed, tapped her chest, and began to read.

> *Someone had taken great care when laying out the body of the girl known as Pistachio. Although her legs were broken, bent back like the legs of crickets, a circle of flowers adorned the space around her head where a halo would have been, had there been anyone left around who believed in the probability of halos or the possibility that Pistachio could have earned one. Her mother watched from the clouds, or so everyone in Gethsemane, Georgia said, and sent down the torrent of rain upon the field. No mother, no matter how bad a job she did, no matter how her baby turned out in the world, can bear to see her folded like an origami swan in an open field, waiting for the birds to come and do their work. No mother, not even Mary the Mother of God, who had to believe, surely had to believe, that her son's death was for a larger good, had to look away when her baby, sweet little brown-eyed boy, sputtered and died and was left for the birds and the flies.*
>
> *Word by word, whisper by whisper, news of Pistachio's death moved around the town. It would settle a moment at one clapboard house and then move to another with renewed energy. "She is dead! She is dead!" whispered the*

words. "She is dead." And those who thought they would be relieved found themselves wondering what would happen next. Where would Pistachio's soul have gone? And they shuddered a moment, outside the view of others, when they wondered whether or not their beliefs could actually be true. The world had been coming to an end at least four times in Pistachio's short life. One preacher predicted it down to the hour and the day, his flock joining hands and singing praises in the church cemetery so they could be on hand to greet their deceased loved ones when they were raptured right out of the ground. That didn't happen, of course, but the preacher was undeterred.

When the world ended for Pistachio, that preacher was nowhere to be seen, though he had lived down the street from Pistachio all of her short time in Gethsemane, and more than once had taken note of her unusual beauty, and more than twice noticed her audacity and was both repulsed and excited by it. On the day the world ended for Pistachio, there was only her body, a ring of buttercups around her head, and a drop or two from the tears her mother shed from an invisible and unreachable heaven.

All of Gethsemane, Georgia knew this day would come, though not one of them would dare admit it lest they'd seem to be suggesting they knew the will of God. The citizenry took the will of God very seriously, and though His ways were mysterious, each member of the community secretly thought he or she understood them.

Pistachio had been a test for all of them, and now that she was dead, they each thought they had passed the test, all for different reasons. Pistachio made them bring out the kinder, gentler Jesus. The one that didn't bring folks in for Sunday sermons. The fire and brimstone Jesus made much better copy, but they knew because of the way Pistachio found her way into their town, the way she found herself at their services, their family picnics, their Easter egg rolls, that she was there to test their compassion. Many of them failed the test over the time Pistachio lived among them, but when news of her death spread from house to house, each resident remembered only a moment of compassion, real or imagined, that they'd offered her. This delusion helped them make peace with the way she died, helped them move it quickly to the place in their minds where they filed away everything that didn't make sense, everything that didn't fit with their world order, so they could sleep soundly at night, knowing they did everything they could, although in the end of course, God's will be done.

28

There were notes all along the margins of the pages. Elise hadn't thought her mother one for marginalia. She always seemed to know exactly where she was going and what was coming next. "Why did she die?" was one of the notes, along with a crude drawing of a rock and a bird. "Meaning in no meaning?" was another. "Who walks out?" another. She was surprised by the number of strike-throughs. She'd thought her mother wrote one word and then the next and then the next, each in its preordained perfect order. The idea of her struggling in her turret, grasping for the right word or question, made Elise feel a bit of joy. Her mother didn't know everything before it happened. She had to figure out what to do as well.

She turned the page.

> *Moss had never grown on the Rock of Golgotha in the town of Gethsemane, Georgia. The story goes that some seventy years ago, Preacher Billy McGivens, known to his flock as Billy Mac, stood on that very rock, hissing snake in each hand, and officially declared that rock the Rock of Golgotha, right in the center of Gethsemane, to be the heart of the town and the burning bush of the Lord.*
>
> *The snakes laid off Billy Mac for most of his lucrative career under the big top. He dunked and duped and buried and resurrected just about as many people as died in Sherman's march on Atlanta. He was undeterred in his*

righteousness and undeterred in his faith in the snakes. Even after the bite, one swift strike right on his jugular, Billy Mac refused to have the snake ripped away from him.

"Behold!" he is said to have said. "The will of God! Satan (and here his voice got quiet) Satan, get thee behind." And those were his last words, or so the legend goes. Whether it's true or not, there's still no moss on this rock. You make it what you will.

Billy Mac's family had roots in Gethsemane since before the Reconstruction. Most of the family had been no-account, but Billy Mac saw opportunity in religion, plus, he really loved snakes and figured God and snakes and his chiseled chin was bound to be a ticket to somewhere. He'd have never believed he'd have died back in Gethsemane. He would have appreciated the irony, though; the creation he put the most faith in (the snake, not God) is what got him at the end. No one knew what to do with the snakes after Billy Mac's death, (they couldn't just set them free if they were some sort of holy now could they?) so one day a young orphaned boy who'd been tagging along with Billy Mac because it was less work than the traveling circus and more fun than wandering from farm to farm helping with cotton and corn, quietly slipped into Billy Mac's tent and opened the canvas bag that held the pair of snakes and watched them slip under the tent flap and disappear into the grass. The town and the congregants thought the snakes had disappeared into thin air because God had exacted vengeance on them for killing his humble servant, but that wasn't what happened at all, and the snakes lived out the rest of their days in peace. Some nights, long

long afterwards, the orphaned boy would think about the snakes and wish them well.

Pistachio was found on that rock on an exceptionally sunny day in 1969. Although no one was left alive who had seen Billy Mac and his snakes, everyone knew about the rock, and perhaps because of that they were a little more inclined to give her a chance before they called the county to come and cart her away. She appeared walking, talking and moving like an adult, but she was barely four feet tall.

Maybe she's a fairy? Some said. A forest sprite. A wood nymph.

"She's just a midget," said John Jacob, the town's meanest kid.

But Pistachio wasn't a midget, nor, sadly, was she a fairy, a forest sprite, or a wood nymph. She was just short and she was tired of fielding questions about who or what she was. Her name was Carolyn Pistachio P. Simmons and she was eighteen years old and she was all alone in this world except for the baby growing in her belly. This wasn't how she'd imagined it, but beggars couldn't be choosers, and though Pistachio was not yet a bona fide beggar, she could see one day being one and thought she should practice acting like one now so it wouldn't be so much of a surprise when the inevitable day came.

The town would say the earth opened up and Pistachio appeared because that was a far better story, but really she had taken the Greyhound from Montgomery, Alabama, with her hat box of clothes that made her feel French. Her husband, Vick, (well he was going to be her husband when he came back) had been killed in Vietnam. She saw his name roll by while watching television and drinking a bottled Coke. She took a moment after reading his name, looked at her empty ring finger and the dark single-wide with the double mattress on the floor, and decided she and whatever was coming next would be better off outside of Montgomery. Her mama had kicked her out when she found out she was pregnant, and so Pistachio had appropriated Vick's trailer, assuming that's where they would be living when the fighting was over. She didn't know if he knew she was pregnant. She'd sent a letter two months ago, once she felt sure she wasn't going to lose the baby by accident, but he'd never written back. Everyone knew it could take months for letters to find their recipients, and some never did. She wasn't sure how he'd feel about it, but at least having a baby would join them together forever.

Vick had, in fact, not received the letter. When he was shot, he had been thinking not about Pistachio, but about a woman he met in Hanoi on his last leave. He never saw the bullet coming and he never saw the letter. If he had, he would have slipped into the jungle like so many others. Not because he didn't love Pistachio; he was actually fonder of her than most. It wasn't that he didn't want a kid—someday he saw that future—a wife, a kid, a dog, a '65 Mustang in the driveway—but not right now. He hadn't foreseen this war and he hadn't foreseen that he would be killing other people and he hadn't foreseen that he wasn't going to get to grow up. The world had made his decision for him, while Pistachio held tight to

the fantasy that he was thinking of her and their family
when the sniper blew his head clean off.

29

Pistachio was crying. She wasn't sure the woman could tell, but she pulled the hat down lower over her face to hide her eyes anyway. She remembered. She hadn't thought of how the experience might translate into words, but when she heard them again, she remembered Vick, his dark eyes and dimpled chin. He had been with someone in Hanoi? Where was Hanoi? He didn't want the baby. He didn't want her. Even if he hadn't been killed, he wouldn't have come back to her. He wouldn't have come back. That was a mean thing, and she felt the slice across her heart that Mrs. Abigail Fisher had given her when she wrote that scene. A mean thing. When she'd first emerged from the pen's nib, she was on the Rock of Golgotha. She didn't know it then, but the coldness and ruthless exposure on the white paper gave her the necessary vulnerability to sit there on that sacred rock, pregnant, waiting for the judgment of the town. It had been humid that day. The words leaked into each other on the paper, but Mrs. Abigail Fisher had kept writing.

30

Elise continued to read.

Gethsemane, Georgia was not like Montgomery. It reminded Pistachio of the towns in snow globes where everything lined up on a grid and all the trees were of complimentary heights. There was only one main street with only one stoplight. To its credit, the street had not been named Main Street, but rather Centre Street, with the reversed "r" and "e" to imply it was something more than it was. Three churches were on Centre Street: a Baptist, a Methodist, and a Presbyterian.

Pistachio had read about Gethsemane in the news. Four Negro boys had been shot and drowned in the Tuskcahawnee River that ran behind the town. Everything had been such a mess when the Civil Rights marchers came from the North. Trouble had always been there. Someone, somewhere (was it Martin Luther King Junior or Rosa Parks?) had lit the match that set everything that had long been simmering exploding. No one knew what the rules were, and folks tend to do all kinds of terrible things when the rules they took as solid turned out to be as unstable as a seesaw in a hurricane. Even though Pistachio knew about the killings, she couldn't help but think that a town with the same name as the prayer garden Jesus used had to have at least one redeemer in it. Pistachio didn't really place a lot of stock in Jesus, but she'd always thought his eyes were kind, and she believed that whether or not his praying made any difference, he prayed with utmost sincerity.

The doors to the Methodist and Baptist churches were locked, but the Presbyterian (Garden of Gethsemane Presbyterian Welcomes You) doors were open wide, and as luck, or fate, or Jesus would have it, Mrs. Honeycutt, the organist, had thought she might should stop by for one more practice session before the big 150-year birthday celebration of the church. As usual, Reverend Franks asked her to do something that just outspread the width of her nimble fingers. She swore he did it on purpose, but he couldn't read a note. She'd figured out over the years a way to improvise by playing only the top or bottom note of the chord progression. Took some dexterous digits, but it was worth it just to keep proving to him that she could do whatever he needed. Mrs. Honeycutt worried every night about her aging face and fingers. Mrs. Lackey, who'd been the organist over at First Baptist for forty-seven years had just been replaced by a skinny blonde woman with fingers as long as chopsticks. Mrs. Honeycutt refused to have that happen to her, so when she finished the final bars (with an extra twirl and trill of the final C chord) and heard clapping in the back of the church, Pistachio's face could only appear to her as that of an angel.

Mrs. Honeycutt let herself listen to the lone applause one minute longer than humility should allow. It was so lovely—a sonic response to her own humble servant's attempt at a joyful noise. When she played in church, no matter how good of a job she did, no matter how much the Holy Spirit moved through her, her efforts were always met with silence. Maybe a rustling of the bulletins, a clearing of a throat. Once she heard a snore and it was all she could do not to cry.

"That was beautiful, ma'am."

Mrs. Honeycutt took in the waif of a girl. She had the air of harmless desperation about her. Mrs. Honeycutt decided that though her eyes were wild, they were kind, an assumption reached, not the least because of her applause or the way she stood in the nave of the church shifting from one sneckered foot to the other. Right then and there, Mrs. Honeycutt resolved to like this child.

"I bet you're the most favorite member of the whole congregation," said Pistachio.

"Why, well, I don't know about that. Reverend Franks is quite revered."

The waif seemed to consider this for a moment. "No offense to him, ma'am, but I suppose he doesn't make music like that."

Mrs. Honeycutt was in love. She even saw a resemblance to herself when she was younger (well, not all that much younger she assured herself). She'd once crept into a black church when she was a girl. Well, not really into it, but outside of it, to listen to the music. They applauded in that church when the music finally decrescendoed. They applauded and shouted and stomped and Mrs. Honeycutt, who was only June then, was in awe. The

Presbyterians did not shout and stomp. Pistachio had finished applauding and looked at the floor. Her hands rested on her belly.

"Well, who might you be?" Mrs. Honeycutt said after the last vibration of applause moved through her body.

"My name is Pistachio."

"Stacy?"

"Pistachio."

"Anastasia?"

"Pistachio."

"Pistachio?"

"Yes."

"Well. That is indeed a noble nut."

They both laughed and Pistachio felt the baby laughing too.

Mrs. Honeycutt stated the obvious. "I haven't seen you here before. Are you visiting?"

"I don't think so."

Pistachio had left behind a goldfish in the single-wide trailer in Montgomery. It was probably dead by now. Its name was Freddy.

"Looks like my little brother, Freddy," Vick had said. "See those bubble eyes? Freddy always looks like he just inhaled a bunch of helium."

The thought of Freddy floating upside down, orange and black scales falling into the red rocks at the bottom of the bowl, was too much for her, so she pushed it into her belly right on top of her laughing baby.

"Well, who you staying with honey?"

Pistachio shrugged.

"The Beans?"

"No."

"The Murphys?"

"No."

"Miss Ida?"

"No."

Mrs. Honeycutt saw herself, crouched on the steps in front of the black Baptist church. Someone had to have seen her. It wasn't safe; she knew that. It wasn't safe for her or them, but she came whenever she could and crouched and listened and secretly hoped that one of the women with the gorgeous wide-brimmed pastel colored hats would scoop her up and take her to a life she'd imagined was filled only with music. One woman did see her.

"You lost little girl?" The brim of the Easter-grass green hat obstructed her eyes.

"No, ma'am."

It was 1946. "What are you here for?"

"Music."

The woman smiled, did not scoop June (not yet Mrs. Honeycutt) up and take her home. "You be sure and listen good." The woman left her on the stoop and entered the church and June just marveled at the strength of the woman's calves.

"Do you want to stay with me?" Mrs. Honeycutt blurted out without thinking that her husband would surely object because he did not like anything out of the ordinary, especially other people in his home. Mrs. Honeycutt couldn't even invite the circle ladies over for tea without clearing it so Mr. Honeycutt could make plans to be

somewhere else.

"Yes," said Pistachio, without thinking about what it would mean to settle into Gethsemane, to settle into another family's life.

Mrs. Honeycutt held out her hand. "Then come along, dear. I live just down the street."

Elise had read all her mother's books, and she didn't remember this part from the published novel. There had been a Pistachio character, but she figured only briefly in the backstory of the protagonist, one Ms. Judy Jenkins. Elise thought Pistachio had been the required crazy-aunt-in-the-attic character, or maybe a random runaway Judy was helping to show the readers she had a charitable heart and wasn't all soap opera vile and venom. It hadn't worked though. Ms. Judy Jenkins was one of the most love-to-hate characters in contemporary literature.

For her mother though, the story ran a little bit differently. *The Garden of Gethsemane, Georgia* marked a distinct turn in her mother's work. Where she had once been a serious writer, addressing social issues and complex character arcs, *Gethsemane* took a different approach. It was almost-parody of Faulkner and Agee. It was a swipe at the pillars that had held her up, the very ones she had gone to study and work with when she, in an act even Elise had to admit was brave, left Georgia for upstate New York's famous writer's colony, Zanzibar. Sales for *Garden* were unprecedented, leaving her early work unread on remainder carts. The reading world loved the new voice, the sharp edges and simple plots. They loved knowing what was going to happen, and her mother was rewarded with advance after advance for the next in the "series everyone is talking about." Elise was beginning to realize that the book her mother published was not the book she had intended to write, perhaps not even the book she should have written. The book had been released two years after her father left, two years after her sister left. Elise set the notebook down. The hat and shawl were resting on the floor.

"Where did you go?" she said to the room. The hat and shawl were still. The porch was silent. Henry was somewhere else, probably on his way back to North Carolina if he had any sense at all. He would pack up his shirts and request a new hat from the Sheriff's Department, and he would probably even take the gray cat, Smeek. He would leave her a note, some form of explanation so she wouldn't worry, and he'd rent out a room at the Blue Ridge Inn close to his office. She'd come visit him a few times; they'd say they'd remain friends, but within a few months they'd dodge each other in the health food store, pretend they didn't realize they were waiting side by side at the same stoplight, and before a year was up, he'd be transferred to another small town outpost in Kentucky or Arkansas, and she'd climb to the top of the hill where they'd looked out at Oz and remember that she had once been a woman who had loved somebody.

31

Pistachio had crept out of the room while Elise was reading. She couldn't handle the onslaught of scenes that filled her mind. She wished Elise could see her. She was becoming quite a sight, a roundness in her belly and a form to her nose and ears. She imagined she might be beautiful, if given the right story. When she inhaled, she felt the rise of her shoulders, the expansion of her ribs. When she exhaled, she felt freedom. The flesh on her bones was becoming a pale pink. When she touched her arm, the skin bounced back, full and new. She remembered Mrs. Honeycutt, but she also remembered her Mr. Honeycutt and the cramped attic room with angled walls. She remembered the smell of Barbasol and Dentyne, and the snippet of song "I come to the garden alone, while the dew is still on the morning" that Mrs. Honeycutt would play on the downstairs organ over and over while Pistachio lay in the attic room in angles. That was not how it was supposed to be. She had things left to say. Things to do. She had things to say to her creator that would have changed everything.

Pistachio found the gate in her mind to the Cemetery of Books. Harold had first shown her how to get there. "It's my favorite place to wander," he'd said. "It's important to remember the stories that came before us." They stepped through a rusted iron gate. Two damp gargoyles peered down at them. The decayed leaves were brittle beneath her feet. He pointed to a moss-covered stone. *The Beginnings of Mrs. Penelope Hatchett by Claudia Z. Holmes. 1872-1890.* "No one's read that book since 1890," he said. "It's still here though. It's marked so we can all come and visit it. That's what's important, don't you agree? Even though the author is gone, the book is still here. Waiting."

"Waiting for the author?" asked Pistachio.

"No. The author just goes one day. It's how it's meant to be. She gave the book as a gift. Sometimes books wait a long time to find the person they're supposed to be with. It's harder for them, I think, especially as time moves by to find their people. Some books find lots and lots of people, others only one or two. We can't know when we're in a book how it's going to end up. Maybe one day someone will find *The Beginnings of Mrs. Penelope Hatchett* in a stack of yellowed books in an antique shop in a tiny town. And maybe they'll pick it up and maybe they'll start to thumb through it and a phrase will leap out at them, and they'll reason that the book is only fifty cents and so they'll buy it, slip it in their laptop bag, and leave the store. That's how it works. Readers arrive one at a time in silence and sometimes secrecy. They wander around the shelves, gaze jumping from spine to spine, picking up a book, reading its jacket, as if all that we are can be contained in fifty words of back copy. If we're lucky, they may read the opening page or two before putting the book back on the shelf if they don't feel that synthesis, that moment when they know and whisper, 'you are the one I've been waiting for.'"

Pistachio had wandered off into the cemetery. Every step she took uncovered a new stone. On the newer graves, she could still see the book cover design on the granite. There were so many.

"Sorry, love," said Harold. "I ramble. I know. I always go on five lines too many. Mrs. Abigail Fisher always cuts me back. I have so many more lines just waiting in my throat."

"It's fine, it's fine," she said. "I just can't believe there are so many." She couldn't see the edges of the cemetery. Every direction she looked, the book covers stretched in front of her. Some of the stones were flat, some were upright, some had edges falling away, and others still were giant monoliths—*The Grapes of Wrath, Gone with the Wind, Harry Potter*. The stone for *Jaws* was a giant great white, full fanged and fearless. "How can anybody find readers?"

"It's magic," said Harold. "Books have a little scoop of magic to help them find their readers. Can't put that in a spreadsheet."

Pistachio smiled. Harold had been railing against spreadsheets lately. His last performance was in the ill-fated *Searching for You,* a book Mrs. Abigail Fisher had been strong-armed into writing by her publisher. It was loosely based on Patsy Cline's life story. "If I'm going to write about a troubadour, let me write about someone who had the good sense to stay alive," she'd said to her editor, who told her she had a contract and she needed to deliver the books they asked for. "Sometimes the books you ask for are not the books I write," she'd said. Her editor was unmoved, so Mrs. Abigail Fisher wrote the story, but she left out the element of magic, so the book was unable to find its readers. Harold had played Patsy's road manager in the tale, and he had given it his all. He loved the music, and caught himself whistling the tunes while waiting for his next scene. The spreadsheets had turned against him, though. The sales figures for *Searching for You* were small towers in the sea of larger towers, which represented the trajectory of Mrs. Abigail Fisher's career. He'd even been mentioned in the *New York Times,* and not in the flattering way in which he was accustomed. The critic, whose name Harold had permanently stricken from his mind, said that his character resembled several other characters in Mrs. Abigail Fisher's recent work, and he questioned whether or not Mrs. Fisher had lost her edge and was now recycling stock characters from other, more successful, novels.

"No, you can't put magic in a spreadsheet," said Pistachio.

Harold wrapped his arms around her. "It's nice here, isn't it? All our friends are here."

Pistachio wished Harold was with her this day as she stepped again into the Cemetery of Books. It was a comforting place, she had to agree. There was so much energy underneath the soil just waiting to *become*. She easily found Mrs. Abigail Fisher's plot. Twenty-one titles had stones with the book's first publication date. Some had end dates too. Harold had told her the end date could be the date the book was finished, which didn't make sense to Pistachio because the book had to have been finished before it was published. Maybe the end date was the last time someone had read it.

Harold said sometimes a book wasn't finished until long after it was published, but Pistachio didn't understand what that meant. At least not when he'd said it. Now, she realized she was a part of a book that wasn't finished, though it had been a mega-bestseller. Her character was the reason the book wasn't finished. She wasn't supposed to have been cut out. This was her new driving question: What would happen if she had stayed in the story she was meant to be in?

And then she found her book cover. The stone was tall and narrow, the title etched deeply in an Old English font. THE GARDEN OF GETHSEMANE, GEORGIA. 1978 - ________. There was no end date. She glanced around the cemetery. All the other stones she could see had an end date. Harold would know the answer. She was afraid she'd never see him again. Her creator was clearly very sick and dying, and everyone knew that the story they were involved with when their creators died was the story they'd be trapped in for eternity. She didn't want to be trapped, unfinished book or not, without Harold. When had that happened? When had she fallen in love with a crazy romantic hero? And what if she could never get him back?

She brushed some leaves from the base of the stone and sat down, resting her back against the dates. The Cemetery of Books had a sickle-moon all the time because stories were always in the process of growing. There was never a time a character could come into the Cemetery of Books without potential or possibility. Sometimes a story was unearthed that had been buried for centuries. Sometimes only scraps of the scenes were legible, but it was enough to revitalize the characters, help them draw in breath through their shuttered tracheas. Even the longest-dead characters never lost hope. The moon never went dark. Pistachio didn't know what to do. Elise was probably still reading from the book. It was odd that she could remember having lived those scenes although they ended up not being part of the final book. It was less the action of the scene that was haunting her than the emotional impact. She'd been genuinely afraid. And the smell—the minty Dentyne breath—it touched something she couldn't name.

Mrs. Abigail Fisher had turned mean. Somewhere during the writing of the novel, she became consumed by anger. Pistachio remembered cowering in the corners of the pages, hoping to be spared the knife. Mrs. Abigail Fisher snapped pens in two. She ripped pages out. She changed ink colors. As she changed, the type of writer she was also changed. The interest in the deeper questions that had peppered her early work, sparked the interest of Truman Capote and the jealousy, although he would never admit it, of Norman Mailer, waned and she became interested only in the cheap shot, the easy out, and because she was quite talented, her cheap shots still came across as better than most. But she knew, and she couldn't seem to stop herself. No matter how many pens she snapped or how many pages ended up in the wastebasket, she no longer had the courage to write into the neck of uncertainty. She no longer had the courage to pose the questions without answers, and though her career stretched long and lucratively in front of her, she never became the creator she had intended to be, and consequently, Pistachio never became the character she could have been.

Pistachio leaned her head against the stone. It was cold, but comfortable. She appreciated its solidity. No matter what else might go wrong, she at least had a home with this stone, with this story. Who was she to think she could have had the best and brightest of lives? Some characters are only walk-ons. The books need them too. The leaves crackled behind her. She was too tired to turn around. She could just sleep there awhile. Maybe Harold would come. Maybe everything would sort itself out with Elise and her mother. Maybe the music chair would start to play again.

A spider with thin long legs walked across her calf. She held out her hand and it walked onto her palm, her dimensional palm. She was still in awe of that space she now took up. Someone was behind her. It must be Harold. He would surprise her in just a moment by saying something hilarious about whaling in the Pacific or coffee growing in Peru. In just a moment, he would tap her on the shoulder and she would pretend to be afraid because that would be the reaction he'd been hoping for, and then they'd lie down among the book covers, their old friends, and sleep under the sickle-moon. If it were Harold walking up to her, she would grab his hand and make him do something brave to stop this climax from happening. Mrs. Abigail Fisher was dying. They had to claim their final story. There was no more time for adventures and subplots and false starts.

The footsteps stopped. Pistachio closed her eyes. Any minute now, he'd speak. She heard the backside of the book cover stone being brushed clean. The feet turned away for a step, and then the body let itself down onto the earth, resting against the other side of the book cover stone. It let out a sigh.

"Harold?" asked Pistachio. "Is that you?"

"It is I," but the voice wasn't Harold's. "We have to talk."

"Abbey," said Pistachio. "How are you here?"

"Don't turn around. Just let me speak, and then we can decide what to do next."

"How did you get here?"

"Child, I told you not to speak. You have never, not once, done what I asked you to do."

Pistachio held a rebuttal in her mouth. She was the one who had promised never to give up her longing for the sea. She was the one who lied when she said she surrendered. She'd thought her creator knew. She was supposed to know everything. The whole universe depended on that.

"Are you not talking?" asked Mrs. Abigail Fisher.

Pistachio remained silent.

"Good. Let me talk. You watch the moon. Which, if you notice, has become the setting sun."

Pistachio felt the heat on her shoulders. Impossible. This was not a place of sun. It was a place of moon, of germination and incubation. But there it was, washing the cool blue light away with its fire. Where was Harold? Where was anyone?

"You still hear her reading down there, right? My daughter. She thinks she's found something, and I suppose she has. But it's not what she needs. I am going to ask three things of you, Pistachio Plat-Eye. I want you to answer them honestly, and then you can ask three things of me. I promise I will answer them truthfully. Are we in agreement? You may speak."

"Yes." Pistachio felt her skin stretch. Surely no character had ever entered into direct conversation with her creator before. There was always something between them—the texts, the dimensions, the fighting of wills. She heard additional footsteps in the Cemetery, but she dared not turn around. If it were Harold, he would know to watch and wait. Black birds, ravens most likely, hovered on thick tree branches. She felt their anxious flapping.

"Good. Tell me when you realized you were different."

"I don't understand."

"You're not like the others. You tormented me. I thought I ripped you out, but here you are, and maybe it's because I'm getting so very old and tired, I actually am willing to listen to you. I have never forgotten you, Pistachio. You were my end."

"What do you mean? I was the one who ended up on the closet floor! I was the one who missed out on the biggest selling book you ever wrote!"

"Biggest selling, maybe but not the best. Never the best."

"It could have been the best," Pistachio said softly. "I could have made it the best."

"I know."

"You do?"

"I do."

"So you do know everything."

Mrs. Abigail Fisher laughed softly. "I most certainly do not."

Pistachio was puzzled. She felt a cracking. The crunching of leaves continued. "But that's not how it works."

"And what do you know, Plat-Eye, of how it works?"

"Is that the second thing you're asking?"

"Well done again. You are formidable."

"I don't want to be formidable," said Pistachio. "I want my story."

"I do too," said Mrs. Abigail Fisher. "I lost it somehow, and then I—" The footsteps stopped. Her creator coughed. "And then I couldn't bear to do what I had to do to find it again. And it appears, judging from this most unexpected turn of events, that I am not going to be allowed to leave this rock without figuring it out."

"I want my story."

"You have to tell me mine," said Mrs. Abigail Fisher. "You know something. You've known something, and it's been so long that I can't remember what it is. I knew you were trying to say something important to me and I couldn't stand to hear it. I couldn't let you write the words, so I cut you out. I had to. You had arrived far too soon."

"Too soon for what?"

"Too soon for me to let go of being angry."

Pistachio was confused. "But you weren't angry before. You were full of questions and you were committed to us and you were excited to be writing. Every morning you wrote with the drapes open, and then when it was my turn—finally my turn—you started closing the shades and the doors. The room was so dark the paper seemed to glow. You weren't angry until then, and from that moment on, we were all afraid of you."

"You were afraid of me?"

"All of us were. You would not believe the carnage on the closet floor! Every time we'd patch someone up, you'd toss another one in. Sometimes whole families! We didn't know what to do."

"Yes you did." Mrs. Abigail Fisher's voice was weary.

"I did. But you wouldn't let me."

"Alright. We're going to start the game now," said Mrs. Abigail

Fisher. "I need for you to tell me what you remember."

"What I remember about what?"

"What you remember about when I was Abbey. About Zanzibar," and then she paused. "You said you and all my characters have been around since before I was born. If that's true, tell me my story. Tell me about when I wasn't like I became."

Pistachio heard the shaking in Mrs. Abigail Fisher's voice. She wanted so much to turn around and touch her, but that had never been allowed. That could never happen, could it? When Abbey was at Zanzibar, Pistachio had just met Harold. He'd been riding elephants in lower Burma and somehow found himself crossing into an Orwell essay quite by accident. Abbey had yanked him back, and there he had been, still swatting giant green-eyed flies. She had been drawn to his bewilderment. "I had been about to be somewhere special!" he declared. "Something was about to happen." And then he turned to her and said, "Do you have my elephant?" And that was when she fell in love. Pistachio and Harold had been part of the golden cloud that hovered around Abbey. They saw nothing but the future, dreamed nothing less than symphonic.

"That was 1949," said Pistachio. She remembered, though. Oh, how she remembered. "I'll tell you the story. I'll pretend to be you like you pretended to be me."

"Pistachio, I did not pretend."

The footsteps started up again. "It doesn't matter. Let me tell you your story. You asked."

"I did. Please use the third person, dear. I can't bear the familiarity."

32

Pistachio settled herself in to tell the story.

Before Mrs. Abigail Fisher was Mrs. Abigail Fisher she was just Abbey and she was going to be famous. She had been making the plans for her life since she was a girl. She would tell you she was born knowing the trajectory of her life. She spoke in active verbs from her very first sentence.

"Father," she'd said, after opening the envelope with the gold stamped address. Zanzibar, the invitation-only artist's colony in upstate New York, had invited her, at the formal request of Flannery O'Connor. She hadn't dared to hope, even though she was sure it would happen. "Father, I am going to New York."

He took his pipe from between his lips. "When?"

"In a month."

He opened the evening newspaper and raised it above his nose. "That will be good."

She didn't know why she expected he would ask more. She traced the embossed letters on the paper. This was the door. Life was beginning. Her life. Not the life she stole from her mother by being born. "You took her last breath," her father always told her, before raising the newspaper shade between them. "You took it." As a young girl, she tried to remember doing that, tried to remember tunneling through the birth canal grabbing buckets of breath so that when she pushed into the sunlight in 1929—the year of the crash, the year of the panic, the run on the banks, the year of men in bowler hats jumping from windows on Wall Street, and women, after their men jumped to the sidewalks or jumped into bottles or opium dens, packing what remained of their family and their belongings into wagons and moving west to an unknown and open frontier—she would have enough air to breathe herself. She tried to remember whether or not she knew if she had taken the breath on purpose, if she'd been trying to steal from her mother, but she couldn't recall. Couldn't honestly recall her first breath in this world, but she made up the story of it, because that was what she did, Abbey Scruggs, that's what she did: make up stories. It was a better story if she stole her mother's breath than if her mother was simply not strong enough to bear her weight. Abbey Scruggs, throughout all of her life, could tolerate many things, but weakness of spirit was not one of them, and to her, unless she made it so that she stole the life from her mother's lungs, her mother had given up, had succumbed to a needless and unnecessary death, and Abbey Scruggs, Mrs. Abigail Fisher, could forgive her mother for losing a fight with her, but not for surrendering. Never for surrendering.

Abbey had been scratching out her stories in notebooks with a fountain pen every evening. She didn't see a way out of Georgia on her own. She had one day, in a bout of courage that she sometimes mistook for bravado and arrogance, sent her story to Flannery O'Connor, % Robert Giroux, and for some reason that Abbey will never understand but will be forever grateful for, she wrote back, and the two of them began a correspondence.

"Dear Miss Scruggs," said Ms. O'Connor's first letter. "Imagine my surprise to have found your story passably good. I can tell you are a young writer, who will benefit from practice and patience. I don't care, generally, for stories set in the South. Possibly because I want mine to be the only ones. You have seen something in the

South that I have also seen and rarely note its appearance in literature. I can tell that you hear this place, Miss Scruggs. Please keep listening to what it says. If you ever wished to send me another story, I would receive it. Most Sincerely, Flannery O'Connor."

Abbey read the letter over and over again on her single bed with the iron headboard. She placed another piece of paper over top of it and traced the letters lightly with a pencil so there would be a copy in case, heaven forbid, something should happen to the original. Abbey Scruggs did send Flannery O'Connor more stories, and when the letter came after the one she'd been most proud of and most concerned with "All Saints Day", Abbey carried it around unopened the entire day. After dinner, when her father had retired to his study with his dark alcohol and darker mood, she sat on the edge of her bed and slowly slid the letter opener between the folds of the envelope.

"Dear Miss Scruggs," Abbey whispered. She scanned the letters, looking for hope. "I do not feel this is your best work, but that is because I can tell that you do. This is something a writer must always be wary of. Confidence is essential. Blind love is neither helpful nor desirable. There are many things in this story which work; namely, the descriptions of the landscape of New Orleans and the dialogue between Peggy and Al. You have a strong ear. There is no movement, however, in the story, no progression from one essential place or state of being to another, and so without that, you have painted a postcard, but not yet a moving picture. We strive, as writers, to create that moving picture. I know that you can accomplish this, so I would instruct you to return to your own books and examine them for movement. You may also wish to spend some time at Zanzibar in upstate New York working on your craft. I would write a letter of recommendation for you should you be interested. You may be a writer of the South, dear one, but most of the time, we must leave the places we write about, at least for a time, so we can see all of the edges. Please advise if you would like this recommendation. Yours sincerely, Flannery."

Abbey didn't understand the movement comment. She did know that everything wasn't working in her story, but she so loved Peggy and Al and she could touch the walls of their shack in New Orleans. At this time in her writing career, people and places were enough for a story. But Zanzibar! New York might has well have been in Europe. She had never let herself think that she could ever go to a place like that. She didn't even go to college where she could meet some of the writers who might be able to help her. She wanted to shout for her father, but she knew better and stopped the words before they could exit her lips. The anticipation of something she could not yet see was tantalizing. She could taste the iron of it on her tongue. What would New York be like? She never questioned the invitation, never once doubted that she should be there, never entertained the thought that she would not be loved, her talent glorified. Never once.

When Mrs. Abigail Fisher, who was only Abbey then, arrived at Zanzibar, a part of her expected to be greeted with a brass band. This was special, was it not? This was an opportunity not afforded everyone. It was special. She was special. But there was no brass band. There was not even anyone to greet her, just a vast expanse of deep green grass, well-manicured curlicues of flowers—golds, oranges and blues—and a squawking blue jay. The taxi driver helped her lift her trunk and carry it to what she assumed was the main house, a sprawling dark wood mansion with a wide wrap around porch. A brass plaque—Zanzibar Est. 1872—was anchored on a white pillar. Abbey tipped the driver, though she was hesitant to send him on his way until she was certain she was in the right place.

The letter of invitation was in her handbag. It was real. They had asked for her. She rang the bell, one ear listening to the retreating footsteps of the taxi driver. There was no answer. She rang again. Nothing. Her right toe tapped nervously. Where was anyone? Thoughts of a brass band retreated to thoughts of sleeping on the porch. How cold did New York get at night?

"Why hello, my dear," said a voice behind her. She turned, startled. "I'm afraid if you're waiting on someone to open that door you're going to wait for a very long time. It's all for show."

"For show?"

"For appearances." The man wore thin round spectacles and had a fine line of a gray mustache. "For photo ops."

"I see."

"You must be Abbey Scruggs? I'm Freddy Cleaver. I look after things. We weren't expecting you until cocktail hour."

"I wasn't aware that—"

"Oh not a worry at all, Miss Scruggs. Let me take your trunk."

Abbey had been unaware that she was standing in front of it, one hand pressed firmly to its top.

"I will take you to your rooms."

"Oh, of course." Abbey swallowed a thick throat full of air, the depth of what she was unfamiliar with surrounding her with heavy arms.

"It's overwhelming isn't it?" said Freddy. "All this beauty. All these grounds. Just put aside so people can create things. What a wonder."

"What a wonder indeed."

"Your first time here?" Freddy easily lifted the trunk with one arm. "Must be. You tried to ring the bell. I keep telling them they need to put a note there, or at least send you information in a letter, but they don't listen to me. They're kind of pranksters. I think they like the confusion it gives people. Puts them in a different frame of mind, I guess."

Abbey struggled to keep up with him. She was suddenly very tired and wanted nothing more than to be back in Georgia in her old room. "Who are you speaking of?"

"Oh, sorry. Zorro and Penelope, of course."

"Zorro?"

"Not his real name, I assure you. But none of us knows what his real name is. They own the property. It's been in Zorro's family since Revolution times."

"I see. And you?"

"I ferry folks from the porch to their rooms and back. I keep the yards, stock the food, tend the stables."

"Stables?"

"Just over that hill. Fine thoroughbreds and an Arabian or two."

"That's a lot for one person."

"I manage. I have nothing else to do."

Abbey felt like all the rules of living she'd previously learned were not valid here. "Where are we going?"

He pointed north. "Just over there. Your room is on the second floor. I trust stairs are not a problem?"

"No, thank you."

"You're the only lady here right now, so you have your own bathroom and sitting area. Of course, you're free to join everyone at night in the common area, but during the daytime, no one speaks to anyone. You can come to the dining hall for your meals and you can take them in silence there or bring them back to your room, but under no circumstances are you to speak to any of the guests during daylight hours. That's just about our only rule."

"I prefer the quiet," she said.

"Well then," said Freddy, opening the door to her room. "Here is where you shall have it."

The door itself was a good foot or more taller than a standard door, the handle a polished brass. Inside the room was a bed at least twice the size of her bed in Georgia, and the bay window through which she could see the horses had a thick cushion for reading. A small parlor area with a fireplace and a writing desk was to her right through an arched doorway, and a fully equipped bathroom was to her left.

"Do you smoke, Miss Scruggs? I can bring you an ashtray."

"Yes," she said, though she'd never touched a cigarette. "Thank you."

"Dinner is at eight back in the main house where you arrived. Enter through the back. There's a blue door. You can't miss it. You can talk then. Meet some of the rest of us. There's a cocktail hour at six if you wish."

"Perfect, thank you, Mr. Cleaver." She felt that strange tug of being both adult and child. No one knew her here. The tingle of that was irresistible.

"Freddy, please."

"Abbey."

"Good afternoon, Abbey. I will leave the ashtray outside your door so you can be at peace."

She nodded and he was gone before she could extend her hand in thanks. The silence of the room and the hallway were louder than any brass band could have been. Her own breathing echoed, her reflexive swallowing trumpeted. She snapped her fingers. Cleared her throat. Stroked the edges of the tightly made bed. Freddy had placed her trunk on a low table next to a dresser with a vase of freshly picked violets. They were a deeper blue than the ones in Georgia. Or maybe they were the same and they just looked different because they were New York violets.

New. New. Everything that will happen next has never happened to her before. Everything she will eat. Everything she will smell. Everything she will hear. Every path she will walk down, every conversation she will hold. New. She wanted to call Flannery and thank her again, but they'd never spoken, and she didn't know how to reach her.

She slipped her shoes off, her dress, her slip, and reclined on the handmade quilt. She would not wear a dress again during her time in New York at Zanzibar. She would be a woman who wore only pants—wide legged ones at first, then later cigarette pants with T-strapped shoes. She would wear lipstick and not cross her legs and she would swear occasionally around the edges of her cigarette holder. She would blow smoke rings and dance with everyone who asked and she would not have one single regret. Not one.

She hadn't brought a typewriter. It was too heavy with the rest of her items. She had brought stacks of paper and fountain pens and ink jars. A passing, frightening thought occurred to her: She had no project to work on. No story. No novel. It would come, she reassured herself. The words and worlds would come. The stories would come. She was young. She was away from home. She was an hour away from the best city in all the world, and she was going to be famous. She was going to meet the best writers of her generation and she was never going to find herself stuck again. This was the moment. Her moment. A soft breeze fluttered the curtains, tickling her cheeks. She would just take a quick nap until dinner, or cocktail hour. What did one drink at a cocktail hour? It didn't matter. She would say yes to it all. She would feel it all. Just a short nap. A quick rest, so she could greet the rest of her life with dewy eyes and moist lips.

She didn't wake until the next day. Freddy had left the standing ashtray outside her door as promised. She, of course, had no cigarettes, but vowed to remedy that. She was hungry and hoped she could find her way back to the main house for breakfast. Silent. She had to remember. She splashed some water on her face, pulled on her dress from the day before, then took it off, remembering she had brought pants. The button and zipper were on the side, and the leg openings flared wide like sails. She was ready for breakfast.

It turned out there was no one in the dining hall. She poured coffee into a white ceramic mug. She toasted bread, spread it with butter and apricot jam. She plucked a banana from the fruit bowl and two pieces of bacon from a cloth soaked with grease. The dining hall had floor-to-ceiling windows along the east wall. Picnic-style tables and benches were sprawled at odd angles throughout the room, and a sitting area consisting of a divan, a few stuffed chairs, and several ashtrays was in the far corner near an unlit fireplace. It was already seven a.m. Surely everyone would be up by now?

"You're the early riser, aren't you?" She hadn't noticed Freddy standing in the archway that led to the kitchen. "Most don't make it down for anything until 10 or so."

"Oh."

"Not to worry. Takes all kinds. You'll always get the fresh coffee."

"I thought this meal was silent."

"Got me," he said. "I just thought you looked a little confused. I'll leave you to your thoughts."

He had vanished into the kitchen before she could ask him to stay. Her thoughts were the last place she wanted to be this morning, this unfamiliar morning. She hadn't found a place to sit yet, and she noticed her legs were spread farther apart than usual, her feet more solidly on the ground. Pants. A wonder. When she sat, her knees opened to either side slightly and she smiled before biting into the thick, crisp bacon.

After breakfast and two cups of excellent coffee, she decided to walk around the grounds a bit and get oriented. She thought briefly of the blank pages in her room, but rationalized that until she knew where she was she couldn't very well write anything. The air didn't smell the same as Georgia's. It was humid, to be sure, but not as much, the fragrance not as sweet. She had thought of New York as being silver—steel and concrete and thick black smoke from factories. She had assumed that all of New York State was New York City, and so the quiet continued to surprise her. Birds and butterflies, just like at home only slightly paler in color, dotted the sky. Squirrels with flattened ears and longer, thinner tails than those she knew ran up and down the trees. She heard the bubbling of water but couldn't see it. A horse whinnied. Could there really be this much quiet in the north? She needed a shower. It was probably nine already. Half the morning and she still hadn't seen another soul besides Freddy. How was one supposed to write in so much solitude?

She had a three-month invitation. Three months to change the course of her life. Three months to create the life that would reflect the one she'd always seen shimmering in front of her. Three months to catch the sounds she'd heard from birth. A crunching of the leaves behind her. A bowing of trees in a darkening storm, thunder almost but not quite rumbling, the tree branches shaking in anticipation. In her short life, three months seemed more than enough time to accomplish those things.

When she returned to her room that first morning, still having seen no one but Freddy Cleaver, she pulled the ashtray into the room and positioned it beside the bay window. She'd have to inquire about where to find cigarettes. She made the bed, fluffed the pillow, folded her clothes and put them in the drawers. Someone had come and replaced the flowers with marigolds while she'd been out. The water pressure was perfect, the hot water plentiful, and after she'd bathed and redressed, she had nothing left to do but write. The blank pages shouted, but she couldn't hear their words. The fountain pen dripped but she couldn't see its marks yet. She sat in the bay window and pretended to smoke. It was nine forty-five. She exhaled invisible smoke, cleared her lungs, and inhaled again. She ground out her invisible cigarette in the real ashtray and tried to imagine what the other writers were doing. She thought of men with handle bar mustaches pacing and shaking their fists at the ceiling. In truth, the men were all still sleeping, cocktail hour having extended until the morning, their words from the day before still shuddering on the pages, their hearts both broken and open. It was nine fifty-one. She supposed she'd better get started. Nine fifty-two. A stack of paper. Two fountain pens and one jar of ink. Nine fifty-three. Well then. Life. Start.

Abbey was certain there had never been a longer day on earth than that first day at Zanzibar. The sun slowed. The clouds did not scurry from one side of the sky to another. Her breath haunted her rather than held her up. The blank papers rustled in an imaginary breeze, but no words appeared from the pens she'd brought especially for this time. She pinned her hair up and took it back down. She brushed her teeth twice, counting the up and down strokes on each tooth. She waited for her stomach to rumble and her bladder to fill. She wondered—for a brief second—where the stories went that had been so loud in Georgia. There didn't seem to be a moment at home when she wasn't followed by something—that incessant crunching of leaves, the bending branches of trees, the shouts from the tops of abandoned barns and church steeples. Everywhere, a voice. Everywhere, a word, and when there was one word there would be another. It was the nature of words. They did not like to be alone. But here, in New York, the land of all opportunities and all languages and all peoples of the world, the words fell silent.

It was only the first day, she told herself, aloud so she could be certain that she still had at least her own voice. There were eighty-nine more days after this one. There was plenty of time left, but the reassurance felt as hollow as it was. Abbey Scruggs had never experienced writer's block, didn't even have a name for it. She had simply assumed that there would always be a story because there had always been one. This was the first of many lessons she would learn at Zanzibar, and the only one that had anything to do with writing.

By the time six o'clock came, Abbey was ready for a cocktail, though she'd never had one in her life. She was ready for something to do with her hands, her lips, her voice, and she was more than ready for something to happen with other people. She had spent less than twelve hours in solitude and it was twelve hours too much. She knew this was a devastating thing for a writer who was supposed to revel in solitude, rail against noise and sounds and company, but she hadn't realized how much the company of others fueled her work (the folly of it now, making such sweeping judgments about writers and about her writing process off of just one half of one day in a new environment in a young body). She hadn't realized that writing might be more than taking dictation. That it might involve listening. Waiting.

Patience had never been one of her strong suits. She had believed that there was no work to writing. That there was a perpetual state of flow, a never ending stream of characters and situations, and she had been certain that she was wiser than her age (and perhaps she was, but she was not nearly as wise as she'd assumed) and that she had the heart and soul of a visionary. She had believed there would never be a time any different from the way she began, and this was another lesson she learned at Zanzibar, though it was most unpleasant. She didn't take into account that if she didn't change she couldn't improve.

Apparently cocktail hour began before six. When she arrived back at the main house, there was rolling rich male laughter, clinking of ice cubes into glasses, and a thick cloud of pipe, cigar, and cigarette smoke. She remembered that Freddy had told her she was the only woman staying at Zanzibar. There might be no one who wanted to speak to her, men being what they were, wanting their own smoking rooms and caves of testosterone and bravado pockmarked with the heads of large mammals. Back home, men and women kept their distance from one another, both out of respect and fear. She needn't have worried about the lack of company. She was too young to have realized how men, though they may harrumph and spread their peacock feather tails, needed the company of women far more than women needed the company of men.

She hadn't noticed she was standing in the door watching them, their mustaches wet with scotch, their bellies full of hot air. But they had noticed her.

"Well," said a bespectacled heavy man holding a stogie. "She has arrived."

The rest of them laughed, though Abbey did not know why.

"She's plain," said another, also holding a cigar. "But give me one more of these and she'll be fine."

More laughter.

"Tell us your name, honey," said a third, the most handsome of them all, with hair just an inch too long and eyes just a hint too blue.

"Abbey," she whispered.

"Abbey," said the first man. "Like a church."

"No, like me," Abbey said.

They laughed again. At her, she assumed.

"Like me," said the handsome one. "Isn't she a jewel? I will rename you Sapphire."

"She's no Sapphire," said the middle man. "More like Graphite."

"Graphite?" said the handsome one, crossing the room to Abbey. "Far too lovely for Graphite." He touched her cheek and Abbey recoiled more from reflex than intention. "My name is Phillip, Abbey Sapphire. I am proud to know you."

She didn't know what to do. She'd never been so much as on a single date at home. The men weren't interested or interesting. They either were full of the arrogance of escaping death in the Pacific and desperate to find a bride to help them make an instant family and forget what they will never be able to talk about or they were even more awkward than she was, unsure of how to talk to her, how to raise their eyes to meet hers. She was certain that neither type of man would have touched her cheek and given her a nickname within seconds of meeting her.

She met his gaze. "Pleased to meet you, Phillip." She extended her hand. "I trust we'll be fast friends." Who had said that? She had a disturbing moment of observing herself engaged in this conversation. She thought she liked her new persona, but she was still foreign, an invader.

"Fast friends," said the first man, stubbing out the stogy. "Well, Abbey Graphite, you are indeed from some other place."

Two more men had entered the room.

"Any scotch?" asked one, a small, pale man who spoke as if he'd just inhaled helium.

"For you, Tru? Always," said the first man. "We're just talking with Abbey Graphite here. She's new." Abbey did not like the smile that crept along the edges of his lips.

"Abbey Graphite," said Tru. "Don't mind any of us. We're lost, all of us."

"Capote's a fatalist," said Phillip. "He sees the blackness in all of us."

"Only you, Phil," said Truman. "Only you. Me? I see nothing but rainbows."

"You're Truman Capote," said Abbey.

"I am, and I can tell by your charming voice that you are also from the great South. These men are boors. They're all Yanks, every last one of them. You'll tire of them soon enough and realize the gift of your birthplace." Truman bowed slightly and left to fill his glass.

"You've read Capote?" asked Phillip.

"I have."

"You've made a friend for life then. He's convinced he's a literary giant and bemoans the idiocy of the world for having not yet taken notice."

"Fuck you, Phillip," said Capote, but he was smiling. Abbey had never been sworn in front of before. "Pardon me, Abbey Graphite. I was not raised to speak that way in front of a lady."

"Fuck you, Truman," Abbey said and the whole room burst into laughter and applause. The Abbey-watching-Abbey was pleasantly horrified. Her tongue tingled with the power of the word.

Truman laughed the loudest. "Welcome to our lair, little darling. We've been waiting for you."

And that was the sentence Abbey had been desperate to hear since she first got out of the taxicab. The absence of the welcoming brass band was soothed by the tiny queer man holding a very full glass of scotch. He sounded like home—not his words, but his very voice. He sounded like home and he had approved of her.

"Can I get you a drink, Abbey Sapphire?" asked Phillip. "Name your pleasure."

She didn't know what to ask for. "Yes. But you choose."

"Phillip is feeding you a load of manure, little darling," said Truman. "We've only got scotch, at least until the next shipment."

Phillip blushed and Abbey noticed his blushing began at his forehead and traveled down his face under his shirt collar. "Leave it to Truman to ruin everything. Just because he's not into the ladies—"

"Tsk, tsk," said Truman. "I'll thank you to keep your envy to yourself."

"Scotch will be fine," said Abbey. "On the rocks," she said because she'd heard that phrase before.

"As you wish," said Phillip.

Abbey was suddenly hungry. She hadn't gone down for lunch. The smoke stung, but she moved into it like a pro. She was used to the cigarettes from home, but the cigars were new to her and harsh. Phillip returned with the drink. "Where are you from, Abbey Sapphire?"

"Georgia," she said, and that felt leagues and leagues away.

"Chicago," said Phillip. "I can't hardly bear all this quiet sometimes. Can't hear myself self-destruct."

"I thought that today," she said. "The quiet was so loud and long and I didn't know what I was supposed to be doing with it all."

"That's the nature of this place," said Phillip. "It's in the middle of nowhere so we've got nowhere to run to but inward. The owners believe that all art comes from inside. I agree with them most of the time, but sometimes a guy's just got to get out. Do you agree?"

"I've only been here one day. I'm not sure I'm qualified."

"You got here somehow, didn't you? Someone thought this would be good for you. That makes you qualified."

Good for her? Like she was an errant child and this was punishment? No. She would be good for Zanzibar. She would be good for the world. "I am a writer," she said.

"God help you," said Truman. "God help you."

"Why?" asked Abbey.

"Because if you're a writer the quiet will never be still."

"That's why you have me," said Phillip. "I'm a saxophonist. I make jazz. Jazz will hold your writing up."

"Phillip has an unfounded sense of worth," said Truman. "He seems to think music is the superior art. We argue this nightly. I tell him that unless he makes his instrument every single day from thin air, he's got no claim on writing. None at all."

Abbey had never heard a conversation like this. She was used to stock conversations about the classics, about the Bible, and about the wars (any of the wars would do—the War of Northern Aggression, the Great War or the Second One). It was as if Georgia had no room for any creators besides God Almighty. New York. What a wonder. She swallowed the scotch and though it burned her throat, she kept her face stoic. She was in an entirely different zoo and she was going to ensure that she survived.

The other men seemed to give Phillip room. Abbey had never been the subject of any male "operation", so she did not see it unfolding. Had she thought to ask, had she perhaps taken up smoking or swearing or been just a few years older, she would have seen that Phillip was just charming because he was charming. Her presence had nothing to do with it other than to provide an object for it. He had been a musician from the age of six, starting first on the street corners of Chicago with his brother who played a mean trumpet before he lost a hand in a meatpacking accident. He learned early the art of seduction, how both he and his instrument were the vehicles for it. If he seduced and his instrument was mediocre, the tip jar was empty. If his instrument astonished but his own body was cold, the tip jar was empty. The merging of his own flesh with the life of the music was the secret, and once he discovered it, he did not know how to separate the two. He was either completely on or completely off, and whenever he was in the presence of a lady, he was always one hundred percent on.

"Come, Abbey Sapphire, and sit awhile and tell me all about yourself," said Phillip. He was on his third drink. Abbey was still nursing her first. "I want to know everything. What brings a woman away from hearth and home to the wilds of New York to spar with a bunch of arrogant men?"

Abbey sat on one of the overstuffed chairs, enjoying the ease with which she could sit wearing pants. It didn't matter what she did with her legs. She stood back up, folded her left leg under her at a right angle, and then sat again. The freedom was delicious. "I have never cared much for hearth, and home is just a place I live."

"Bah! Place is everything," said Truman.

Phillip cleared his throat. "Stop eavesdropping. Go visit with Newton."

"He's not here this week," Truman said, sighing loudly. "Whatever shall I do?"

"Please continue, Abbey Sapphire. The natives are ill mannered."

"I didn't think I was coming here to spar with men. I was coming here to write."

"Ah, a virgin!" said Truman.

"Shut up and have another drink," said Phillip. "You don't have to be mean to everyone the first time you meet them."

"How ever will they know how it will end up then?" asked Truman. "Best to be up front."

Abbey found she rather liked the little man Truman, but she was aware that if she said so, he would devour her. She was learning the rules of this zoo faster than she would have thought. Besides, she was a virgin, but she felt that Truman wasn't talking just about sex.

"And what do you write, dear?" asked Phillip, holding up his hand to block out any stares from Truman.

"I don't know."

"Why is it the women never know?" asked a man who had just entered the room. "Ask a man what he's writing and he can tell you, down to the comma. Ask a woman and she is always waiting. Always waiting for her writing to arrive. No offense, my lady, but that is why women will never become great novelists. Writing a novel is not about waiting. It is about doing." The man raked his fingers through curly blond hair, then pantomimed jabbing a spear into an animal. "It's about nature, not nurture." Phillip opened his mouth, but was interrupted. "I'm not being callous. I know what you're going to say, Phillip, because you've got that look in your eyes of conquest. You're on the hunt too, my friend. Don't deny it. Nature, not nurture. It's just the truth."

The man stabbed the imaginary animal a few more times before he was satisfied the creature was dead.

"Norman, you are such a bore," said Truman.

"Better a bore than a dandy," said the man. "Madam, I am Norman Mailer. You hate me already and that is just fine. We'll get along swimmingly." He extended his hand and when she took it, he pulled her off her chair and kissed her. "See," he said. "Nature. It can't be helped."

Abbey wiped her mouth with the back of her hand. She did not know what to say, but she knew she had to say something. If this moment passed unanswered, she would be the one cowering every time Mr. Mailer swaggered through. "It seems to me that your definition of nature is one-sided. I do not see how nurture is not also a part of nature, for without it, nothing would live. It follows suit then that your definition of women writers is also one-sided, but it is easy for me to see how you have come to that conclusion. Your goggles are strapped on quite tightly and you have prewritten the script for what you will see. Fortunately for you, there is nurture, for in your definition of nature, a blind creature must surely be destroyed. An unlucky fate for one as pretty as you."

Truman began clapping first. The Abbey-watching-Abbey was stunned. She hadn't known she could say these things, perform this way. Getting away from one's home, away from one's places of comfort, was apparently essential to understanding what one is capable of becoming. If one never leaves, one can only be the type of plant that grows in the area of one's birth. She knew who Norman Mailer was. She knew who Truman Capote was. She may have been from Georgia, but she hadn't been living under a rock. She did not know anymore who she was and that was tantalizing. Norman's eyes blazed. She was ready.

"Tell us again what you are working on?" he asked.

"I will not," said Abbey. "I would hate for you to steal it."

"Let it go, Mailer," said Phillip. "Let it go."

Norman's face cracked into a Harvard-portrait smile. Abbey saw the snake underneath it. "You can name your first born after me," he said. "And you can tell him about the time you spent swimming with the big fish before you had to go back home and make babies. Nature, miss, wins every time. I'm sorry, I didn't catch your name?"

Reflexively, Abbey started to speak.

"It doesn't matter," said Norman. "I won't need to remember it." He strode out of the room through the open double doors. Abbey sat back down and reached for her drink. She knew she was shaking by the clinking of the ice.

"He is not a gentleman," said Phillip. "Please don't pay him any attention. That's what made him so angry. You didn't acknowledge his greatness."

"That's not it," said Truman. "She got to him because she spoke. He's going to be pissed for days."

Abbey's vision of the way Zanzibar would be had deflated. She hadn't realized how high her expectations were, how much she was counting on a community. Folly, she said to herself. Folly. She didn't have a community in Georgia so there was no need to have one here. The alcohol was taking its effect. No one here behaved as people did back home, where a modicum of manners, hats in hand, was present. Men and women might not interact in daily life, but when they did come in contact with each other, they knew how to be. She saw that as the cage it was. Here, everyone was free.

She didn't have to be any particular way here. She didn't have to be the one to prepare the food or clear the table or mend the clothes. The starkness of that awareness stung. The rooms, the buildings, the grounds of this place were perfectly manicured, the epitome of civilized society, but inside the walls the humans were unleashed to their essential selves. Abbey wished she had a friend she could write to about this. Flannery had been here several times. Surely, she knew.

"Well, darling," said Phillip. "You're here now and all the natives have sprayed their territories. Where is yours?"

When Abbey returned to her rooms that evening, her mind was buzzing. She wasn't as angry as she might have thought she'd be. She had never felt the current in her body as vital as that night. Phillip had tried to accompany her, but she had declined to his promises of another night when he would bring his saxophone. Truman had walked her partway back before ducking into the woods with a "Do join us all tomorrow. It's ever so much more exciting with you here." She didn't know what that meant exactly, only that in one day she had interacted with two of the most influential young writers and even if the outcome was less than desirable, she'd done it, and that was something that would have never happened in Georgia.

As she ascended the stairs to her room, the Abbey-watching-Abbey was intrigued by the fire the sparring with Norman had evoked. But then, when she closed the door, confident no one else was going to speak to her or see her that evening, she sat daintily on the edge of the bed and tried to lengthen her breath which had quickened to the speed of a hummingbird's.

The stacks of paper were still empty. The fountain pens still clean and sharp and the room as silent as a tomb. She had spoken the truth—she wasn't sure what she was writing. She had been certain in Georgia. She knew the stories before she wrote them. Was that how it was for these men? There seemed to be no doubt in what they were doing. The world was theirs to dispose of and dismiss at whim. In the darkness of her room, their words and movements took on grandiose proportions. They competed with the crickets and tree frogs and won.

The paper rustled. The grandfather clock at the end of the hallway outside her door chimed midnight. She was exhausted and still a little bit hungry, but she was afraid to sleep. Nature never stopped and she was aware that the sheer persistence of it was what made it enduring. Even when it appeared to be waiting it was moving. She had to figure out how to do that. She had to figure out how to both move and be still. These men didn't know how to be still and that, she was certain, would be their undoing. Nevertheless, she remained frozen, which is not the same at all as still, and even though she longed for sleep, she stayed sitting on the edge of the bed breathing shallowly.

It turned out that no one was at Zanzibar to make friends, nor, did it seem to Abbey, that many were there for their work. They were there to avoid day jobs, or families, or grown up responsibilities, and though Abbey wanted to judge them for that, she was doing much the same. She may not have a family of her own, but she was obligated to her father in a way that was stifling, and she was destined to become a school teacher and a spinster and she had almost accepted that fate before coming North.

Being a spinster had undeniable allure, but she didn't think she could be a teacher. She simply didn't like children all that much and wondered what she would possibly do with them all day long. If she could make something great at Zanzibar, maybe she could avoid both fates. She raised the Make Something Great flag and let it hang limply in her room. She'd hoped for the fierceness of her breath to send the flag aloft, but that did not happen. Her breath continued in bird-gasps. Her papers were not entirely blank, but they didn't say very much. She wondered what Norman did in his room when he was alone. Did he actually slay the sentences every single day, or was he curled up more times than not in a fetal position on his bed scratching at the darkness? She'd have asked him about his process if he'd have been a different person. Maybe she'd have had to be a different person, too. Regardless, she did not ask—not Mailer or Capote—but she had found herself drawn to Phillip, who as promised, brought his saxophone to their next meeting and did what he knew how to do. He used both instruments at his disposal, and he piqued Abbey's interest, though she did not say so right away. She remembered what he'd said the first day they met: Jazz will hold your writing up. She didn't know what that meant at the time and she wasn't sure she knew now what it meant, but she had found herself alone in her room with the Make Something Great flag decidedly not flying until she hummed a bar or two from the notes Phillip had given her the day before. The way his whole body moved when he played captivated her.

If her instrument was language, how could she move that wholly with it? How could she make writing move her body? She'd never considered these types of questions in Georgia, and she'd not even known to think of any such thing. Could one art form enhance another? She'd always thought of painters painting, dancers dancing, musicians playing and writers writing all in separate but equal corners of creation. There was no communion among the members. When Phillip played, his hips swung left, right, forward, back, and his eyes half-closed like he was in prayer. He didn't always seem to know she was there listening, but he played like he was playing for all the angels, and she responded in spite of her better judgment. His sweat smelled of peppermint and he had started to let his hair grow in a way that would have scandalized her hometown. One night, playing his newest work for her in the courtyard underneath a half-moon, he stumbled on a few of the notes. Backed up. Played again. Backed up. Played again. Backed up. Played again until the bars were seamlessly sewn together.

"I wrote that this morning," he said. "Thinking of you."

Abbey had been at Zanzibar only six days. She had written three paragraphs, one of which was drivel. "Which part was me?" she asked.

"The part I stumbled over."

Abbey had not seen Norman for two weeks.

"He's still pouting," said Truman, who also had been missing for several days.

She had tried not to think of him at all, but his words had gotten inside her bones. She'd thought she could push them out like the rubbish her brain knew they were, but they had taken root in a place underneath her mind that had much more fertile soil. She asked Phillip about it.

"Do you think Norman is right about women?" The moon was full now, the summer warming up. She missed fireflies (too far north, she'd been told). She and Phillip had taken to spending most evenings together. She never tired of watching him play the sax. She wished she could share something with him, read something she'd written and move with the sentences, but she still had much of nothing. She'd taken up doodling, especially drawing the strange flat-eared squirrels. Once, she made a small cartoon starring a squirrel and a butterfly. *What are you doing?* was the bubble over the butterfly. *Gathering nuts for winter,* said the squirrel. *Why? Because it's what I do,* said Squirrel. Argh. She drew a line through it. Nature.

Phillip had been absently playing, the notes dancing with the gurgling of the creek she'd yet to find. Phillip drew a note out long and sweet. "I think it doesn't matter whether he's right or not. It only matters what you do."

"But that's just it. I'm not doing much of anything."

"Who knows what he's doing? What any of them are doing.

Nobody creates the same way, Abbey. The only race is with the art." He touched her cheek and drew a circle on the side of her neck, sending shivers through her. "Kiss me." And she did, her first kiss feeling nothing like she'd imagined. It was soft and hard and living. She felt his mouth clear in her toes.

She had been kissing him more frequently lately. She'd known she was supposed to be doing more—a woman wearing pants would know what to do, wouldn't even think about what to do next—but she was still in costume, still squarely between the girl who left Georgia and the woman who was living alone in New York. Sometimes his lips still held the vibrations from the sax and she imagined that when he slept, his whole body buzzed and shimmered with song. She did kiss him, taking his tongue in with hers.

"Read to me, Abbey," he said.

"I haven't written anything."

"That's impossible. All day you don't write anything? You have to try things out, don't you, before you know what works? I don't just write music—I have to play a lot before I know what I'm saying."

"Yes, but jazz is different," she said. "It's not—"

"Careful, Abbey Sapphire. Just because it doesn't look like Mozart doesn't mean it's not music."

"I wasn't going to say that. I was just saying that jazz is more fluid than writing. It's a conversation, right? That's what you've been telling me. With everyone playing?"

His smile was wide but closed. "Yes, jazz is a conversation. But it is more than that. It is a spontaneous response to someone else's art. It can't ever be the same twice." Abbey didn't understand. There was no equivalent in writing that she could think of. "Think about it. What if someone wrote something and read it and then you wrote something and read it back—"

"But that wouldn't really be spontaneous. It's slower, I guess. Writing."

"You're too concerned with how it might come across."

"Maybe." Abbey was no longer sure what she meant. She'd never thought of writing as a conversation, but she supposed that maybe it was. At least with the reader. "Aren't you afraid you're going to play something wrong?"

"You're in your head too much, Abbey Sapphire. You just have to listen. Maybe you spend too much time trying to figure out what you're going to say and then you can't hear what's being said to you."

Abbey thought about the three—well, two—paragraphs she'd written. She'd spent an inordinate amount of time just writing the letters. Seeing how her capital letters looped and practicing her signature—Abbey Scruggs, over and over again—you could never have too flamboyant of a signature, she believed. There would be people wanting to buy her books. People who would cherish them and place them on their bookshelves or coffee tables and think about the moment they met the famous author. It didn't occur to her to think she was getting ahead of herself. That she hadn't yet written a single book, much less one that people would be waiting in line on a snowy evening to purchase. It was easier to imagine after the fact, simply assuming that the premise was true. She had even written a letter to her father, full of fictions about her progress. She didn't expect, and had yet to receive, a reply. She thought of Norman Mailer. "You can't listen to writing," he'd said. "You have to create it."

She sipped her scotch, having grown used to its burn. "This is where we differ," she said. "I don't see how you can write anything of consequence if you're the one doing all the talking."

Abbey was not sure how she'd ended up in this conversation, and she didn't even know if she believed that. Nothing was as simple as she'd anticipated. She had no idea who this man was with the piping blue eyes and the dancing saxophone, no idea what this landscape was about, these men with their bravado and fame. Sometimes she thought she had no business here at all; other times she felt this was her destiny. Most of the time she felt very young, and even though these men were also young, they had done things—gone to wars or been in other cities or just been men. The difference between the genders was fiery and unapologetic. How had she not seen that before? When she was feeling too young to be here, she was also uncertain of herself as a writer, herself as a person who had anything to say. Maybe Phillip was right. Maybe that was what the problem was. She was expecting herself to have something of value to say when instead she should be listening. But to what?

"When you're listening, what are you listening for?" she asked Phillip. The night was cool. She pulled her sweater tighter around her neck. She thought about the footsteps crunching on leaves.

"I don't know. Sometimes it's a note. Sometimes it's a feeling and when I open my mouth it comes through as a sound. I can see the notes sometimes. Not all the time, but when I can, I know I'm playing something real."

"Because you're in a conversation?"

"No. Because I've become the conversation."

Abbey didn't understand. She was nineteen and had thought she knew what she was doing. She had thought she was ready for this place, but Phillip was talking in riddles and she knew if she were wiser, more talented, more something she clearly wasn't, she would know what he was talking about. She would be able to inhale her cigarette smoke smoothly and she would be able to drink scotch until the late hours of the early morning without missing a beat.

Abbey Scruggs did little writing at Zanzibar, but she did do something she had never thought herself capable of. She fell in love. Not sort of in love. Not in lust. Not in heat. She actually fell in love, and she was embarrassed and thrilled by it. She felt herself succumbing to nature and she didn't care. Her father had not written to her and she had been there over thirty days. With each day she saw Phillip, her father's absence faded into the rustling leaves. While Abbey sat in her room and watched the breeze toss the leaves around, Phillip was in his room sweating and dancing and humming. His saxophone was never cold, never idle. He walked around the grounds with it as the sun was rising, skipping a little bit and then waltzing into the next series of sounds.

Abbey watched him sometimes from her window on the second floor, when she was supposed to be writing (those pages! Those blank and rustling pages!). She liked to see if she could spot his shadow among the branches of the trees. Sometimes when he moved, it was as fluid as the way the wind blew the branches back and forth. She never told him she watched him dancing with the sunrise. There were things you don't speak about, and she knew that watching his private conversations with the music was one of them.

She should at the very least have taken notes—if for no other reason than to see if she could write the story of a man alone in the woods with a saxophone in the pre-dawn of summer. That was a story that would surely hold mystery and great sensuality, two qualities she hadn't thought she could bring to her writing. For now, it was enough to watch the young man walking in the pre-dawn dancing, wasn't it? Only enough for a moment, not a whole life.

"I'm writing about you," she'd say when he asked, and he told her she should not do that, though she could tell he was flattered.

She should write what is only hers to write. "But that is you," she'd say, and he'd shake his head and say that was not true, and he was right though she did not believe it.

She wrote a story about a dove and a story about the babbling brook she never found. She wrote a story about Norman Mailer and Truman Capote, but even then she knew it was just mean and written for her own amusement. She wrote lines of poetry about Phillip—about watching Phillip, listening to Phillip, touching Phillip. She could get only a few lines before she ran into a thick place, as if the paper had swelled with moisture and trapped the pen's nub. It was the paper, she'd say, the paper that kept me from writing anymore. But she knew it was because there was nothing else she could say. There was nothing else to follow the moment, and she was quickly learning that holding a moment would kill it. Maybe she was a poet and not a fiction writer. Maybe the novel would never wrap its long arms around her. For the moment, she seemed only able to write in staccatoed phrases and pauses. What she wrote was dependent on what happened next with Phillip, and the same was true of Phillip's music, only she was fueling his and he was stalling, albeit unknowingly, hers.

On the forty-seventh day at Zanzibar, Phillip Fisher, a white Jewish jazz musician from Chicago, got down on his knees in the courtyard and played her a proposal. His eyes were closed the entire song, and his body swayed and pumped and bent. She was crying and he was crying and his lips were tingling and the brook was babbling and Abbey said, yes, yes, yes she would go with him, play with him, and he stopped to take a breath and kiss her. This was why she had come to Zanzibar, she thought, not to write, but to find him. Now that that had been accomplished, she thought she could return to the words and the stories, her life firmly on a course now, a girl now fully grown up.

"You'll come to Chicago then?" he said.

"Of course not," she said. "I live in the South." She hadn't meant to say that, but the words were true. She couldn't go to Chicago could she? Her father, though he still hadn't written, needed her there. He would be alone without her. What would everyone think if she, the only daughter, the daughter who had taken her mother's life in birth, abandoned her father to cold ham and greens for the rest of his life?

"I can't go to Georgia, Abbey Sapphire. They'll kill me down there." That was only half a joke. "You know I'm Jewish."

She did and she hadn't really thought about it, religion not being the foremost thing on her mind those past days. "There's not much of that where I live," she said, and they both knew what "that" meant. "More in Mississippi, Alabama."

"I need a city, Abbey Sapphire."

"I won't go to Chicago," she said, and she did not know why she was so adamant. She had never been to Chicago, had never even been to New York City. She'd been to Atlanta a few times and she didn't like it, but she couldn't remember why. He wiped his eyes, put the saxophone back in its case, and touched her cheek.

"I have to think about this," he said, and she knew she'd spoiled the moment, the only moment a girl like her was bound to get, and she didn't have a good reason why. She just didn't like his assumption that she would leave her home. She tried to remember the way his proposal song had sounded, but she couldn't. Jazz was for the moment, he always said. If you capture it, you'll kill it. If you try to remember it, you'll only hear the echo, not the notes.

"OK," she said. "I'll go back upstairs."

He nodded. "Good night, Abbey Sapphire."

She was too young to see how sad he was, how much he wanted to hold her and take her into his world. He was too young to know what to do next either, so he left her there, did not even walk her back to her room, and took his silent saxophone back to his quarters where he tried to avoid running into the other men, but it was impossible.

"Go to Georgia with her," said Truman. "Every artist needs to hear the South."

Norman poured him a drink and refrained from saying the obvious, but that was only because he didn't need to. *You're a musician, Phillip. There will be so many others you can't even imagine.*

The night Phillip proposed to her, just before the residency was to end, was rainy. "Where did you get this?" Abbey asked, the 'yes' still wet on her lips. Phillip had opened a palm to reveal a sterling silver ring, the top a raised blue enamel, the design a starburst of marcasite.

"We went into the City the other weekend," he said. "I saw it in the window of a jeweler. I know it's supposed to be gold—and the marcasite is supposed to be diamond—"

Abbey took the ring from his hand and held it to the new sunlight dancing through the window. The marcasite glimmered. Not diamond, but deeper. A heavier, more serious sparkle.

"Put it on your finger," he said.

"You do it."

He slipped it on her ring finger. The rich blue enamel held the possibility of the future. When it was on her hand, the silver band disappeared, leaving only a blue sky and sparkle rising from her finger.

"You sparkle like that," said Phillip. "You're not flashy. You're just there, always, holding up the sky. Flash burns out, you know. But your light is eternal. It's not special, and don't take that the wrong way," he added when he saw her eyes simmer. "It's just you. You don't have to try."

The ring was heavy. She'd never been one for jewelry. She liked a single strand of pearls or occasionally earrings, but jewelry was fussy. This ring, however, wasn't fussy. It was solid. And sparkly. A combination she'd not entertained before.

"Do you like it?" he asked.

"I love it," she said. "I'll never take it off."

"One day I'll get you a better one, I promise."

"This one is perfect." She ran her fingers over its raised center, shimmering stones. "It's like it's growing out of my finger."

Phillip kissed the ring, then her hand, then the inner hollow of her elbow.

"It's almost time for breakfast," Abbey said. "I'm starving."

Phillip sat up, propped himself up on a pillow. "I mean this, Abbey."

"Me too. I hardly had any dinner last night."

"Not food. This. You. Us. I mean this. I will come to Georgia."

Abbey had not understood jazz. Not that night or any night since. She didn't understand the fluidity of conversation. When you put words on a page (not that she had written many), they stayed unless you took them away. In jazz, the conversation stayed only until the breath was finished and a new word took its place. That next word could be, indeed quite frequently was, the exact opposite of the one just uttered. But she didn't understand that then, and they skipped breakfast, and she grew hungrier.

33

"Is that really how you saw me?" asked Mrs. Abigail Fisher. "I can scarcely believe it."

"That's the story," said Pistachio. "That's the story I remember."

"I like it. I'm not sure I would have told it that way, but you're a decent storyteller."

"Well, the point of view is everything."

"You are a saucy one," said Mrs. Abigail Fisher.

"How did you remember it, then?" asked Pistachio.

"I remember Norman and Truman, of course. I miss Truman. Did you know he and I wrote to each other for years? After *In Cold Blood*, he was quite undone. I kept all the letters, of course."

"Where are they?"

"With the rest of my papers. My daughter has them in her hands right now. But you know that, don't you?"

Pistachio didn't know at all what she had given Elise. She had simply found the notebook on the closet floor. It seemed important because of how deeply it had been buried.

"And now that I suppose my time is actually ending, I can tell you I remember Phillip. I made him leave, you know. I think he would have stayed. Now that I can let that idea in, I think he might have stayed."

"What do you remember about Phillip?"

"It was easy for him, his art. He was somehow able to let note lead into note without getting too much in the way of it. He could have helped me, I think. I had to control most things."

Pistachio wished she had the fireplace poker so she could bonk her on the head. Lightly, of course. "I could have helped you."

"It has been a strange and odd delight to be with you again, Pistachio. I can't stay any longer."

"But what about the game? We've still got questions left."

"Let my daughter read to you. And then I suppose we'll all know what to do. We have to make the stories together, I think. I'm sorry I cut you out. You scared me, and I had had enough that year."

"I just wanted to show you something."

"What?"

"I can't remember anymore. It's been too long. But it could have all been different. Maybe not Phillip, but your stories, your books, they could have been different."

"Yes, well, I am the coward, aren't I? I feel a bit drunk here. My tongue is too loose. I must leave."

"How did you get here? This place is just for us."

"My baby brought me. Turn around now and look. You can see her here, can't you? My daughter brought her back. I'd love the irony if it weren't so terrible."

Pistachio pushed onto her knees and stood, brushing the twigs and leaves from her legs. The figure she saw was pink and fleshy and round, and it carried a green bear. "That's Katrina? That's who Elise brought in?" What happened to the feral creature with the tail?

"It's who Elise brought in. But she's not Katrina." The figure held out a tiny hand and Mrs. Abigail Fisher took it and rose. "I'll be back soon, I fear, Pistachio. This is not how I imagined my ending, but I am at least still interested in how it will work out." She smiled for the first time at her character. "And Pistachio, darling, did you honestly think there was a place anywhere that I could not go? We are linked."

"Don't go! Where is Harold? You can't go without giving him back to me."

"I didn't take him. I promise you."

"But when you die, I'll be trapped without him."

"Not if he finds you, child. There seems to be a myriad of unexpected possibilities on the table this week. What story do you want to write?"

"Mine?"

The figure and Mrs. Abigail Fisher had descended the hill toward the setting sun. Their shadows stretched lean behind them.

"Wait!" screamed Pistachio. "What am I supposed to do now?"

"Go read the story," said Mrs. Abigail Fisher.

"I can't read!"

"Why do you say that? You don't strike me as the kind of character who would believe the limitations someone else set for you."

When they had disappeared, the waxing moon reappeared. The ravens fluttered their wings and jabbered at each other. Pistachio's book cover stone had the end-date started now. 2-0-0. Only one number missing.

34

Pistachio crept back into the parlor where Elise sat with the green notebook open in her lap. She put Henry's hat back on her head, wrapped her shoulders with the multi-colored shawl and cozied up to Elise again.

"You came back," said Elise.

Pistachio nodded, the hat rubbing Elise's thigh.

"It's been very quiet on the porch," said Elise. "I wonder what has happened to my mother."

Elise left the notebook on the end table. Through the window, she saw her mother sleeping sitting up in the porch swing, Katrina curled into her lap holding Mama Bear close. Her mother's shoulders rose and fell. Katrina breathed through her mouth. The air was still. The stench that had welcomed Elise and Katrina just yesterday morning to the house had softened into more of a stale odor of unwashed skin and fermenting food. The glass between Elise and her mother was pitted. She remembered when she was only as tall as the lowest pane, and she would stand at the window to wait for her father to come home in the morning. She wasn't sure where he worked. Mother said he worked in the dark and she worked in the light, but Elise had always felt the opposite was true. The sun might be out when her mother worked in her room, but the curtains were closed, the lights dimmed. He'd come back smelling of cigars and whiskey, his eyes wet and gleaming. When he'd see her waiting for him, his mouth stretched into a smile, the edges of his mustache twitching.

"Daddy!"

"Elly-Fish!"

"I waited for you!"

"I'm so glad!"

And sometimes he'd snap open his saxophone case and play her a morning song, which he said was quite different from an evening song. You could tell the difference, he'd said, by how the progressions danced with each other. "Can you hear it?" he'd ask, and she said she could, but she really wasn't sure. The notes didn't seem to have a beginning or an end to her. They layered on top of each other until they had a life of their own. Before he finished, he'd draw out the final note, wipe off the mouthpiece and say he had to go get some shut-eye before "your mother" wakes up. He'd wink though, and she would know that things were peaceful between her mother and father. She'd know they would probably have dinner together before he left that evening for his night work, and if it was a particularly good day, her mother might read chapters to them in front of the fireplace. There were those days, she reminded herself. There were.

She pressed her palm against the lowest pane of glass, wishing she had a handprint of her little girl palm to compare it to. She had a brief thought that maybe he would come home that morning. It was a day of oddities, a day that was not at all like any other day, and if she could be reading a novel draft to an invisible book character wearing her fiancée's hat, then surely it would not be impossible for her father to come walking up the stairs. She wished. She murmured the wish. She closed her eyes, but when she opened them there was only the window, with her mother and Katrina on the other side.

She'd never watched her mother sleep. Her mother's room was off-limits, whether the door was closed or not. She stopped trying to go in after her father left and Courtney Lynn left. Her mother had stopped closing the door to keep her out, but the energetic barrier was far too great.

Her mother's eyes opened. She touched Katrina's hair. Pushed against the floorboards to rock the swing. Elise raised her hand, pressed it against the windowpane, this time a higher one. "Mama?" she whispered.

Mrs. Abigail Fisher nodded and waved back. "Come outside," she said. Or that's what Elise wanted to believe she said as she read her lips. Pistachio had taken the green notebook. The pages were flipping back and forth. How odd that this is not odd, Elise thought. But it had always been this way. There had always been creatures living in and around their family. She wondered what might have been different had she seen them more clearly sooner.

Katrina's flesh was no longer dripping from her bones. She seemed comfortable with her mother, and that was something Elise could neither understand nor stomach. Her mother's fingers stroked Katrina's hair, not deliberately or because she knew someone was watching and so she had best appear to be a good mother, but just because she wanted to and it was a natural extension of affection. Elise felt jealous. She opened the door.

"Get up, Katrina," she said. "Where have you been all this time? I'm tired of you playing tricks."

"Did you drink the coffee?" asked Katrina, who didn't move from Mrs. Abigail Fisher's lap. "Mama Bear and I made it special just for you to keep you warm."

"I dropped it out by the honeysuckle."

"Well, you best go and get it." Katrina kissed the top of Mama Bear's head. "Take her with you if you want. She can help you find what you lost."

Elise did not want to touch that bear, that spinning, jumping, button-eyed thing. She didn't want to leave the porch, leave her mother who was demonstrating compassion. Mrs. Abigail Fisher raised her hand to Elise. "Daughter," she said. "You and I need to go to Benjamina."

"You know Benjamina's name?"

"Of course I do."

"But we never—"

"I know."

Katrina started to hum the lullaby.

"It's a strange song for a baby, isn't it?" said Mrs. Abigail Fisher. "Why would a person want to sing a child to sleep with images of falling out of a tree?"

"The world is cruel, Mother. And babies fall out of trees all the time. Sometimes they even go to sleep and don't come back."

"I want you to be warm," said Katrina. She sat up, held out Mama Bear. "I want you to be warm now, Lissa."

Elise stepped back. The bassinet had appeared in front of her, looking just like she remembered. The image shimmered for a moment and then vanished. The bassinet was threaded with a pale green ribbon. She had liked the way the ribbon felt when she rubbed it with her fingers, and after Courtney Lynn left, she pulled the pale green ribbon from the bassinet and carried it with her, tucked into a pocket or, when she got older, in her shirt. She didn't know what became of that ribbon. She had looked for it more than once. Katrina untied Mama Bear's neck scarf.

"Here, Lissa." She held out the ribbon. "Take it."

Elise did. The ribbon was faded, worn through on one end where she had rubbed it over and over for years in the dark of her bedroom after everyone had gone. Her index finger and thumb made the instinctual movements. They still soothed her.

"Take me on the wagon," said Katrina. "Ride me round the yard."

The wagon in which Elise had carted the ghost of her sister had been red, as most wagons were then, and before Elise put the bassinet in it, her Mother had used it for carting pots of just-blooming marigolds and zinnias to line the yard with. The bassinet fit perfectly into the wagon's bed. She hosed it out first, to get all the leftover dirt from the new potted plants out and to make the wagon as comfortable as she could. Silly, she knew. But once the bassinet was in the wagon and she started to pull it around the yard, everything changed. The shadows lengthened or shortened, whatever was appropriate for that particular time of year, and then the sounds stopped and she was in some sort of sound tunnel. She didn't know how to describe it any better than that. Inside this sound tunnel there was only her breathing. She'd cough or sneeze occasionally and the echo of that sudden sound reverberated all around her. When she was through fidgeting, coughing, itching, smacking her lips together, she would have no choice but to give in to what was coming, what was always coming.

It was nothing like a horror movie. It was like a lullaby. The baby, Courtney Lynn, would whisper her name, "Lissa," (she couldn't quite say Elise) and she would say it over and over and over, a mantra. Elise would tingle. She knew people say they tingle all the time, but she really would. She would feel an electric current running from her toes to her scalp. Sometimes the current would be so strong she shook, but most of the time she could hold steady. She liked the feel of it, of her, inside of Elise. "Lissa, Lissa, Lissa," she'd say, and on days when everything was in perfect alignment, Elise heard the thumping of Courtney Lynn's tiny heart next to her own, and on the most perfect of all days, she could whisper back to her and she'd respond.

"I'm sorry."

"I'm sleeping."

"I'm sorry."

"I'm sleeping."

"I didn't want you to be cold."

And then Courtney Lynn would break the spell. "I am cold." And Elise would feel her tears start to bubble in her belly, like when Mother forgot to turn the gas off and left her tea water too long in the kettle. She knew if she let a single tear fall, she'd lose her sister again. Water seemed to make her go away, like the Wicked Witch. So she'd hold her tears back and swallow hard until she could hear her tiny heartbeat in her chest again.

She pulled the wagon around the perimeter of the yard, but she never went by Baby's Creek. Elise wanted Courtney Lynn to see the new baby robins and the bumbling bumblebees and the inchworms inching across the grass. She wanted her to see the pictures in the early summer clouds: elephants, kangaroos (especially the roo) and tigers. She wanted her to taste the first berries from the hedges and swat at the early mosquitoes. She pulled the wagon around and around and around until after many months the grass refused to grow around the edges of the yard. "Lissa, Lissa, Lissa," she would whisper, and Elise would whisper back, "I'm here, I'm here, I'm here," and Courtney Lynn would whisper back, "Me too, me too, me too," and that was the response Elise had been waiting for in the lonely sound tunnel. That was the comfort she needed, the proof that what she was doing made sense.

It had to happen, usually as the sun was setting, when the baby would take her heartbeat back and Elise would be left with the inexplicable loneliness of only one heart. She would be left with the echo of her whispering, and she would be reassured for another day that her sister still loved her, that she hadn't left her, and that (even if she was cold) she would stay as long as Elise needed her to. Mother might have thought Elise was crazy, but she wasn't crazy at all. She was only responding to what she was hearing, and when the baby was there with her, Elise didn't have to play alone. She didn't have to discover the yard all on her own. She could share the coming of summer and mourn its passing. When Elise had pulled all the pale green ribbon from the bassinet, the sheet that had been covering it flapped in the breeze. Soon after that, the bassinet began to collapse and she was growing too big for pulling a rusting red wagon around the yard.

Elise was fourteen the last time she walked around the yard with her sister, many years too old for pulling a rusting red wagon, but she simply couldn't leave her out there all alone, and she was afraid that if she stopped showing up, her sister would find somewhere else to go.

It was not like a horror movie at all. Not one bit.

35

Pistachio held the journal and paced. She could indeed read. Had she always been able to, but just had let herself be told she couldn't? That happened to regular people all the time. Why wouldn't it happen to characters? And what if the character who could read, the one who lived off the coast of Japan being tended to by crones, was just another story? Just another diversion. She was furious, but she couldn't stop reading. Each time the marks on the page became a word, she grew thicker and juicier. Each time the words became a sentence, she breathed more deeply.

Pistachio had never seen the inside of a home like Mrs. Honeycutt's. It was like a TV home. All the furniture matched and clear plastic slipcovers protected the dark brown and olive leaf upholstery. A huge Oriental rug, the biggest rug Pistachio had ever seen, kissed the edges of the feet of all the furniture. The walls were a pale robin's egg blue, the trim bright white. Dark shadow pictures of people lined the walls in oval frames.

"That's the first Pendergrass Honeycutt," said Mrs. Honeycutt, pointing to a man with dark eyes, a face with no hint of a smile. "Sometimes his eyes follow you around the room."

Pistachio took a step back and Mrs. Honeycutt laughed. "They say that's how he was in real life, too. Had eyes everywhere. A body could never get away. Least that's what they say. I never knew him, of course. He's my husband's great-great grandfather."

Pistachio nodded. The carpet was squishy and new and Pistachio wondered if she should take her shoes off. There was no place for her dirty sneakers in such a house.

Mrs. Honeycutt glanced over her shoulder. "I just need to get a few things cleared up before I introduce you. Let me just put you upstairs for a bit and you can get settled in and I can clear everything right up. How does that sound?" Mrs. Honeycutt pushed lightly in the small of Pistachio's back, and, like a well trained gelding, Pistachio stepped forward and began climbing what seemed like an endless staircase. The center of the stairs was covered with the plastic wrap, same as the furniture. When they came to the landing, Mrs. Honeycutt did not release her hand. "Keep going, honey. One more flight." Three flights of stairs? For one family? The second staircase was narrower and spun in a spiral snail's shell. Pistachio felt a little dizzy. "Hold tight, dear," said Mrs. Honeycutt, which was quite unnecessary since the girl had not once let go of the wrought iron banister. The attic room was humid and the furniture not nearly as grand as downstairs, but still, miraculously dust-free.

Pistachio had to stop reading for a moment. She remembered fragments of angry conversations between Mr. and Mrs. Honeycutt. She felt the scratch of sheets over her body in the afternoon. The bristle of facial hair against her neck. She heard the plink-plinking of piano keys in the early morning. The pages in the notebook were slashed through with red ink. Notes, upside down, sideways, in circles, lined the paper. One strike-through was deep enough to cut through several pieces of paper. Who could that have been? Pistachio wondered. Whose death cry arced across those pages?

After the news of Pistachio's death made the rounds, there was only the organist, Mrs. Honeycutt, to sit with the body. "An angel she was," said Mrs. Honeycutt, to no one. "Fell straight out of the sky and then God took her straight back."

Mr. Calhoun, the undertaker, had done a nice job preparing her body, her legs unfolded and straightened, her hair smoothed and washed. She didn't look like she was sleeping, no, that's a big lie, no one dead looks like they're sleeping. At their best they look like a very good paint by number reproduction of someone you might have known.

When you see a dead person, you make that initial comparison between dead and alive, and then your brain begins to deconstruct the living person and rebuild her as the dead person. It's quite astonishing how quickly this occurs. Then there is a moment of relief that you are not the one in the mahogany box and then the brief, albeit irrational thought that you are not ever going to be in a mahogany box because you eat right, brush your teeth, and are overall a very good person. Then you start to unravel the things and feelings and stories that tied you to that person, and for most of us, far quicker than we'd like to admit, the person who had been living just days ago begins to dissolve and we are amazed and more than a little frightened by how insignificant everyone is. We'll put that thought out of our heads pretty quickly, ugly and incomprehensible as it is, and move on to enjoy a nice ham and cheese sandwich with a splash of yellow mustard and potato salad at the funeral lunch.

Mr. Calhoun appeared at the door, stovepipe hat almost touching the top of the doorframe. "Mrs. Honeycutt? Shall I bring in the boy?"

Mrs. Honeycutt did not know what to do. She clutched her ironed handkerchief in her right hand, her left absently touching the strand of freshwater pearls around her neck. How could it be that she forgot entirely about the boy? "He shouldn't see his mother this way."

"Pardon me, ma'am, but he's asking to. He should see her if he wants to. It may not seem so, but it'll help him later on."

Mrs. Honeycutt noticed for the first time the hint of redness around the sunken Carolina blue eyes. At a quick glance, he looked like a caricature of a funeral director—tall black hat, somber suit with a red carnation, slight stoop to the shoulders—but upon closer examination, she saw that the only thing scary about him was that he had the courage every day to stand with death and with the dead. The faint scent of formaldehyde lingered on him.

All by himself, he attended the dead in the basement of his three-story funeral home. Why had she never respected that before? He'd been in Gethsemane as long as she'd been alive. His father was the first Calhoun in the business, and Mrs. Honeycutt, like almost all the children, made up scary ghoulish stories about the Calhouns. One, she recalled shamefully, had a touch of cannibalism in it.

Now, she wanted to hug him. She did not believe she had as much compassion in her whole body as he did in his thin and brittle fingers. "Where is he?"

"In the parlor. I give him a deck of cards to play with."

"He's good at solitaire."

"Ma'am, don't let him get too good at it." A pause. "Pardon me."

"No, no, Mr. Calhoun. Pardon me." She crossed the red and orange thick rug and let herself touch, without looking, Pistachio's cheek. "Of course the boy should see his mother."

Mr. Calhoun nodded, slipped out of the room.

Mrs. Honeycutt steeled her soul and let herself gaze at Pistachio. Her blonde hair was so smooth against her forehead and the pale blue satin lining. If there had been bruises on her face, Mr. Calhoun had erased them. If Pistachio had cried, those tears had dried, even before Mr. Calhoun had touched her. She couldn't remember if Pistachio's eyes were green or blue, and for a full five seconds, she pondered lifting up the lids, one last time, so she could be sure. Madness, she thought, but Mr. Calhoun was gone and the boy hadn't yet come. A quick lift. No one would know. Right eyelid—and instantly Mrs. Honeycutt was sorry. The eye was glassy, reflective even, but it was distinctly green. The lid stayed up. Mr. Calhoun returned with the boy.

"My. Oh my—I—" Mrs. Honeycutt did not know what to do. The boy held his deck of cards, head bowed to the floor. Could he be only five? He seemed so much older. He held himself with such reverence—such solemnity.

"Mr. Calhoun, if you don't mind, could I see you for a moment?"

"Of course." He motioned her to the hallway.

"No. No, up here. Please. If you don't mind."

"Of course." A lifetime of working with the dead had given him more than a few tools for dealing with the living.

She leaned in and to her surprise, he did not smell of formaldehyde, but rather Mennen. "Ah. Mr. Calhoun, I—you see I couldn't remember. I suddenly couldn't remember." She thought she might cry, but her throat felt stopped with cork. She pointed, instead, to Pistachio's open eye. Without a word, Mr. Calhoun lowered the lid, almost seeming not to touch her at all.

"It's OK, Mrs. Honeycutt. I always thought it one of God's great cruelties how quick we forget. Seems like the least He could do was let us hold just a bit."

Mrs. Honeycutt couldn't speak.

"Her eyes were green, ma'am. Like a Christmas tree."

"Thank you."

"Anything else you want to see? Touch?"

She shook her head. "I just couldn't remember and I got afraid I wouldn't be able to tell the boy about her. He'll go on, right? He'll forget her."

"Boy never forgets his mother. Whether she was good or evil or something in between. He's never going to forget."

Pistachio's son, still clutching the deck of cards, approached the coffin.

"He's not said anything since the news," said Mrs. Honeycutt.

"It takes time."

Mrs. Honeycutt was suddenly frustrated. What exactly did that mean—it takes time—and time to do what and time to understand what? Nonsense. She wanted to hit Mr. Calhoun hard enough for him to shout, but those emotions blew away when the boy approached the coffin and peered at his mother. He could barely see over the side of the box. He slipped the cards into his front pocket, and reached into the coffin, and unconcerned with protocol or manners or the opinion of anyone else, he put his tiny hand on her belly. He looked up at the two grown-ups, who had become oddly quiet.

"My first home is gone," he said, removed his hand, and left the room.

"A boy can't ever forget his mama," Mr. Calhoun said again. "It's just plain impossible."

The preacher would be there soon, and even though Mrs. Honeycutt knew very few folks in town genuinely cared about Pistachio, she knew the church would be packed. You can't beat a mixture of curiosity and Christian obligation. "Who could have done this to her?" she asked.

"I surely don't know, ma'am."

When the boy left the viewing, Mrs. Honeycutt did not know what to do. The room, suddenly overcome with the sickening sweetness of too many flowers in stagnant water, wrapped its fragrance around her throat. "I'm very sorry," she said to the kind undertaker. "But I must go."

"Very well, ma'am. What, then, shall we do with her?"

Mrs. Honeycutt was supposed to play the organ. Her husband would come, if for no other reason than to give her one less thing to argue with him about. The pastor would talk about charity, perhaps, compassion for those less fortunate, he'd likely share the parable of the sheep and the goats, only he'd be sure to leave it ambiguous as to whether or not Pistachio made it safely into the pen by nightfall.

"We should let her rest," she said. "That's the very least we should do."

"I'll bring her on over to the church this evening. Service is tomorrow morning, right?"

"Thank you."

"Forgive me ma'am, but you'll not forget. Not the part that matters. It's not God's way."

The funeral parlor was as generic as a hotel room. Inoffensive, muted colors. Piped in music that meant nothing to anyone. Cellophane wrapped white peppermints. Benches with cushions that were just comfortable enough for an hour or two, no longer. Grieving holds to a tight schedule.

"Do you think anyone else will come see her?" asked Mrs. Honeycutt, who suddenly could neither bear to remain in the sterile room nor leave it.

The undertaker was an honest man. He knew grieving people were like children—they could spot a lie from across the room. "I don't know, ma'am. The curious, perhaps."

She was grateful for his truth. "Maybe then, I'll stay with her? Until you want to take her on over?"

36

Pistachio had been reading! She had fallen into the story and the rest of the world had vanished! She had transformed the marks on the page into ideas and scenes and feelings and she shouted for Harold to come quick before remembering he wasn't there.

No one was there. Elise was on the porch. Everyone was on the porch now and she was alone in the house. Then the scene she just read took root. She had died anyway. Even in the part of the book that didn't make it into the final version. She had still died. She didn't feel anything for her son, though she could feel his hand on her body, on her womb. She could feel he was missing something that he couldn't identify; the absence of which would define his life. She'd never seen Caleb in the closet or anywhere else. Had he been conscripted into another novel? Sent on one of Mrs. Abigail Fisher's tragic missions that no one ever returned from?

Harold called those missions the Plank Stories because they required the characters to walk off of some sort of plank into oblivion. Every character dreaded that possibility. Some creators, he told her, have militias that arrive in the night and remove the troublemakers or the rebels. They always come when it's darkest, and they use clubs and tasers to take away the characters. He didn't think Mrs. Abigail Fisher commanded a militia, but you could never be completely sure. The Plank Stories were kept in an airtight vault under seven different lock combinations. Each story had a combination lock as well, and some of the stories, the ones that no one dared imagine, had only one character, trapped in a monologue for all eternity.

Pistachio could imagine Mrs. Honeycutt—her long organist's fingers and her Woolworth's perfume—and she knew now where the Dentyne and Barbasol smells came from. Mrs. Honeycutt no doubt bought the products her husband used and then somehow played the downstairs piano loud enough to honestly not hear what he did. Pistachio was struggling with whether she could remember something that she hadn't yet finished reading. When did a scene become real? When it was written or when it was read? She thought she could ask Mrs. Abigail Fisher. This could count as one of her three questions. Mrs. Abigail Fisher had started the game in the Cemetery of Books but walked away, as usual, before Pistachio could ask what she needed to.

Pistachio had a flash of a memory, but maybe it wasn't a memory. Maybe it was a story or something she made up to make some meaning. She had been so very young, not even defined yet, but she spent many of her days at the creek, which was now behind Benjamina the Bottle Tree Vine where little girl Elise went every night. She remembered Abbey, who was not yet Mrs. Abigail Fisher, kneeling beside the icy creek. Abbey liked to dangle her fingers in the clean water and see how long she could keep them there before she no longer felt the tongues of the water spirits lapping at her skin.

Ever since Abbey could leave the perimeter of her yard, she had come here to watch the silver sparkle of the minnows, the waving branches of the algae on the rocks just below the water's surface. Sometimes a water snake swam by. Sometimes monarch butterflies grazed the surface. Mostly she came here because it was quiet except for the sounds of the animals and birds that lived there. In the quiet, she could wait until the people living in her head began to speak. For Abbey, it was like going to church was for others—this going someplace out of her regular life, her regular surroundings, into something extraordinary, with movement going on at all sides, above and below, left and right, front and back. Sounds that she could only hear when she let herself slip underneath the dominant sounds—beneath the crow's demands, beneath the thunder behind the next hill, beneath the dynamite of the coal mine and the whistle of the Southern Pacific's 4:00 train. When she let those things slide away, she could hear what was really happening—the air bubble conversations among the fish, the rock's whisper to the earth beneath it, the buzzing of the ants' mandibles.

She could sit there for hours, her body so unlike the other eight-year-old girls' bodies that needed to run and climb and sweat even as their mothers tried to press them into domesticity, ironing, washing, cooking, milking. Abbey could spend hours, legs crossed, watching the earthworms wriggle in the afternoon sun.

She enjoyed playing a game with the sounds—letting the loudest become the quietest and then ratcheting it back up again. Sound level wasn't static. It could be manipulated just by her mind and attention. She could do the same with sight, focusing intently on the three-part body of the fire ant, no longer seeing the running creek, the mile high pine trees, the thunderhead brewing to the north. She could see the tiny head on the tip of the ant's antennae. Then, she could close her eyes tight and in her mind back away so that the ant became just a part of the scene around her, not the entire scene. The sky now had a role, the grass, the trees in their broad circle around the creek. She noticed different things, depending on where she placed her attention. The story changed whether she was up close or far away. The soundtrack shifted based on where she narrowed or widened her gaze.

For a time, a few truly golden years, Abbey thought she was a magician, a sorceress, a high priestess. She thought she'd uncovered something previously unknown in the world—relativity. The clarity or blurriness of something depended on where she was in relation to it. The importance of something had nothing to do with the thing, but rather who was viewing the thing. She couldn't articulate that, not yet at eight; she was too enthralled by the different things she could see simply by opening one eye and closing another.

Pistachio had felt giddy watching Abbey watching the world. That was when she first whispered. "Hello? Abbey? It's me!" And both she and Abbey had been filled with delight.

"Who are you?" asked Abbey.

"I don't know yet," said Pistachio.

"Me either," said Abbey. "But we're in such a beautiful place, how can we not be magic?"

37

Pistachio was troubled. For all of her life, she had thought she was separate from Abbey, that she and all the other characters in the golden orb were more like associates or colleagues who, when called upon, fulfilled their roles in narrative. But she was starting to see that the relationship was more like that of a tree to fruit. Abbey was the tree and she and all the characters were fruit. Or maybe nuts. Pistachio preferred nuts. In any event, the fruit, the fruition, of the tree is *of the tree,* and even if the fruit is picked and eaten, it still brings with it the nourishment and heart of the tree from which it originated. Maybe it's more than fruit. Maybe it's a branch, or, if she could dare think it, the roots. What if the characters held up the creator? Blasphemy. She could hear Harold now. "What are you saying? Do you know the danger we'll get in if talk of this gets out? You could end up burning on the stake forever in some medieval novel. Why, Pistachio, why can you not just accept?"

She wanted to, she really did, or she told herself she did, and now she's just pacing back and forth and back and forth, holding an unpublished draft of a story that used to star her, watching her creator and her daughter walk off toward the Bottle Tree Vine, and she thought she could shout to them, "I know what happened there! I know what needs to come next!" But she still couldn't leave the house.

The most astonishing and troubling things were the memories. Her memories, which by all rights and agreements and contracts were supposed to be hers, were merging, and she was beginning to not only remember things from early in her creator's life, but she was beginning to remember her creator's experience itself. What sort of narrator would this be? She had been content (OK, not exactly content) with being a peripheral narrator. It was safe. She could watch from behind the curtain and she could keep a modicum of self-control. But if she could slip inside Abbey's thoughts and if she could direct the story—if she could be the filter—Harold would be positively verklempt. He would pass out right in front of her, in the most dramatic of fashions, and he would shake his fist at the sky and lament the changing of the guard, the nullification of tradition, the threat to the cannon. He would writhe and wail and squirm and squiggle, but Pistachio knew at some point, the possibility of the story would capture his eye and he would sit up, dust himself off, and say, "How on all that is holy have you done that?"

It made her smile to imagine Harold in that way, and even more to imagine how he would feel about her if she were able to control the narrative. She'd never send him off to fight in ridiculous wars, or fall in love with irredeemable femme fatales. She'd keep him with her. Close.

Abbey had written once about a schizophrenic character. The woman's mind had split into three distinct voices after the death of her son in Vietnam. The transitions between one character and the next didn't happen like in movies where the actor will bow her head and look up with the eyes of a demon. They happened within the sentence and the character's voice sometimes shifted mid-breath. There was no line, Pistachio witnessed, between one voice and the other. They swam together, fish in the whirlpool, and switched dominance with each wave. Madness wasn't about angles, she realized. It was a spiraling, a circling down and up and down and up.

Had she gone mad? Or had she just stepped into her ultimate role?

The notebook lay open on the floor. She squatted and read some more.

The boy, Caleb, was far from the mortuary and farther still from the church where tomorrow he would find himself sitting in the front row in uncomfortable long britches and collared shirt, looking at the box that held his mother's body. Caleb, never one to run unless it was absolutely required, had been walking steadily toward Golgotha, where his mother was said to have appeared in town for the first time, pregnant with him. He had always loved his mythical beginnings and had never thought until this day to ask about his father. Now he would never know. Now he was free to set out on his own, though at five he was not sure what that would mean. He knew he didn't want to stay with Mr. and Mrs. Honeycutt, but he was old enough to know he had nowhere else to go at that moment.

The bugs were out in force and after a time he stopped trying to swat them away. He liked the rhythm of his feet against the asphalt. He liked the solidity of the earth rumbling through him like a train. Sometimes he wished he could catch that rhythm, jump on the train and jump off somewhere new, just like his mother had done. Everyone told him he was too old to be so young, but he didn't know what that meant. He had always been just the way he was.

When he reached Golgotha, he knelt before it, digging his knees into the moist earth. A woolly caterpillar inched across a decaying leaf. He stroked its arched back. It froze under his finger. Its back was soft like a horse's muzzle. He clasped and unclasped his hands. He knew he was supposed to cry. He knew he was supposed to feel something profound, but he didn't. The sun still looked bright and awake, the clouds still made cloud pictures and the caterpillars still inched across leaves on the ground. Life kept moving.

His stomach growled. It wasn't the right thing, he knew, to be hungry on the day of his mother's wake, but his body did what it wanted. He thought he would like a ham sandwich with yellow mustard and a tomato. He couldn't remember when he last ate. The caterpillar had gone. There were different cloud pictures in the sky. The rock where his mother was said to have appeared was just a rock. He stood and ran his palms lightly over the surface. The rock was a slate granite; it left a dusty film on his palms. He tried to remember the way his mother's hands smelled, but he couldn't, and he knew that should make him sad, but it didn't. Something was very wrong with him.

Caleb turned his back on the rock and began the return trip to Gethsemane. He would stay for the service tomorrow and when Mrs. Honeycutt put him to bed in the evening, he would climb out the window and be gone. She would worry for a time, but she would forget because he wasn't hers. He could never be hers.

Caleb kicked a smooth stone most of the way back to Gethsemane. It was no longer the brightest part of the day, and his hunger increased. He tried to remember if his mother's hair was brown or blonde, but each color seemed right. He could remember her both ways. There seemed no actual answer. His hair was blond, so maybe that was the right answer. Mrs. Honeycutt's was gray. So that meant it was impossible that she could be his mother, even in a pretend sort of way.

A truck rattled past him, the driver lifting his hat to Caleb, but not stopping. Caleb was sure he had some sort of disease that made everyone in the town soft and nice around him, but never warm and friendly. He thought he remembered his mother saying folks had their own ways of doing things around here. They looked at Caleb strangely, not like they looked at the girls and boys from other families. He felt like a new insect species under their microscopes.

He still planned to leave the next day after the funeral but his hunger was getting sharper and he had forgotten that he would need to eat, would need money of some kind, would need some help. He had forgotten that he was a little boy. His heart so often seemed so old.

The funeral was empty, as the funeral director had predicted. There was the preacher (a good man, everyone said, but Caleb didn't trust him. He saw him rolling the quarters from the offering plate into a cardboard sleeve and pocketing them.) Mrs. Honeycutt, of course, Mr. Honeycutt chose not to attend (a headache, a sudden attack of colitis, something—please explain to everyone, dear), the resident mourner, Mrs. Evelyn Tibbs, who came to every funeral because it was her duty to God and the deceased, and a reporter from the Atlanta

Journal-Constitution, who was there on a hack assignment about the strange murdered girl-child who had been named after a nut. The journalist scribbled pictures in his notebook during the service.

Caleb, handsome in pressed gray big-boy pants and shiny black shoes, sweated throughout most of the service. His mother, he knew, was in the box in the front of the church. He was thinking of shells, of husks of things, like corn. You peeled back the husk and you got all the yummy corn and then you threw the husk away but all the yummy goodness stayed inside you. His mother was a shell, a discarded coat, an empty bird's nest. What had happened to the yummy part? Mrs. Honeycutt dabbed at her eyes with a yellowed but clean handkerchief, and when it was time for music, the preacher nodded at her and she stood and went to the organ.

"I was practicing this number the first time I saw her," said Mrs. Honeycutt, who promptly blew her nose. The journalist looked up briefly, then returned to his drawing. Caleb realized that Mrs. Honeycutt had loved his mother, though he couldn't figure out why. She was not hers either. Caleb closed his eyes and listened to the music. He liked music. It made different pictures in his mind, sometimes pictures of things he'd never seen in his actual life. The pictures moved and danced with each other like colors in a kaleidoscope every time the music changed direction or tempo. He saw his mother, braids flying from one side of her head to the other, singing to herself as she hung up the laundry or helped him get ready for bed.

Mama.

"Such a tragedy," Mrs. Honeycutt said. She had finished the song. No one, of the few people in attendance, had made a sound. "I just wish you could have known her. She was one of God's best angels."

But that wasn't true, was it? Caleb had seen what had happened. He didn't make a step to help, but it wasn't because he didn't care, it was because his feet wouldn't move. He had seen his mother with Mr. Honeycutt and he had been holding her hair, which he must have unbraided, and she was laughing for a moment before she kissed him, or he kissed her, Caleb was too young to know for sure. Mr. Honeycutt made a strange noise, like a surprised animal, and then he snapped her neck. Just like a chicken's. Caleb must be a very bad person because he didn't make any sound when he saw it. He just watched, and then when Mr. Honeycutt had left, after arranging her body so she would be found soon, Caleb began to cry and run back to town. "My mama's dead! My mama's dead! My mama's dead!" And then, the good Christian people of Gethsemane were very interested in speaking to him.

Caleb had heard the sounds his mother would make when she was with Mr. Honeycutt. He was much too young to understand the significance of those sounds, but for the rest of his life, whenever he thought of his mother, which was not often, he remembered the thin wail she would make, a wounded animal wail, and then there would be whispers and sometimes shouting and then sounds he could not identify. His mother would come back to his room, where he had been sometimes sleeping and sometimes pretending to sleep, and she would stroke his hair and sing a song, the words of which he could not remember, but the tune, a minor key, never left him. Sometimes his mother would curl around him in the boy-bed, and he liked that, but he would not admit it. He didn't like it when he could smell Mr. Honeycutt on her skin. He would ball his hands into tiny fists and clench his anger to his belly.

Pistachio's own belly ached, its fragile fleshiness a shock under her thickening fingers. Caleb's hair had been the thin blond of young wheat, and his neck had smelled so new, like a stuffed toy she'd just brought back from the store. He had his father's nose and hands, she could tell even at such a young age. What had happened to him? Where did he end up? Could he be in the Plank Stories in the vault? "My boy," she said. "Oh, my boy."

The journal had a series of crosses and scribbles and the next few pages had been ripped out. Caleb? Where did you go?

Re-visioning of final scene in
The Garden of Gethsemane, Georgia
by Mrs. Abigail Fisher

Pistachio had thought the house was too tidy. Even the walls were spotless, no art work, no family photographs, not even a cross-stitched reminder that God was love. When Pistachio moved up and down the stairs, washed her dishes in the sink, dried her clothes on the taut line, she felt the tidiness growing branches, stretching its arms out to envelop her and pull her into the blaring white of it all.

The house could have been featured in a magazine. Everything was perfect but perfectly no one's. Anybody could have slipped into the house and made it theirs. In the beginning, Pistachio was grateful for the clean sheets, the food on the table, arranged by color and always precisely distributed, and the almost constant music coming from the piano room. When her son was born, she was grateful again for the clean sheets, the food on the table, and the almost constant music coming from the piano room. But only a few weeks after Caleb arrived, the clean sheets, the food on the table, and the almost constant music coming from the piano room began to exact their fees.

Mr. Honeycutt smelled of Barbasol and Dentyne gum. He had unruly hair at the base of his skull that traveled down his back. Pistachio used to imagine that Mrs. Honeycutt had one day, once, loved that hair, maybe even twisted its longer strands around her fingers and kissed the small bumps on his spine. Maybe she once looked forward to his return home, to his heavy fingers on her shoulders, to his sleeping breath.

Mr. Honeycutt came home from work at four sharp, went upstairs, took a shower, and then climbed the final set of stairs to Pistachio's attic room. The first time was an accident, or so Pistachio had believed. She thought he maybe drank too much from the hidden stash Mrs. Honeycutt kept underneath the kitchen sink behind the cleaning solutions.

Pistachio was silent, tried to be in fact gracious; after all, he had allowed her to stay in his house for so long. She had let herself believe it was a one-time thing, a single incident that he would either forget or regret the next day. But it became his ritual, and after he was finished, he would leave the room and take another shower and then sit across from her at dinner, staring uncomfortably at Caleb.

Mrs. Honeycutt always dressed for dinner, no matter if it was just the three (or four if you count Caleb) of them. She wore a dress with a pinched waist, a full pleated skirt, and pantyhose and heels, no matter how hot it was. Her hair was pin curled to its most unnatural wave, and her orange lipstick reflected the dearth of color choices available at the Woolworth's, not her poor taste in make-up shades. Mr. Honeycutt never noticed the thinly cut ham (she'd trimmed away the fat for him), the perfect arrangement of cauliflower, carrots, and fresh broccoli, the violets in the thin crystal vase that had been a wedding gift from Mrs. Honeycutt's mother. He never noticed the perfume she was wearing, a heavy floral, or the tight tips of her manicured fingers. But she kept preparing the meals every night. She dressed for him every night, and then most nights Pistachio would find her sitting in the dark at the pea-green breakfast table nursing a glass of something dark and strong. Sometimes she held a choker-length strand of pearls in one hand like a rosary, the glass of alcohol in the other.

Pistachio watched her frequently in the dark, but she never said a word. The woman sitting in the midnight kitchen was more interesting to Pistachio than the polished, smiling organist. Pistachio sat watching Mrs. Honeycutt longer and longer each night in hopes that she might turn around, and rather than being angry at being caught, would be relieved, and would then perhaps talk to her, woman to woman, and they might could see what could be done. But that never happened.

Mrs. Honeycutt knew that Pistachio was in the shadows behind her. She saw her reflection in the window above the sink. More than once she'd wanted to invite her to sit in the other chair, drink a glass with her, and say everything, or nothing, depending on what the night was calling for.

Pistachio wasn't particularly pretty, though she did have youth on her side. She was too angle-y for Mrs. Honeycutt's taste, too sharp-edged, but maybe that was what he preferred, and her own wider hips and softer belly wasn't what his body longed for. There were moments she knew she should cast Pistachio back out into the world, maybe even poetically take her back to Golgotha, but now there was Caleb, and even she, childless, unwillingly, could not tear apart a mother and a child. Besides, and this was the piece that made no sense to her, she actually liked Pistachio, maybe even loved Pistachio, and each day brought less and less animosity and more compassion. And then this part, the even deeper part underneath her heart, whispered to her that she was just a bit relieved that Mr. Honeycutt was no longer sweating up against her at night. These thoughts banged around inside her, cracking open fissures in her bones. She didn't know what sweet Jesus would think about all of that, about what was going on underneath her roof, and how she was too weak to stop it.

One thing Mrs. Honeycutt had never considered was that Pistachio was unwilling. Mrs. Honeycutt was ashamed of many things in her life, but after Pistachio's body was found bent and broken, she was most ashamed of that. She had simply not thought that Pistachio didn't want to do it, and when the position of the body, the slight whiff of Barbasol that Mrs. Honeycutt noticed right away, pulled the shades up on the awareness that had gnawed at her gut in the dark, she collapsed to the floor like a good Southern woman, only she was not grieving, not yet, that would come much later; she was ashamed that a woman she had honestly tried to give refuge to had become a prisoner in her attic.

At her dinner table, the night Pistachio died, Mrs. Honeycutt fed Caleb all the vanilla ice cream he could eat, and she did not remove the fat from the pork loin for her husband, and she did not provide him the freshest vegetables or biscuits. She sat, back to him, and fed the child spoonful after spoonful, trying to pre-sweeten the life she was sure he was now going to face. Her husband didn't say a word. He cut the fat off his own meat. He forwent vegetables all together, and he looked at the Dowager's hump forming on his wife's spine and wondered how it had come to this.

Pistachio felt sick. She remembered Mr. Honeycutt and his rough beard on her skin. She remembered the plink-plinking of the piano in the living room, the sound track to her silence. She remembered that she had wanted to tell Mrs. Honeycutt, who had been so kind to have brought her into her home, but then she couldn't find the words, or Abbey didn't give her the words, and when she really thought about the softness in Mrs. Honeycutt's eyes, the way she carved the meat for her husband at dinner, the way she polished the silver and arranged the table so he would feel like he was a king rather than a clerk in a shoe store, the way she always applied lipstick a shade too orange in the oval hall mirror right before he was supposed to return home, when she really thought about these things, she couldn't tell. She should tell, but breaking the heart of the only character who had shown her kindness was more than she could do. So she listened to Mrs. Honeycutt playing the hymns: *In the Garden, Rock of Ages, Softly and Tenderly Jesus is Calling* and she told herself as she lay beneath his dead-weight, that she was doing this for love of her.

Pistachio caught memories of both writing and living the words. She didn't need to close her eyes to find the images. She sat down. She stood up. She felt breath expanding in and out of lungs and pressing against a rib cage that had never been open. She reached to her head and there was hair, silky and thick. Hair.

It was no small thing to shift point of view in a story. Readers, Abbey had always talked about the readers, readers expect things of you once you set up a world. They expect that you have the sense enough to follow your own rules about things. It makes the reader feel safe, so you can take them to scary places. That's the writer's job, Abbey would say to classes at universities and bookstores. It's the writer's job to make the reader feel safe so she can then slice them open and allow them to feel. And point of view—well, point of view was the puppet master. Point of view was the great and powerful Oz. It gave the story focus. It filtered out and held in what mattered to a particular question.

But the questions have changed! Pistachio thought. I have changed the questions. I. Oh dear. Now she'd shifted person, too. Could that be done? She thought of Millicent again, the schizophrenic woman from *I am Thou*. Anything could be done. The imagination's limits were always self-imposed.

I have changed the questions. I am assuming the story. I am going to walk along the ocean's edge and I am going to dance with Harold under the fullest full moon and I am going to take my story back. She rifled through a drawer for a pen. She was going to write her end. Wait until Harold found out!

Actual Final Scene from
The Garden of Gethsemane, Georgia
by Pistachio P. Simmons

The reporter from The Atlanta Journal-Constitution left town without getting any answers, though he did manage to snap a poignant shot of the orphaned boy staring up at the altar cross. He noted that the boy did not cry during the service, but felt it cruel to write about that. Before too long, the mystery around what happened to young Pistachio Simmons faded into the background as tomato plants began to ripen, azaleas began to bloom and schools let out for summer vacation. Boys rode bicycles over the spot where Pistachio's body was found, imagining one day flying, pedaling just fast enough to lift into the air and travel to as yet undiscovered places.

Mr. and Mrs. Honeycutt started their days the same way they'd started them the length of their marriage. Some mornings they both almost spoke. She would stir her third sugar cube into her coffee and start to ask him;

he would put down the business section of the paper, clear his throat, take a bite of toast and began to tell her something; but they ended up never quite meeting in the middle. After a time, there was no need to speak at all about any of it. The clink of her spoon on the china cup's lip, the rustling of the paper was enough conversation for the both of them.

The spot where Pistachio arrived in town and the spot where her body was found became the stuff of legends, the mythology of Gethsemane. It's just a story, people would say. Just a story. No meaning whatsoever. And so that's what people would believe after a tsk-tsk or a snicker over the plot. It's just a story, and so it doesn't matter.

Abbey seemed frail to Pistachio now. She seemed old and fallible and dying. Dying not like the way Harold dies in every book. Dying in the way that Creators do. Forever. Pistachio put the pen down. Her hands were cramped. She'd thought the pen would have slipped, maybe even refused to write, but it was just a pen and it did what pens do no matter who was holding it. "Harold," she said to the air. "You have no idea."

Then she had an epiphany. No, no. Too much. Not allowed. Ridiculous. Silly. Absurd. Won't work. Can't work. Balance of the universe. Stop. Don't. But once she'd held the pen, it was impossible to put it down again. She'd written her ending. One story. If there was one, there was another, and another after that. All it took was letters. She picked up the pen, a ballpoint, unusual for the Fisher house.

Harold. There is a secret in the yard. We know what it is. We watched together behind the bay window in the parlor, do you remember? I know you do. I see you, wearing suspenders and wingtips from your most recent story in Ohio during the Prohibition. You look handsome, your hair slicked back, your wire-rimmed glasses perched just so. I am calling you home today, darling. We have work to do.

And then she closed her eyes and she imagined Harold, just as she described him, waiting for her outside the house. He'd be amazed, indignant, maybe even angry, but he'd soon feel the fresh air and see the depth of the dimensions and he'd wonder how he ever stayed contained within the hard covers of a text.

"Abbey," said Pistachio. "I am coming for you." And she took the deepest possible breath and stretched her full arms up to the ceiling, grabbed Henry's hat in case Elise still couldn't see her, and walked, on wide solid feet, out the front door toward the Bottle Tree Vine. "Abbey," she said. "I am coming."

38

Pistachio's big feet crunched the fallen leaves beneath them. When she emerged into the out, she stopped a brief moment to take in the bright. So bright, this sun on the outside, even on a hazy day. It could slice a person. A person. Character. Pistachio meant character. Where is Harold? Could he survive this sun? There were deeper smells in the out, too, dirt smells that were also life smells. How did Abbey describe these things? Pistachio had only simpler words—alive, dead, in-between. Those words meant everything to her, but she could see how they would not mean anything to a reader. Abbey must have loved her readers very much to take the time to find all those right words.

A thick crow swooped in front of her and she ducked. In the house, in the stories, the crows swooped, but they didn't just come out of nowhere. They had a narrative purpose. This out-world was random and loud. The crow had crow-friends, and they circled the yard waiting for someone to toss something away that they could fight over. Abbey and Elise and the feral thing were a few yards ahead of her, the space in-between them a cavern. Pistachio couldn't call Abbey Mrs. Abigail Fisher anymore. The formality was false, now that she had seen her thoughts, felt her heart.

Her footsteps were so loud. She was unaccustomed to weight. Her ankles shifted and then stabilized. The yard was filled with debris that Pistachio recognized from various books. There's the one-armed wheelbarrow that served as transportation for the ill-fated

Nicodemus in *Flights of Fancy*. There's the fragile apple tree that never took root. It had a feature role in *Beneath the Earth,* Abbey's least popular but most risky book, about the creatures that had been buried beneath the apple tree—fish, snails, frogs, the occasional bat—and the world they made down there together. She'd been intending to make it a children's book, but her editor thought it too ghastly for children. "Nonsense," Mrs. Abigail Fisher had said. "Children can handle anything. It's adults who cower at the first sign of the dark."

The sky in the out moved. That alone was amazing. The clouds drifted and darted, swelled to belly shapes and stretched into tendrils. No wonder humans felt so rushed. They were always trying to keep up with the galloping sky. Abbey and Elise's heads had sunk beneath the tree line. They must have begun the descent to the creek. When Pistachio and Harold had watched Elise when she was a girl, they couldn't see anything after the hill. Elise just seemed to walk into the world and disappear. She and Harold had done a great deal of speculating, but that's all their talk was, just stories.

"Hello!" Harold leaped from behind a weeping willow tree. He was indeed dressed in 1920s regalia. His suspenders were red and white striped, his shoes spit-shine polished, his pinstriped jacket decorated with a white carnation. "I am here!"

Then he stopped, pulled his jacket closed and cowered.

"Don't be afraid," said Pistachio.

"Pistachio! I was just about to ambush a bootlegger, Pinetree Pete, the most feared bootlegger along the Ohio River. I thought I'd been killed when I was tumbling out of the scene into the water. I can never be completely sure. I—oh—you should have seen us, P. We were waiting underneath a drawbridge, just like a merry band of trolls. Of course, we weren't particularly merry because we might get killed, but we had some jolly laughs nonetheless. William Jackson was in a particularly good mood because his sweetheart Annabelle had just said yes, but what he didn't know was that Annabelle had also said yes to George Inskeep, who was also under the bridge with us. We were just about to have the big reveal when—"

Harold was sweating. His neck was pink and dripping. His arms flailed wildly as he told the story. Pistachio held up a single hand. She loved how fully-formed he was. How he was of flesh. "Stop, love. You're here with me."

"But Pinetree Pete was just on the other side of the bridge. We could feel the rumbling in the earth, you know? We put our ears right flat down on the ground."

"Shhh."

"I always get yanked out of stories right when something is about to happen. I never get to have the climax. Never." He stomped his foot and Pistachio laughed. "It isn't funny," he said.

"No, no," said Pistachio. "Not funny at all."

He took his jacket off. "It's really hot out here. What story is this? It looks different."

"This is my story."

"Hey, that-a girl! I told you you'd get the right role one day. Patience and perseverance, that's what I always say. Patience and perseverance!"

"It's not a role, Harold. I wrote you here."

He stepped back, wiped his sweating hands on his pants. "Impossible."

"Possible."

"Impossible."

Pistachio's patience was wearing. She had to get to the Bottle Tree Vine. "Come with me. I wrote you here. I took the story. It wasn't nearly as hard as we thought. Certainly not impossible."

"You picked up a pen?"

"Yes."

"Where are the burns?" Character-lore contained volumes of warnings about touching pens—any pens, quill pens, calligraphy pens, ballpoint pens, fountain pens, roller-ball pens—there was a particularly fierce warning about Pentel 0.5 purple pens, but no one knew why. To touch the pen was to invoke all manner of judgments and firestorms and brimstone tumbling.

"It was just a pen, Harold."

"No! It's magic."

"I didn't say it wasn't magic. I just said it was only a pen. The magic isn't the pen. The magic is us."

He turned to run but slipped on the sandy path. Pistachio was beside him instantly. "Get away from me!" he shouted. "You've gone south! You've gone south!"

"We could go farther south," she said. "This is only Georgia."

"You can't go farther south. You're completely crossed over. Stay away!"

"Harold!" She slapped him light enough to calm him. "Listen to me. I wrote you here. We can be together now. No more conscriptions. No more wondering where you were or who you were with. I'll always know now."

"But I don't want you to always know," he said. "If you always know, then why would you wait? Why would you think about me at all if there were no more questions?"

"Because I love you."

"That's not enough," he said. "Haven't you read all the stories? It's never enough."

Pistachio had to admit that was most certainly the truth.

"Don't sulk, Harold. Look at where we are! We're in the garden. We're in the out. Doesn't it feel different?"

"You're different. Look at you, all thick and round and full. I'm still a paper doll."

"You're not. You're sweating. Your arms jiggle. I can write you fatter. I'll give you better hair."

"What's wrong with my hair?"

"Nothing's wrong with your hair. You know what I mean. I can make you into anything."

"What if I don't want that?"

Pistachio hadn't considered the possibility that he wouldn't leap into this new world with her. She felt a spark of anger. "Of course you want that."

"I just wanted to be in a story with you. But if you make the story, then where do I fit?"

You do what I want, she thought. You say the right thing. You're always here when I need you, not gallivanting off with some long-haired floozy in the Reconstruction. You're with me. But she didn't say any of that. She was hearing something in her head that wasn't her. Someone in her head. She shook it, tapped at her ears, clicked her solid teeth. The voice kept on. There was no pen out here in the garden. No way to write this down. Maybe this was something Abbey should have written down. Maybe it would have helped them all.

"Oh, Harold," she said. "I am becoming."

"Becoming what?"

"Becoming *her*."

"Don't be silly."

"I. Remember. *Her*. Listen to me."

Harold put his hands in his pockets. "Fine. But just for a minute.

Pinetree Pete is coming."

"Just for a minute," said Pistachio, and began to tell him her new point of view.

The moon was only a yellow pencil curve, like the moon you always see in picture books with cows, dogs, or little girls and boys reclining on it. Mrs. Abigail Fisher hadn't dared to bring a flashlight although she felt certain her neighbors were asleep. The shovel was heaver than she'd imagined, harder to wield. She had always thought the Georgia clay to be soft and pliable like sand, but it was not. Each crack of her shovel on the ground created a hairline fracture. No one was watching. A school night. A work night. Respectable families, and this was a respectable neighborhood, were in bed, having turned off the television, washed the last dish, packed the final lunch. The children firmly in REM sleep, the parents facing towards or away from each other, depending on whether or not they'd had sex that evening after the 11:00 news—highly unlikely, work night. School night. Girdles. Valium. Too many things are in the way of such intimacies.

How long could it take to reach six feet down, and was that really necessary? She was a baby after all, just a baby. Mrs. Abigail Fisher had not known what to say to Elise, all red faced and swollen nosed, when the great author finally came down the stairs for a nightcap. Now after she had given Elise the drink that had been meant for her, she hoped her daughter was at least sleeping soundly.

She had thought it would be to her advantage to wait until the clouds covered the almost new moon. If she waited until the Milky Way was a bale of stretched cotton backlit by the rising moon, she would be safe. She'd waited until Elise was asleep in the single bed covered by her pale pink sheets. She'd waited until she thought she could stand steady, hold the shovel, move through the motions and keep moving through them until it was done. Until the clay earth was stroked smooth back into shape. Until the honeysuckle vine stretched its arms out into spirals over the disturbed earth. She whispered a prayer, something older than she could remember learning. "Go to rest, little one. Go to rest. The animals of the woods watch over you. Go to rest, little one. Go to rest. I will see you when the work is done." She couldn't utter a Christian prayer. She couldn't invoke a deity, couldn't beg for forgiveness from the earth, from the honeysuckle, certainly not from the sleeping creature under the ground. Not sleeping. Not sleeping. But hadn't she just told that to Elise? Courtney Lynn is just resting now. She will be all right. Don't you worry. Don't you worry. But even as she spoke the words, she regretted the lie. What was the better choice? To say, "Go to sleep, my daughter. Your little sister is dead? She is dead because you gave her too many blankets? No. She is dead because I was not watching. I watch everything but my own family." Which is the better thing to say? She chose the lie. She was a novelist, after all. It was all she knew.

The owls watched from the woods. They saw 340 degrees of the story. They saw the woman carrying the bundle wrapped in too many blankets. She was one of those ageless women. In the dark she could be thirty or fifty. Her steps stuttered as she climbed the hill. Could she be seventy? No. She was too strong with the shovel. Too sure of the movement. Her hair, once comb-clipped snugly in back of her head, hung in tangles around her face, the breeze gently pulling at each strand. After the first crack of shovel into dirt, the woman made a trapped animal sound. Then she made no more sounds until she whispered to the honeysuckle plant, inhaling its scent deeply before standing straight and returning to the house, dragging the shovel behind her. The honeysuckle plunged its fragile roots deeper into the ground, it wrapped them around the sleeping, blanketed bundle and began to feed.

The moon was waxing the night Mrs. Abigail Fisher brought the first cobalt bottle to hang on the swiftly growing vine. She'd also brought a stone in the shape of a heart from the creek. It was supposed to be a gift, something solid that wouldn't turn into anything else, at least not during her lifetime. She hung the bottle on a top branch with twine, gave it a spin and watched it sparkle in the evening glow.

She planted the stone without gloves, wanting to feel the coolness of the soil, the slickness of the earthworms, beneath her skin. She wanted to reach deeper into the earth and touch the bundle wrapped in the quilt she had pieced together, poorly, from scraps of her maternity dresses for a different baby. She no longer remembered the young girl who made that quilt. Could she still find her daughter's fingers? Could she slide her own finger through an eye socket, and if she did that, would she feel anything at all in her heart or would she still be granite? Would she still be frozen? She tried to write the sentence: Underneath the layer of topsoil, the worms and beetles and larvae, the flesh had indeed begun to decay, to return to the soft belly of the planet, had begun to... had begun to... Mrs. Abigail Fisher, The South's First Lady of Letters, had no words for what came next.

Pistachio had found her way to the earth. The memories pressed her shoulders down, her shoulders that now were capable of bearing this weight and this responsibility. Was it like this for Abbey? Did the weight of all the stories break her?

"P, what happened?" asked Harold, feeling more comfortable

now that he could potentially rescue someone.

“Did you see it? Did you see the story?”

“I didn’t, I’m sorry, but I see what it’s doing to you. We’re not supposed to be out here. Let’s go back inside and wait. She’ll come back in and then she can write us into a story together. Like it’s supposed to be.”

“Nothing is like it’s supposed to be, Harold. Can’t you see that? Can’t you feel that? This day—this day alone has stretched on for much longer than twenty-four hours, hasn’t it?”

“I don’t know. I just got here.”

Pistachio wanted to scream. She wanted to kick him back to the Prohibition or the War of 1812 or the signing at Gettysburg. She could do that now, if she wanted to. She could. And she suddenly realized that was exactly what Mrs. Abigail Fisher had done to her. She’d kicked her out. One strike-through and that was that. She had done it because she could and well, wouldn’t you know it, and Pistachio would have laughed except she was too overcome with the memory, you can’t really kick someone out. They have their own agenda. They have their own desires and motivations and they might one day when you least expect it come knocking back on the door.

“You didn’t just get here. You’ve always been here. Just like I’ve always been here. At least as long as Abbey has been here. But we get to live beyond her, Harold. We are written larger.”

“You’re getting grandiose, my dear. Please send me back to Pinetree Pete. I’m worried about my friends there. Who knows what can happen in a story.”

“Is that what you want? To go back to her story?”

“It’s not her story, P. It’s my story. All these stories I’ve been in are my stories.”

“But she sends you everywhere. I never know where you’re going to be or how you're going to end up. I thought you wanted to be with me in my story."

"Our time together is in-between the stories. I thought you knew that."

"Knew that? We knew that characters couldn't read, but we can! We knew that characters couldn't write, but we can! We knew so many things that turned out not to be true. What if we didn't have to wait until we were both free?"

"Well then," said Harold. "There would be no story because there would be no more yearning."

"At least come with me to the Bottle Tree Vine. Maybe that's the story you're supposed to be in. Maybe it's supposed to be like this."

"Oh, so now you believe in predestination," he said, but he was smiling. He held out a chubby hand. "OK. I will accompany you to the Bottle Tree Vine on one condition."

"What's that?"

"Don't write the story down there. Let them be."

"What if I'm a part of the story?"

"Then be a part of the story. Don't be the queen."

Why wasn't Harold excited by all this power? Why wasn't he impressed by her? By all she had to do to get here?

"You thought it was easy," said Mrs. Abigail Fisher.

"What? Where are you?" Pistachio couldn't see anyone but Harold on the path.

"I'm in your head."

"You are not."

"I am too. Isn't that what you figured out earlier? You were going to take back the story or some sort of nonsense. You found your point of view."

Pistachio's heart pounded.

"Don't say that, dear. It's clichéd."

"Where are you?"

"Where aren't I?"

"Harold!"

Harold was already a few steps down the path. "Yes? Aren't you coming?"

"She's *in my head.*"

"Well of course she is. You didn't think you were separate, did you?" He made some soft comment about youth and individuation and blah-blah find-their-own-path.

"I heard you."

"No you didn't. You just summarized what you thought you heard."

"Not so easy, is it, dear?" said Mrs. Abigail Fisher. "I confess this is truly not how I thought it would end for me, but it is ever so much more interesting than I could have imagined. I thought I would die alone in the turret and it would be weeks before anyone noticed the smell. Now, it seems, I shall die alive. And that is the greatest gift, wouldn't you agree?"

39

Elise and her mother and Katrina had been walking together but not together in silence for several minutes. "I hear the creek running," said Elise. "I love that sound. I used to hear it in my dreams."

"Baby's Creek," said Mrs. Abigail Fisher.

"That's not its actual name," said Elise.

"No."

Elise stopped walking, held her hand up to the honeysuckle vine, brushed its yellow-white petals. The sweet smell would be overpowering to many people, but Elise had grown up with it, slept wrapped in it for years, maybe even took it with her when she thought she left home.

"I used to think about the story of Moses in the bull rushes," said Elise. "I'd come down here—" and she stopped. She didn't want to reveal anything more. Her mother would turn on her, use it on her, trick her into somehow being the one who did everything wrong. What was the point anymore of keeping anything precious? "We've got to get the house cleaned out, Mother. We've got to get you someplace safer. Maybe you can come to North Carolina." The sentence came out before she could stop it.

Mrs. Abigail Fisher smiled. "Why Daughter, I didn't know you cared."

"Forget it."

Katrina threw Mama Bear on the ground at the base of the tree. Maybe she hadn't thrown it down so much as let it slip through her fingers, which were disintegrating in front of her. Her skin was slipping from her bones, the veins and ligaments stretching long and popping, then sliding to the earth. Katrina knelt down, covered Mama Bear with her body, and sank.

"Can you see that, Mother?" asked Elise.

"I have seen it every night for more years than I can count." The vine shook, the bottles clanked against the branches, black birds erupted from their nests into a swarm in the sky.

"I assume my not-son-in-law is not coming back," said Mrs. Abigail Fisher.

"Doubtful, Mother. Isn't that what you always predicted? I lose everyone."

The ground opened and welcomed Katrina in, pulling her bones and skin into its roots. Mrs. Abigail Fisher knelt and reached into the damp hole. "Don't go again," she whispered. The blackbirds squawked and spun. The bottles twirled. Stars, Elise thought. They are almost like stars.

"I'm sorry I killed her, Mama," said Elise. "I just didn't want her to be cold."

Mrs. Abigail Fisher pulled her hair loose from its sloppy bun. She was wild, like Katrina had been; her bony shoulders peaked, then shuddered.

"She's going to tell," said Pistachio, who had been trying to keep her mouth shut, but it was all too much, the birds, the bottles, the bull rushes.

"Don't say anything," said Harold "This isn't yours."

"It is," said Pistachio. "This is why she hated me."

"Your father has to be dead by now, doesn't he?" asked Mrs. Abigail Fisher.

Elise couldn't say anything. Katrina had buried herself. The bear was gone. The bottles clinked softly. Her father had died, of course he had died, because he had never tried to come back for her.

"Harold," said Pistachio. "I can help her!"

"Don't interfere!" he said.

"It's not interference," Pistachio said. "It's revision."

Pistachio found the backstory and merged into Mrs. Abigail Fisher's mind and went to work.

Yes, Phillip had to be under the earth, Mrs. Abigail Fisher thought, no longer hearing the sounds, no longer remembering he and Abbey on a swing in a small Southern town, no longer feeling the saxophone swell through his body and no longer hearing the sounds it made as they broke her heart.

Who would have notified her had he died? She was surprised to be thinking of him like this on this very noisy day. The strangest things had been happening. Conversations with characters who were supposed to be ghosts; conversations with ghosts who were supposed to be long crossed over; conversations even with her daughter, a hint of friendliness under the cauldron's churning surface. Who would have notified her had he died?

The bottles shook. Sometimes the sounds that traveled on the back of the wind sounded like his saxophone. Sometimes those sounds even made her a touch sad, an emotion, for him anyway, she long ago thought she'd lost. Someone, a reader she had thought was just being insensitive, told her at a book signing that she'd seen Phillip performing in a jazz club in Chicago. She didn't know what to say to this reader, who was holding out her book to the appropriate page, handing her a thick black marker with which to sign, and smiling, coffee stained teeth yellow and proud.

She wasn't exactly surprised—he had always wanted to go back to Chicago, and she couldn't leave her home. She had believed, perhaps mistakenly, that her ability to write came from being in Georgia. She had based this only on her experience in New York at Zanzibar, where try as she had, she couldn't make the words. Maybe it was a mistake to have blamed it on Zanzibar. Why not blame it on youth, inexperience, falling in love (oh, the shudder of those words). Why not blame it on Norman Mailer and Truman Capote and the Arabian horses that were just over the hill? Maybe she could have been a different writer in the city. An urban woman. But there was so much competition there, and as fierce as Mrs. Abigail Fisher liked to think she was, she much preferred to be the belle of the ball she knew rather than a wallflower at the biggest party in the country.

Maybe she should have agreed to Chicago, or Memphis, or Detroit. Wasn't it true that a writer should be able to write anywhere? That playing music required other musicians, an immediate audience, not an amorphous reader ten years and ten states away. She knew that, but she wouldn't go with him. He had asked. She had told Elise that he had left them, and had deflected all the questions that had come since. But he hadn't just left, and now, standing in the dust and the dark (or is it dawn—they look so similar) she knew that she had not only contributed to his leaving but forced it. Maybe it was wrong for him to ask her to compromise her art and maybe it was wrong for her to expect him to do the same. Whenever a battle of wills ensued, Abbey was certain she was going to win—not because she should win, but because she would not back down.

She pretended she heard him playing from the ground as she pressed her hands against the hole where Katrina sank, where she had buried Courtney Lynn. She remembered the way he moved with the sax, the way his lips had tingled on her cheek that first night, the way his art had helped make hers better, and he had always said her work did the same. What had happened between them? It was so far away now it didn't matter, only that he was probably dead, and she was definitely dying, and right now, there was no one living or dead, she would rather talk to than her most darling ex-husband Phillip Fisher.

It would make far more sense for her to speak with the ghost of her husband than to speak with Pistachio. Maybe she could trick Pistachio into thinking she'd finally slipped into madness. Pistachio hadn't shown up yet this day, but perhaps that was a ruse and her thinking so much about Phillip was another trick to prick her armor.

I'm right here, whispered Pistachio. *I'm right here with you.*

Her limbs had once moved fluidly, her arms once intertwined with Phillip's in a morning bed, her legs used to run (had they really gone butterfly catching? With a net?)

Phillip's shoulder blades had reminded her of angel's wings. They were prominent, sharp, and she was certain that she could see the feathers in the air around them. When they lay together, there was a breeze, even if the windows were closed, the furnace off, and she had been convinced the breeze came from his wings shuddering on top of the bedclothes. Holding his saxophone for so many years had built those wings. The bones made a temple. When he slept on his stomach, sometimes they raised the back of his pajama shirt. Funny how the reasons they began to roll away from each other in the darkness had disappeared somewhere.

"Phillip," she whispered to the darkness of the earth. "Phillip." And when he didn't answer, she was more than a little bit surprised. She had so, suddenly, wanted to speak with him.

"I will always find you," he had said to her on more than one occasion when she'd been hiding in her bedroom underneath her papers trying to shut out his music, which had somewhere along the line shifted to noise. “I can see you.”

And perhaps that was true, and perhaps that was why he had to inevitably leave. Abbey couldn’t bear to be seen without a persona or a mask. Phillip had slipped underneath it before she knew how essential it was to craft it, but that vulnerability had been a continued source of irritation for her ever since. She resented that when he played and made his music, he could perform it and share it right away. He could wear the cloak the music allowed him. She could not do that with writing. She was alone with it or she was in public with letters and sentences that she supposedly wrote but no longer had any attachment to. There was no moment of merging that she experienced that could be shared with an audience. The intimacy that Phillip needed—that he mysteriously thrived on—frightened her.

I am right here, said Pistachio. Harold couldn’t hear her. This was between Mrs. Abigail Fisher and her. It has always been between them. The Cemetery of Books emerged around the honeysuckle. Harold gasped. Stones towered above them for a moment, then settled into their natural sizes. The stone for *Garden of Gethsemane, Georgia* had an end date, and the earth in front of it was turned, waiting. The shadows in the book cemetery were so long and thick they could be mistaken as ground cover. The sun was a thin red watercolor splash along the horizon. The moon would return to the cemetery soon.

“Daughter,” said Mrs. Abigail Fisher. “I have one more story, if you’re willing.”

Elise had picked Mama Bear out from the earth. Her arm had been reaching up from the grave. Without Katrina, the bear didn’t move or dance or make her drop her coffee. Without Katrina, the bear was lonely. She pressed it to her heart.

"One time," said Mrs. Abigail Fisher. "On a singular trip to the west coast with Phillip, we had watched the sunset at a tiny beach in Encinitas. California had not set well with either of us. There was too much sky, too much space for anything to be safe there. But the beach had been lovely, albeit cold, and I had been fascinated by the snowy egrets who waited every day in the same places, sunrise to sunset, to run into the cool silver surf as the waves crested. They were like pelicans, only much smaller, more dainty, and I'd wanted to name them.

"Your father had laughed at me. 'Abbey Sapphire,' he used to call me Abbey Sapphire, 'You can't tell one from the other. How can you name them?' But I could tell one from the other, and I could tell who was in charge of the rest of them, who was lonely and who was old. I laughed at myself too, believe it or not, child, though I said goodbye to all the snowy egrets when we left (Good-by Sam, Goodbye Delores, Mary Louise, Martin and Professor Q).

"This trip was part of our honeymoon, a road trip in a big new car with fins. I liked to think of the car cutting through air like a fish cuts through water. I felt at home in the car on the open road with your father. The sunset we watched on the beach was quick. It seemed like the sun was still well in the sky, an easy thirty minutes before it vanished, so we had kissed a little, the sand sticking to our cheeks, and when we opened our eyes again, the sand was gray, the ocean a deepening indigo, and the sun in its final blink to darkness.

"'It fell so fast,' said Phillip.

"'I thought we had all the time in the world,' I said, brushing strands of hair out of my mouth. "I forgot to pay attention.'"

The blurred line of sun edging the Cemetery of Books was holding its breath.

"He called you Abbey Sapphire?" asked Elise, trying to reconcile this woman, this mother she had known, with a woman who could have taken a road trip in a car with fins and named the snowy egrets on a southern California beach.

"He did."

"He called me Leesy-girl," she said, and clutched Mama Bear tighter.

"I know."

"I didn't mean to make him go," said Elise, so softly Pistachio thought only she could have heard.

No, no, said Pistachio, but she said it in her head. Harold kept a hand on her back. The Cemetery of Books was gray. The honeysuckle vine was a brilliant yellow, blue bottles spinning, yes, Elise, like stars.

"There was a bassinet," said Mrs. Abigail Fisher. "Courtney Lynn slept in it."

Elise was motionless. They had never, not since the day of the funeral, mentioned her sister's name.

"It belonged to me and to my sister, Giselle."

"I didn't know you had a sister," said Elise.

"Because she's gone," said Mrs. Abigail Fisher. She's gone.

I can't, said Abbey to Pistachio. *I can't. You do it. Can you give her this?*

I can't, said Pistachio. *But look up. The end is waiting.*

I heard footsteps behind me all of my life. I thought it was death.

I guess it was me, said Pistachio.

"My father had kept the bassinet where Giselle had slept, and I had always found it unnerving to walk into the cordoned off room at the top of the stairs and see her first bed, which had been my first bed too, draped in yellowing white. Sometimes I would peer into the room and imagine my mother, who of course I never knew, beside it, stroking my cheek or singing softly to me. My father kept no pictures of my mother, or if he did, he hid them well, so I imagined a woman with long flowing hair, the kind I was never to have, and the green eyes that Courtney Lynn had gotten."

Elise choked.

"Where else could they have come from? Phillip was dark and my own eyes were gray, even as a girl." Abbey, still pressed against the earth, reached a hand for Elise's foot. "Yes, Elise, I remember, I remember her eyes."

"I don't think I do, Mama."

Mrs. Abigail Fisher rose to her knees. "You didn't do it, Daughter. It just happened. Babies just stop sometimes. I wasn't watching. I was working. It was me. I thought you would be strong enough to carry the story. But no one is."

Elise felt a cracking in her belly that spread to the base of her spine and traveled up to her shoulders. Crick, crack, pop. The framework of her life split apart.

"I spent many many days watching nothing after Courtney Lynn died, Daughter. Phillip had gone two days after the funeral. I thought I'd managed to convince you that he was away on a trip to Chicago and would be back just as soon as he could, but I never thought you were gullible enough to believe it. But you pretended to pretend, good girl that you were, until you stopped asking and I could stop talking about it. You were a strange girl, Daughter, always so quiet, always so much in the shadows. I sometimes forgot you were there at all. I don't want to count how many times I forgot about dinner, even something as simple as hot dogs and boiled greens. But you would always manage. I was certain of that. You were born resourceful.

"In the days and months after Courtney Lynn died, you would

take the bassinet and put it on a wagon and pull the empty bassinet around the yard. You would talk to it, and maybe you put a doll in there, I never asked, but the talking seemed to give you some brightness from time to time. Sometimes you would sing, and sometimes you would skip a little bit, your bare feet turning green from the dew. I cried, Daughter, for what it's worth, during those times when I watched my only living daughter dancing with my only dead one. I knew I should want to stand up, go outside, and rock both children, here and gone, in my embrace, but I just couldn't, and over time, the tears froze up inside, and over time you stopped singing and dancing (zip-a-dee-do-da-zip-a-dee-a) with your ghost sister and you grew quiet, too quiet for a young girl, but quiet enough so that I, your mother, did not ever have to raise my voice in either praise or reprimand and could return to my bedroom to work."

Pistachio jumped up and down. Harold tried to keep her still. *Don't stop, don't stop, don't stop,* Pistachio said. Abbey had stood up. Elise held Mama Bear between them. Her face was wet. Her throat was closed.

"Daughter," said Abbey. Elise shook her head. Abbey nodded. "That is how I had imagined it."

Elise stepped back, knocking one of the spinning bottles with her head.

Pistachio watched her Creator, the woman who had sliced her and cut her and left her in a dusty silverfished closet to rot, collapsing from the inside out. She wasn't slipping like Katrina had been; she wasn't sleeping like Courtney Lynn had been; she just was falling inward. The air that had held her up was leaking. Pistachio cried out, *Mama!* And Abbey looked up, smiled weakly. *Wait! I have something I can give you!*

"No!" said Harold. "You're interfering! You can't interfere! Look!

Her grave is open. It's time. Don't stand in the way of that."

"I can't bear it. She doesn't have anything. I can give her a story. I have a better ending! Abbey! Abbey! Can I give you a story?"

Abbey extended a hand. "Please, I'm melting. Give me a story."

Pistachio tossed Henry's hat to Elise, who still clutched the green bear, though not as tightly. Henry, Elise thought. You have gone, haven't you?

"Abbey," said Pistachio. "Listen to me. Let me revise the story." Pistachio leapt from *The Garden of Gethsemane* tombstone, outrunning the shadows of the falling sun, and perched on Mrs. Abigail Fisher's shoulder. She leaned into her ear and spoke her ending.

"Dear Phillip,

I am not sure how to address you—dearest, beloved, my love—it has been so long and I imagine you have rather wished to forget me. I had thought I wished to forget you, but it appears that now that I can no longer remember where I put my slippers or where I am or who I am, the memories of you are dancing around my edges.

"When I have pen in hand, I have some modicum of my old self back, still. When I have the smoothness of the paper beneath my palm I feel soothed, stable, though my handwriting is legible only to itself, I am afraid.

"I don't know how to ask this, other than to outright speak it: Are you dead? I can't help but think I would have heard something, but I am not much for following the papers and I am even less inclined to ask another. So with that approach, it is little wonder why no one would have tracked me down.

"I don't think that I have moved very much farther

along in the thirty years I've been away from you. That I can't blame you for, and I am reasonably certain I can't blame you for the rest of it, either. What was I writing this to you for? Oh, yes, I was going to write the scene of your passing.

"I will pretend that I was there, that you had asked for me and that I had responded (although in all likelihood I would not have, had you actually asked for me, but if you called today, I would come.) The room is bright, lots of sun, open curtains, open windows. It is spring, for it is too much to bear to imagine that you passed in winter and had to remain so cold for a whole season. I have brought flowers, violets and buttercups, and placed them in a vase beside your bed. We are, remarkably, not angry with one another.

"Your saxophone is in the bed with you. You are at home, where you have lived with your new wife, who is standing on the other side of the bed watching you. She is a good person, as you have said to me frequently. She has qualities I don't, and that's obvious from a first meeting. She is pretty, in the traditional sense, even though she is also over sixty. She has a dog's eyes, and that is not meant as an insult, dear Phillip; they are the eyes of loyalty. She loves you, and I am glad for it. For you both. She has put one of your CDs on the stereo and I am surprised that, even though I am far from musical (a tin ear, you always said) I would have recognized this music as yours no matter where I heard it. I can see you swaying in the moonlight beside the creek we could never find. I feel your lips on my cheek, my neck. You look small, in the bed, Phillip.

I have often thought of you as so large, for when you walked out of our house for the last time the space you left was unbearably huge. Age spots dot your neck, your arms, and the skin on your face falls into the hollows of your cheeks like a limp hammock.

"'He's been like this now for days,' your new wife of thirty years says. 'I can't tell if he is asleep or awake.' She smiles at me and it is sincere and beautiful. I don't know what to do with her grace. 'He would be glad to know you came.'

"'I don't know about that,' I say, and I want to touch you, my hands reach for yours, but I pull back. I am not the wife anymore. You are not my husband. Her hair has grayed in the way that makes her look only that much stronger, more beautiful. Mine has made me appear haggard, weary. 'I haven't heard his music in so long,' I say. 'I didn't know he made a CD.'

"'Someone recorded a show,' she says. 'He didn't think that jazz should be recorded. He thought once it was captured, it died.'

"I feel hummingbirds' wings in my throat. Did we do that to each other, dear Phillip? Did we capture and kill each other?

"Your eyes open and turn their gaze on me. They are young, Phillip. They are the eyes I first loved. 'The music is beautiful, Phillip,' I say, and you smile, your dry lips cracked and lined. You make a sound deep in the back of your throat and your new wife leans in. I imagine your breath is foul, but I won't allow myself the intimacy. It is no longer my right.

"You make the sound again. She shakes her head and shrugs her shoulders The curtains are emerald edged in gold and they billow like laundry on this most fresh spring day. A blue bird perches on the outer windowsill. There is so much life in this room of dying—the color, the wind, the bird, your new wife of thirty years, your CD. That may be the greatest miracle of all—the way the dying and the living dance with each other. You raise your hand and I can see the prick marks on your inner arm from all the blood they've taken from you the last few months you have been dying. Your skin is bruised, purpled, yellowed and greened. It won't be much longer. Your feet are stiffening under the blanket. Your new wife of thirty years has held everything together these past few months but she is cracking now because she knows she finally can. There will soon be nothing left she has to hold together. We might have been friends, she and I, if I were a woman given to such friendships. I am glad that you have found her.

"Your arm falls back to the bed. I know that I should leave, that I should give her this final moment alone with you. Your breathing is gargling and your eyes have closed again, the lashes wet. She sits on the edge of the bed, then lies down with you, curling her body against yours, resting her head on your shoulder. Your saxophone is on the other side, the side I am on, and I suppose that is fitting since I am not the one who is supposed to curl with you. I want to push the instrument closer so it can be touching you. Another labored breath. There will not be many more

"'I love you,' she says to you, and kisses your cheek, your ear, and lets her lips linger. She is crying and she is that much more beautiful because of it, because she is able to cry freely and openly in the room of your dying with the woman you used to love standing beside you. I want to cry. I feel my guts churning, my breath tangling into knots, but I can't. I hear you, so many years ago.

"'Abbey Sapphire, let it go,' you whispered to me the night I told you about my mother, about my childhood and my first pet cat. 'You are more beautiful when you feel.'

"And I came as close as I ever have, that night with you in the magical months before we were married. A few tears snuck out of both eyes.

"'Don't hold so much,' you said. 'It will one day be too much.'

"But I couldn't. I couldn't let you see me shaking. I didn't know what sounds would come out and the not-knowing was more frightening than the holding.

"'I'm not going anywhere,' you said. 'I will be here when you're through. Just let it go.'

"Maybe that was the first time I disappointed you. Maybe that was why I couldn't write with the ease that you could play. Maybe that was why my characters are intellectually fascinating but never quite catch the hearts of readers. My work engages the mind alone.

"'When you feel something, you've got to ride it, like a magic carpet,' you said. 'If you try to change it, you're going to get stuck. If you try to stop the ride, you're going to grind the gears and crash.'

"But I couldn't. I wanted to, Phillip, I did, but I didn't know how. I didn't know how to be like you. I remember the way the house sounded after you left. I'd never taken the time to hear our house before; it had always been so full of you, of your music, of our laughter. I want to imagine your serenading on the porch before dawn, but I dared not. It would bring me too far back into the past, a place I am having increasing difficulty getting back from. Did you even do that, my love? I like to remember it. But not today.

"After you left us, our only other daughter clung to me too tightly. You knew I didn't know how to hold her. You knew I couldn't be what she needed. After you left us, we ate macaroni and cheese and drank cherry Kool-Aid for weeks. She didn't want anything else, and I didn't have the energy to prepare anything else. I was hardly hungry. There were so many reasons I knew I was a terrible person during that time. I missed you more than I missed Courtney Lynn. What sort of person does that? I missed you in the darkness. I missed you in the dawn. I missed you most when I was writing, or not writing, in my room all alone. Suddenly, the all alone that I thought I wanted was too much. There was no place left for me to bring anyone to life, not in a room that was so loud without you.

"Your wife stands and smooths her hair. Your CD has ended. The blue bird is gone. 'Do you want to say anything to him?' she asks, and she means it, and she is not the least bit jealous, the least bit threatened. You found someone who could feel. I am happy for you both. And I

actually mean it. I touch the neck of the sax. It's cold.

"'I loved him,' I say to her.

"'I know,' she says. 'He loved you, too.'

"There is one more breath. The inhale is very long, as if you wanted to take everything in you had missed. There is an interminable pause.

"'Thank you, Phillip,' I say, because it is all I am capable of saying, but I mean so much more. When the exhale comes, we both know it is the last one. I press my hands to my mouth. I have to keep it all in. I have to. She wails and it scares me at first, but then I listen deeply, like you taught me, and I hear the music of it, I see the wave of it, and I try to hitch a ride on it and hope that I can ride her sadness through to the other side. I inhale sharply. I had forgotten for a few moments to breathe. My body is not yet done. We stay in the room together. She is wailing and I am rigid, but Phillip, my love, I am only rigid on the outside. On the inside, I am dissolving.

Until soon, I remain your one and only,

Abbey Sapphire."

Mrs. Abigail Fisher knew this moment. It had been approaching her whole life. The footsteps in the leaves, heavier and heavier, closer and closer. The trees bent forward, the leaves spun in circles ahead of the footsteps. Pistachio held her trembling hand. The fiction had ended and Mrs. Abigail Fisher was left with the only slice of narrative she could not avoid.

"This is the sound," she said.

"Write it," said Pistachio.

"I can't write it. I can't move."

"Speak it."

"You are going to kill me," said Abbey.

"Yes," said Pistachio. "I have to. It's the only way the story works."

"I thought it would be you, Elise."

Elise can't help but choke a laugh. *Mama.*

Abbey saw the boots that were attached to the feet that had been stalking her all of her days. They were dusty work boots, up to the knee.

"We are running out of time," said Abbey. "I am running out of time."

"Lie down," said Pistachio. "There's a place for you. You will be with all your stories."

The heart-shaped rock pillow she had brought so many years ago to mark Courtney Lynn's resting place was hard beneath her head; she imagined the curtains dancing in her turret even though the window was closed.

"What do you imagine, Abbey? What ending can you give?" asked Pistachio.

"I'm inside," she said. "There are voices on the stairs. My daughter, the one who lived, the one who is living, is climbing the stairs. She is holding the banister lightly, fingerprints tangling with the dust. There is a man with her and he is also laughing, at her perhaps, or at me, upstairs in the bed with the dancing curtains. It doesn't end like I thought I thought there would be more."

There was nothing on the movie screen behind her eyelids. No shadows interplaying. No sounds, no sunlight splashes or whispered conversations. No characters touching or fighting or walking away from each other. No words. Where did she make things up from? Usually they emerged from a sense, a texture, a scent, a sound. From there, a whole world unfolded like a pop-up book. But now, nothing. That had never been.

"Where do I make it up from?" she asked. Did she speak that aloud? Where did Phillip make it up from? Phillip. There was a distant whistle. What was she supposed to do with that? Courtney Lynn. Mama is here. I am here.

Elise and Henry were almost at the landing. The blank pages fluttered in her mind. She heard them rustling. Edge blurred into edge, a white out. Pistachio was fading as well, becoming white space, the empty pages at the end of the book. The footsteps grew louder. They were right behind her, behind the headboard and the wallpaper. They were under her, beneath the fading blue half-shag carpet, and then they were beside her. Look. Oh. There you are. Here I am. Here I have always been. Oh! A first person. Why had she waited this long to claim I?

Death did not look like what she had imagined. His boots were waterproof, his jeans tight, his hands white and thin, smooth as a young girl's. His voice was also soft, sweeter than she would have thought, and exactly the right words passed across the lips.

"Mama," said Abbey.

Death was soft, full of milk and smelling of laundry softener.

"You have been stalking me," said Abbey. "You smell like home."

The saxophone began in the distance.

"Keep talking, Abbey," said Pistachio. "What's the ending?"

Abbey struggled for breath. Elise knelt beside her. "Mama," she said. "What?"

"You and Henry entered my room. 'Mother, we heard you fall,' you said.

"The room had gone silent. You saw me on the bed, fingers wound around the top sheet. 'Mother?' You asked about me."

The saxophone grew louder.

Henry stepped closer. He pulled out his cell phone.

"Don't," said Elise.

"I need to call the ambulance," said Henry.

"Don't."

Abbey still breathed, a shallow choppy sea.

"Elise," said Henry.

"Don't."

Elise noticed the bent angles of her mother's limbs. Who had placed her in the bed? When did they leave the garden? Who had wrapped her in the blankets? She pulled a heavy quilt up over her mother, covering her face.

"Elise," said Henry. "Don't."

Elise watched the quilt settle around her mother's nose, thin lips, hollow cheeks. It would take just a minute. She was already almost gone.

"This is the end of the book," whispered Pistachio.

"Yes," said Abbey.

A shadow played the saxophone. It wove over the tombstones and book covers.

"Phillip," she said.

The notes grew louder.

"I thought I had to choose," she said. "Art or love."

"They can't be separated, Abbey Sapphire."

Elise removed the quilt from her mother's face. Henry put his phone away.

"It's almost time," said Elise.

Abbey untangled her fingers from the sheets and reached for Elise. "Courtney Lynn," she whispered.

"No, mother," said Elise. "It is me."

Abbey looked confused. "You smell like honeysuckle."

"She's gone," said Elise. "I couldn't find her."

"I couldn't either," said Abbey.

The shadow saxophone player stopped; the sun had vanished from the Cemetery of Books. The stars were twinkling and Abbey thought of childhood nursery rhymes, and strangely, of Norman. Nature or nurture. Death began to tap its feet. Nature wins in the end. She heard their voices but couldn't see them.

"Can I pour you a drink?" asked Truman. "We've got all the best."

"Leave her be," said Phillip. "She's got much to talk about."

"Elise," said Abbey. "I thought I had to choose."

Henry wrapped his arms around Elise. She wanted to wriggle out of his embrace, but she couldn't. She wanted to wriggle out of the room, but she couldn't. The saxophone sang and Abbey wanted to respond, wanted to dance with it, pull it closer to her, find a way into the remaining notes. Pistachio was barely visible anymore, the pages of her story folding over her. Abbey walked past *The Garden of Gethsemane, Georgia* book cover, stood beside her name, traced the end date with her index finger.

The saxophone's notes gleamed in the forest. The boots were gone, but the crunching remained. Behind her. Beside her. Underneath her. Above her. Elise. My girl.

Elise touched her mother's arm. "She's cold," said Elise. "I think she's gone."

Henry removed his hat.

Elise kissed her mother's forehead. "Well," she said.

Henry kissed Elise's shoulder, felt her sobbing inside her skin.

"She's going to be fine," Abbey said to Pistachio, who was again in brilliant color. "My daughter. She's going to be fine."

"Come on, then," said Pistachio. "We've got us some other places to be."

Abbey took her hand, which was warm and three-dimensional, and the two of them walked out of the Cemetery of Books in the direction the sun had vanished, swaying slightly to the sultry sounds of sax and crickets, inhaling honeysuckle and baby powder and the glue of the spine holding together the pages of her next story.

"That's a fine ending, Mrs. Abigail Fisher," whispered Pistachio as she and Harold gently covered her with earth. "A mighty find ending indeed."

In the After Words

Dear Reader,

You may find it in bad taste to finish the story of my mother, the South's Esteemed Lady of Letters, Mrs. Abigail Fisher. You may think it improper and at worst, dishonest to try and write this story, especially since I had so little information to go on, but I find that there is nothing else that I can do that will honor who my mother could have been, and that feels very important to me somehow—that the world understands who she might have been.

Mama's dead now. Took her a long time to go, but she went peaceful, in a dream. She had her whole life to write her side of the story. This version is mine. I put in sections from her notebooks and her letters so you would know I was playing fair. But every story has a lens. This lens is mine and I've said what I had to say to make the story work out. You can decide what parts you want to believe and what parts you don't. Mother would say it doesn't matter what's true and what isn't. All that matters is the story, and this one, dear readers, is mine.

When I left my mother in the ground, I had thought Henry would be long gone, but when I got back to North Carolina, there was a note on the kitchen table. *Meet me at our rock,* he wrote. I *can see behind the curtain.* And I poured some food for poor Smeek and drove as quickly as I could. It was cold. Winter comes early in the Blue Ridge Mountains. I'd forgotten gloves. I saw his police cruiser parked in the dirt. He still wants to trespass with me, I thought.

He was standing on the rock when I found him. I did remember to bring his hat back. I didn't want to sneak up on him, so I said, "Hey. I think you left this."

His shadow nodded, but he didn't turn around. I reached the rock and pulled myself up. I took his hat off my head. "Do you want still want it?" I whispered.

He pulled his hand out of his pocket, stretched a finger toward me.

"I do," he said. "Damn it all, Elise. I do."

A year later, after we managed to get the old house cleared out, I brought Henry back south. He wasn't any too happy to go to Georgia. We'd married at the old Oz Theme Park in one of those hot air balloons that went straight up in the sky and then returned, rooted always to the earth. We were about to auction the house and I wanted to go visit her, one more time. I brought the only photograph I had of Courtney Lynn.

In the photograph, Courtney Lynn's eyes are wide with wonder, whether it was wonder at her father, at the camera's flash, at the brightness of the sun that day, I could never know. She was taking her first half-step forward. That was how I liked to remember Courtney Lynn, stepping into her future. When I looked at the picture, I imagined my sister had just stopped, just run out of current, and when the right combination of things could be arrived at, she could be wound back up and her life could continue as if nothing had happened. My own shadow darkens the corner of the photograph, angled and too tall, wider at the feet than at the head. The photograph was edged in a white scalloped border, like most of the photographs from the fifties. One of the corners was dog-eared, and on the back, in handwriting I could only suppose was my mother's, *1957, C-L, age 2.*

"This is my baby sister," I said to Henry, handing him the photo.

Henry held it by the edges, turned it over and read the back, then studied the face.

"Well, um, where is she?" Henry shifted his weight from one foot to the other. I noticed the paleness of his eyebrows and I wanted to kiss them. They were translucent earthworms.

"Right outside. Underneath the honeysuckle," I said. "By the creek."

"Elise, you don't have to say any more."

"I do. She brought you here."

Henry tried to speak, but I shushed him. "Not anymore talk now. Let's just go to her."

Henry absently touched the barrel of his holstered gun.

"You won't need that, Henry. She's already dead." I stepped confidently through the worn path on the floor I'd trampled for so many years. Henry followed, stepping exactly in my footsteps. I took him down the three wooden stairs off the porch onto the overgrown flagstone path past the overgrown rose bushes, thorns popping sideways from the stems to Baby's Creek. Henry gasped when he saw the honeysuckle.

"She's something else, isn't she," I said, proud, so proud of my baby sister's growth.

"I—where—I've never—"

"I know."

The honeysuckle, its white petals gilded yellow, was an organism of epic proportions. If one didn't know where to look, one couldn't find the roots. It was a carpet of petals, its fragrance so heavy that birds, bees, dragonflies, and all manner of creatures sought it. In between the white petals were hints of red feathers, glistening wings, and so much sound from the cobalt bottles hanging from the branches. The plant buzzed and hummed and vibrated. The plant had stalks, multitudes of them, stretched out as far as either of us could see around the shore of Baby's Creek. The roots were thick as the roots of eucalyptus trees, gnarled and bumping along the sandy soil. All manner of ants—black ones, red ones, fire ones—marched over and under them.

"Intoxicating, isn't it?" I said, noticing Henry's breathing had become labored.

"What kind of honeysuckle is this?"

"Why are you so surprised? You said you could see it from the road. You saw it last year when you ran off."

"Yes, but I thought it was just a lot of different plants, I guess. Not one gigantic plant that must go on for—"

"Two and a half miles," I said, because I knew. I measured it in footsteps, and it was almost 13,000 footsteps from one side to the other, depending on how wide I stepped. Most days I stepped small, like I was Courtney Lynn on that first half-step morning in the summer of 1957.

"Two and a half miles," said Henry. "That's amazing."

"It is."

The vine curled into itself, holding its own hands as it spread out along the creek bed and climbed upward towards the sky.

"What holds it up?" asked Henry.

"Hope," I said.

I felt my mother's gaze from the dormer window that faced the creek, though it had been a year since her death. I didn't turn around, refused to turn around.

"I want to sit down," said Henry.

"It's the vine. The fragrance is heavy."

"Like the poppy field in *The Wizard of Oz*. Don't let me sleep forever." He laughed awkwardly.

There was a spot under the canopy of intertwined branches where nothing grew at all, where there was only sandy dirt and the imprints of knees and palms from where Katrina and my mother had vanished.

"Come with me," I said, and led him deeper into the vine. The sun spattered our faces with gold flecks. An unusually large robin's nest weighed down the branch above us. I had seen at least five generations of robins born in that nest. Each new family brought more twigs, more pieces of fabric, more fishing netting, more yard scraps. Each new family's eggs were bluer, larger, and produced baby birds with open haunted mouths, shrieking and pointing their thin tongues toward the points of sunlight. Mother always said she saw black birds, but I saw the robin, the bird of spring.

The clearing under the canopy of honeysuckle had been a sanctuary for me. It was hidden from the dormer window and it was a cocoon for me to wait in until I could see Courtney Lynn again; her half-steps before falling, her giggle and her exquisite green eyes. Sometimes I was waiting for her, drawing pictures in the sand with tiny fingers. Sometimes I had to sit a long time before I saw her, and sometimes I didn't see her at all.

I hadn't really expected to see her that day, not on the day I'd brought company, but there she was, in her white christening gown, hair close cropped and fine blonde, playing jacks under the heavy white flowers. Henry didn't see her, but he did know the ground was sacred.

"You must have come out here a lot," he said.

"Most days when I was growing up. If it wasn't raining."

"What did you do out here?"

"I talk to her."

"And what do you say?"

This was private, between me and Courtney Lynn. Between my own small self and Courtney Lynn's even smaller self. Courtney Lynn bounced the red rubber ball, caught it and scooped up three silver jacks. Henry didn't notice.

"I say I'm sorry."

"What happened, Elise?"

"I wanted her to be warm. I just wanted her to be warm."

"Where was your mother?"

"In her room. Working. Writing. I don't know what."

"Where was your father?"

"He had gone to Chicago for the weekend, I think. At least that's what Mother has told me. I don't remember."

"You were how old?"

"Three."

Courtney Lynn stopped playing jacks and turned her face to mine. I knelt beside her, scooped the red rubber ball and jacks into my own hands.

"Want to play again?" I asked.

Courtney Lynn shook her head.

"Mama's watching," I said, because this time it was true. This time, it was true.

"No," said Courtney Lynn. "Mama's not watching anymore. Mama's in a different story."

Henry's hands were over my own, knocking the jacks to the earth. "What are you doing?" he asked. "I don't understand."

"I'm crazy," I said. "You should get away from me. Everyone thinks my mother was the crazy one, but that's not true. It's me. It's always been me."

Courtney Lynn smiled, but it was a sad smile, holding everything she didn't have words for yet. I touched her fine blonde hair.

"You would have been so beautiful," I said.

"Yes," said Courtney Lynn.

"Elise! Stop! Who are you talking to?" asked Henry.

"You don't see her." It was a statement, not a question.

Henry lowered his voice. "I don't see her."

"Do you believe in ghosts?"

"I don't think I do, Elise. I think there are things nobody can quite understand, but ghosts—well, in my line of work I guess the ghosts I see are the ones people make up and carry around with them. Folks' ghosts are about regret."

Courtney Lynn stopped moving at all, gaze fixed to the earth.

"You're saying people make up their ghosts and then carry them around?"

"Absolutely."

Courtney Lynn remained frozen.

"Why would someone do that?" I asked.

"I don't think it's just someone," said Henry. "I kind of think everyone does."

I bounced the red rubber ball, but Courtney Lynn didn't grab it.

"Who is your ghost?" I asked.

Henry shuffled his feet. "You."

I laughed a nervous laugh, but I was also fluttering inside, a different kind of flutter that wasn't fear. I had to pick up the ball. If it rolled away, how could we finish our game?

"She's not here, Elise."

I took his hand and led him deeper under the vine. Courtney Lynn didn't move. The brambles thickened and seemed to reach up from the earth and catch our shoes, our pants' legs, our ankles as we moved deeper and deeper.

"Are we going toward the creek?" asked Henry.

"We're going away from the creek," I said. "We're going into the vine."

I thought about the forest scenes in Disney movies—how the trees came to life and snatched bits of clothing and frightened the heroine as she ran away. Those forests were trying to keep characters in. This time, the branches grabbed at us, but it was more of a swipe, more of an accidental scratch as they opened to us. I couldn't see the sun anymore; the overhead brambles and petals were too thick. The vine, this single vine had expanded into so much twig and scent and nest that I could no longer determine a beginning or an end to it. It was as if the entire world had turned inside out and become only this one buzzing humming organism. I stopped abruptly and Henry stumbled.

"She is here," I said, pointing at the root of the plant. "She's right here. You can bring whatever equipment you need to find her. We should have buried her properly. Mother wanted to keep her near, I guess."

Henry pushed his glasses up the bridge of his nose. He was sweating. "I don't want to do that, Elise," he said. "Just tell me what happened."

I knelt, touching the thick trunk of the vine. Courtney Lynn hadn't followed us. "Mother put her here," I said. "I wasn't with her. She wouldn't let me come." The sob was sharp. "She wouldn't let me come. But I think I'm the only one who's ever come back. I'm the only one who visits."

"I'm sure that isn't so," said Henry, who wasn't sure at all about that, but thought it the right thing to say. He didn't want me to stop talking. He didn't want to leave the strange tomb of branches. He didn't want the sunlight to scare away the shadows.

"I would know if she ever came," I said. "I would see her footprints."

"Not if her ghost whisks them away," he said.

"She doesn't ever come," I said again. "Not until the very end. That was the only time she came."

"OK," said Henry, who saw another set of footprints and the broken branches from a different direction, made by a different sized shoe. "She doesn't ever come."

I nodded. "Never."

"OK."

"I wanted to come," I said. "I didn't want her to be the one to bury her."

"It was an accident," he said. "Whatever happened, I know it was an accident."

I looked up from the ground, pushed a strand of hair out of my eyes and really took in Henry, his strange awkward stance, his skinny body and thinning hair, his glasses that didn't seem to fit his face. "I just wanted her to be warm." And I moved closer to him and then closer and then he took my hands and pulled me to him and wrapped his bony arms around me. His holster pressed into my hip; his palm pressed into my back.

"I know, honey. I know."

"She was my friend, Henry. We were playing house."

Courtney Lynn still had not followed us. I had never been this far in without her.

"She made one hell of a honeysuckle plant," said Henry, and I knew he immediately wished he could take that sentence back, but I burst into laughter and tightened my embrace and so he began to laugh, tentatively at first, then louder and louder, the laugh dancing in his belly, traveling up his throat and forcing his mouth open in the most unexpected of ways. We laughed and laughed and the honeysuckle plant buzzed and hummed and rumbled and our mouths opened and opened until we found one another's, lips on lips, chin bumping chin, tongues traveling, laughing, laughing, laughing until the vine itself shook with the folly of it all.

Love to you, Dear Readers,
Most Sincerely,
Elise Fisher Wakefield

Daughter of the South's Esteemed First Lady of Letters,
Mrs. Abigail Fisher, and saxophonist Phillip Fisher,
sister of the much beloved Courtney Lynn Fisher.

May you keep your characters close.

ABOUT THE AUTHOR

Laraine Herring holds an MFA and an MA and directs the creative writing program at Yavapai College. Her work includes the novel *Ghost Swamp Blues* and *Writing Begins with the Breath*. She also teaches at the Kripalu Insitute for Yoga and Health and online at DailyOm.com. She lives in Prescott, AZ with four beautiful orange cats and whatever ghosts happen to be currently speaking. Visit her at laraineherring.com for updates, newsletters and more.

www.ingramcontent.com/pod-product-compliance
Lightning Source LLC
Chambersburg PA
CBHW050322200626
46810CB00022B/340